Blood West

BLOOD WEST

THOMAS D. CLAGETT

THORNDIKE PRESS
A part of Gale, a Cengage Company

Copyright © 2022 by Thomas D. Clagett.
Thorndike Press, a part of Gale, a Cengage Company.

LIBRARY OF CONGRESS CIP DATA ON FILE.
CATALOGUING IN PUBLICATION FOR THIS BOOK
IS AVAILABLE FROM THE LIBRARY OF CONGRESS.

ISBN-13: 978-1-4328-9265-4 (softcover alk. paper)

Published in 2023 by arrangement with Thomas D. Clagett

Printed in the United States of America
1 2 3 4 5   27 26 25 24 23

For Sally and Raymond Imblum,
my sister and her husband

CHAPTER ONE

Halting in the long shadows, the creature listened to the cacophony of sounds coming from the saloon across the street. A piano played. Laughter and shouts carried into the black night. The creature waited. It was late, but there was time yet. It had not feasted for three days.

A different sound alerted the creature, and it turned its head. A stocky man stepped onto the wooden walkway a few storefronts away and yawned. In his hand he carried a cloth bundle tied with string. It was a drugstore merchant closing up his shop late. The creature watched him lumber away when a deep voice boomed from the saloon.

"The United States, as we understand,
Took sick and did vomit the dregs of the
    land.
Her murderers, bankrupts, and rogues
    you should know,

All congregated in New Mexico."

Boisterous cheers greeted the ditty.

Someone said, "They're right here in Las Vegas, the Territory of New Mexico, by damn! Every one of them!"

Another man said, "Yes, sir, indeed!"

The creature's ears drew forward, alert.

A lean, rough-looking man wearing a black hat with a silver band appeared at the batwing doors, looked out at the street, and draped his arms over the doors. He held a half full bottle of whiskey in one hand.

"Give us another, Jess," a voice called.

"Had enough for tonight," the lean man said, looking back over his shoulder. "Think I'll head on over to Mimi's, spend some of this money I won from you boys. Hear she got a luscious one in today. All the way from Kansas City."

"At least give me a chance to win back some of my money."

The lean man laughed. "If you can't afford to lose, you can't afford to play, you dumb bastard."

"Watch yourself out there, Jess," the barkeep said.

The lean man turned his back to the saloon doors. "What are you worried about? Afraid I won't pay my liquor bill?"

"Well, no, but —"

"But what? You think I'm scared of that wolf everybody's pissing their pants over?" He glanced around the saloon. "What a bunch of little old ladies. I told you that wolf was long gone."

Reaching into his pocket, he took out a silver coin, tossed it high toward the bar, pulled his revolver, and fired at the falling coin. Bottles on the shelf behind the bar shattered, and the barkeep let out a yelp, putting his hand to his bloodied ear.

"You shot my ear!" the barkeep shouted.

The lean man laughed, said he was sorry and to put the broken bottles on his new bill.

"Son of a bitch," the barkeep said low.

The lean man strode to the bar, reached over, grabbed the barkeep, and clubbed him with his revolver. His head bleeding and eyes rolled up, the barkeep fell back behind the bar.

"Apology accepted," the lean man said.

Stepping outside, the batwing doors flapped closed behind him. The man stood there, his fist on his hip, a black silhouette against the light from the saloon.

The cruelty in the man's eyes sharpened the creature's gaze.

The lean man put the whiskey bottle to

his lips. Took a swallow. Wiped his mouth on the back of his hand. He turned, revealing the holster with a revolver hung low at his side, and swaggered up the street. Reciting his ditty again, he chuckled.

The creature followed, keeping to the shadowed storefronts on the opposite side of the street, away from the saloon where horses stood tied to the hitching rail. The horses strained at their tethers and shied away. The creature knew that horses smelled fear as keenly as danger.

But this night the creature stalked a different animal. The lean man was his prey.

The prey continued on his walk. He passed a dressmaker shop, a glassware store, barbershop, and suddenly halted.

The creature crouched behind a large barrel by the doorway of a hardware store.

The prey glanced about, his eyes searching.

The creature watched the prey disappear around a corner. It hurried up the dirt street. At the corner was an alleyway. Slipping into shadows, the creature peered into the dark alley, its eyes seeing as clear as day through the darkness. The prey bent over a bearded drunk, passed out against the wall. The creature heard the soft clinking of coins as the lean man lifted the unconscious man's money.

The creature made a low sound.

The prey turned.

Safe in the shadows, the creature waited.

Satisfied no one was there, the prey shoved the stolen coins into his pocket. The drunk moved, mumbled something. The prey stomped his boot heel into the drunk man's face.

"Shut your mouth," the prey said low.

The creature ran its tongue over its pointed teeth.

Moving down the dark alley, the prey took another pull from the whiskey bottle, then threw it down.

The creature entered the alley. It heard the prey laugh.

Near the end of the alleyway, light from another saloon threw a pale hue on the wall. The prey stopped at the edge of that dim light. Turning, his hand reached for his revolver.

"Come out of them shadows," the prey growled.

The prey's revolver did not clear the holster.

CHAPTER TWO

"I promise, if we find your husband we will send him home," Deputy Sheriff Antonio Valdes told the worried young woman clutching a shawl around her shoulders. They stood in the front doorway of her small adobe house. Valdes wore a dark suit, his badge pinned to his vest. The sheriff of San Miguel County and his deputies all wore suits and ties.

"*Gracias,*" Teresa Analla said, wiping tears from her eyes.

Valdes felt sorry for her. She looked like she had been crying for hours.

"But," he said, "if he is causing trouble again, I will have to lock him in jail and take him before a judge in the morning. He may well order your husband to post bond."

"We have no money for that!" she said, the worry in her voice rising.

"Then he will have to stay in jail for as long as the judge decides," Valdes said.

"*¡Bueno!*" came a loud voice from inside the house.

Valdes saw another woman come up behind Teresa. She wore a black dress, her graying hair pulled tightly back.

"*Mamá*, no!" Teresa said, drawing her shawl tighter.

The old woman gave her daughter a stern look. "You know where he is. He is out drinking and gambling and more, just like he has done every night since he came back." She turned to Valdes. "It is always the same. He is gone for weeks, comes back, and leaves again. And when he is here, he takes the money my daughter makes from washing clothes and spends it on himself. That is not a man."

"Don't say that, *Mamá*!"

"He is no good," the old woman snapped and went back into the house.

Teresa burst into tears and shut the door.

Turning away, Deputy Valdes shook his head. He heard the old woman inside the house tell her daughter to bolt the door and help her bar the windows. Lots of folks had taken to locking their doors and windows at night now. Ever since this wolf business started, folks were scared.

Almost without thinking, Valdes pulled his revolver part way out of his holster, making certain it came out easy. He looked up and down the narrow street, listening closely, and wished the sheriff would get back to town.

Placing his boot in the stirrup, he climbed onto his dun horse and took out his pocket watch. The hands read a quarter past twelve. Another long day. He thought about going home, but there was no need. His wife, Maria, and their four children were away visiting her father in Albuquerque. They would be there for at least a month.

He is no good. Valdes knew that his father-in-law was telling Maria that very thing every single day. That old man never approved of him. Thought his daughter could have done much better than a deputy sheriff. A judge maybe. Or a wealthy landowner. Someone important. Someone distinguished. It made no difference that Valdes was a hard worker and a good Catholic, or that as a boy his parents sent him to the Christian Brothers in Santa Fe so he could learn to speak proper English. The New Mexico Territory was part of the United States, and his parents believed it would be to his advantage to know the language of the Americans. "To better fit in. *Es muy importante,*" they told him. But that old man did not care about any of that. Not at all.

14

Valdes grunted, taking solace in the knowledge that some day soon, maybe very soon, the old man would fall over dead, and that would be the end of it.

Antonio Valdes enjoyed being a lawman. He had been sworn in as a deputy sheriff for the county when he turned twenty — fourteen years ago. And in that time the town had changed considerably.

The telephone had come to Las Vegas, first town in the territory to have them. The wires attached to tall poles stretched from the telephone exchange building at the end of town out along nearly every street. The jail had one. And, once it was finished, the new courthouse they were building across from the jail would, as well. Of course, Doctor Burwell had one in his home. Most of the hotels and shops had them. Even all the way out to the Montezuma Hotel at the hot springs.

There was electricity, too, for those who could afford it. Some businesses had it, including a few big homes. At his house, Valdes still used reliable tallow candles.

Telephones and electricity in Las Vegas was on account of the railroad. The Atchison, Topeka and Santa Fe had brought some good things, and some bad. Like the swarm of thieves, thugs, fakirs, bunco-steerers, and

15

other scoundrels who had descended on the town almost overnight. Vigilance committees threatened to hang them, but Sheriff Romero usually succeeded in calming things down. He was a respected man because he was a fair man. The law was the law, and that was what he ran on in the last election. And he expected his deputies to enforce the law no matter what color or creed a miscreant was.

Dedication to the law was why the sheriff was away in Ohio. He had gone there to bring back a fugitive from justice, wanted for murder. Before he left, he put Deputy Valdes in charge.

Valdes reached the end of the street when a noise made him pull his revolver.

"Don't shoot!" someone called out.

"Who is there?" Valdes said, seeing movement in the shadows. *"¿Quién es?"*

"Amigos. Jim Hobbs and Manuel Serrano."

"Come out," Valdes said, motioning to them with his revolver. The sheriff had instructed his deputies it was always best to be cautious until you were certain.

The two men came into the moonlight, holding their rifles, barrels pointed down. They were part of a citizens committee recently organized to protect the town.

"We can't be too careful these days, can we, Antonio?" Hobbs said.

Valdes chuckled, holstering his revolver. "*Sí, es verdad.* Any sign of the wolf?"

"Nothing," Hobbs said.

"This *lobo* is very smart," Serrano said, swinging his rifle barrel up onto his shoulder. "He keeps away from the traps. Like he knows what they are."

The long howl of a wolf rose off in the distance, and Valdes quickly pulled his revolver as all three men spun around, their guns pointed toward the mournful sound.

"Too far away," Valdes said.

"Might not even be the one we're hunting," Hobbs said.

"Maybe," Serrano said.

Valdes slipped his gun back inside the holster. God, how he wished the sheriff would get back to town.

As Hobbs and Serrano went back to their patrolling duties, Valdes reined his horse around and headed for the jail.

A large, wide wooden building, the county jail sat a block away from Our Lady of Sorrows church, and beyond it was the plaza. Valdes was glad the plaza seemed fairly quiet this night. No sounds of rowdiness. Plenty of places were closing early on account of this wolf business. Not the saloons, though.

Climbing down off his horse, he heard Deputy Cleofus Silva call his name and turned to see him riding up fast.

"There has been another one," Silva said, reining in his horse. Silva held a shotgun in one hand.

"*Madre de Dios.* Do you know who it is?"

He ran his hand over his heavy black moustache. "Jess Culpepper."

"Shakespeare Jess?"

Silva nodded. "Sam is there keeping watch. We will need the wagon. *¿Si?*"

Valdes agreed. The flat bed wagon was around behind the jail. First he would help Silva hitch a team to the wagon, then get on the telephone to Doc to let him know they were coming.

Valdes pulled the wagon to a stop at the alley entrance where Sam Cuddy waited, a lantern in hand. The yellow glow of that lantern cast the only light on the quiet street. The saloon across the way had locked its doors a good hour ago.

"Sure am glad you're here," the wiry-haired deputy said, a look of relief spreading across his weathered face.

Silva tethered his horse to the post where

Cuddy's horse was also tied.

"Tell me what happened," Valdes said, jumping down from the wagon.

"I was making my rounds, and I seen a fellow pissing by the alley," Cuddy said. "He claimed somebody robbed him and busted a couple of his teeth. But I smelled the liquor on him and was about to arrest him for public drunkenness. That's when I saw a pair of boots sticking out from the shadows. Figured I better have a look." He wagged his head. "Ugliest thing I've ever seen. I found an old tarp back in the alley there and threw it over him. Keep anybody else from seeing him. Including me."

Valdes took the lantern from Cuddy, squatted down, and lifted the tarp.

"See, like them other two," Cuddy said. "Got to be one big damn wolf, all I can say."

"I thought there would be more blood," Silva said, standing behind them.

Valdes dropped the tarp and handed the lantern back to Cuddy. "What about that drunk? Did he see anything? Hear anything?"

Cuddy snorted. "He didn't even know there was a body lying where he was pissing. Could barely walk. I told him to git and sober up." Cuddy reached into his trouser pocket. "Here's all the money Jess had on him. A hundred and fifty-four dollars. Can't say I'm sorry Jess is gone. But dying like this just ain't right, even for a mangy scoundrel son of a bitch like him."

Silva grunted his agreement.

Valdes took the greenbacks and the few coins. He figured there was enough to cover Shakespeare Jess's burial and Doc Burwell's fee with some left over to buy blankets and other supplies for the jail.

"You did fine, Sam," Valdes said and asked him to help him get Jess in the wagon so he could get him over to Doc's place.

"You want me to come with you?" Silva asked as the three of them lifted the tarp-covered body onto the flat bed.

"No. You two go and get some sleep. I will see you in the morning."

Climbing up on the wagon seat, he heard Cuddy say, "I don't believe I can sleep, not after seeing that."

CHAPTER THREE

As he drove the flat bed around behind Doc's house, Valdes saw Doc waiting in the light of the open rear door. Near fifty years of age, Doctor Nathan Burwell had thinning hair, though his side-whiskers were bushy and flecked with gray.

Climbing into the bed, Valdes pulled the tarp off the body of Shakespeare Jess. Doc took hold of his feet while Valdes gripped Jess under his arms, and they carried him into the house.

Valdes turned his head to watch where he was going as he was walking backwards down the hallway. Just as well. He did not care to see Shakespeare's wounds and the blood soaked front of his shirt anymore than need be.

They laid the body on the table in the examination room. Doc rolled up his sleeves while Valdes told him what Deputy Cuddy had said about finding the body.

Slipping on his spectacles, Doc examined the wounds.

"Same as the first two," he said. "The throat is torn out, nearly down to the spine. Something ripped it out. Used its teeth. You can see bite marks on the skin here. Something else I better check."

Doc pushed up one of Shakespeare's shirtsleeves. Valdes felt certain about what he would find. But it did not make him any less uneasy.

His face grim, Doc took a scalpel from a tray next to the table and made an incision across Shakespeare's exposed wrist.

"I swear," he said, "I saw my share of men maimed in the war, but this . . . I've never seen anything like it in my life. Just like the other two." Doc peered closely at what remained of Shakespeare's neck. "A wound like this, he was dead within moments. How was he lying when you found him? On his back?"

Valdes nodded.

"Help me roll him over," Doc said.

Valdes did as Doc asked and watched as he pulled up the back of Shakespeare's shirt and then yanked his trousers down some.

"Blood ought to have pooled in his back and his buttocks." He removed his spectacles. "I just don't understand. First it was animals found torn up like this and now three men."

Valdes heaved a sigh. "I wish the sheriff would get back."

"It's been a good two weeks now, hasn't it?"

"Fifteen days. He sent a telegram yesterday. A lawyer got a judge to hold up Ennis Kinsall's extradition. I am glad I do not live in Ohio."

"Any word from Brodie or Linares?"

"No," Valdes said. Linares and Brodie were two other deputies, but they were away collecting taxes. Riding the circuit around the county, they were not expected back for another week, at least.

Reaching into his pocket, Valdes took out the greenbacks and counted a hundred dollars onto the table.

"What's that for?" Doc asked.

"This should cover your fee, and his burial expenses," Valdes said. "I kept some for expenses, for the jail. It was Shakespeare's money."

"Oh. Well, I'll see to it," Doc said, rubbing the bridge of his nose. "When the reporters come asking, we still tell them it was a wolf attack, like the first two?"

"We have to. What else can we say?"

Doc grunted. "Saw Isadore Stern the

other day. Said he's sold every trap he had in his store. Charlie Ilfeld says he's sold out, too."

Valdes nodded.

"And some folks already left town," Doc said. "Mrs. Maxwell over at the Summer House says she's had more than a dozen guests leave."

"It is the same at all the hotels in town."

Doc sniffed. "Molly Brennan left, too."

Valdes stared at him. "When?"

"About a week ago."

"That will look bad for the Montezuma."

"I tried to talk her out of it. She came by on her way to the train depot, bags in hand. Said she was real sorry but she couldn't stay here any longer and was going back home. She also said some of the hotel guests had packed up and left after they heard about that first attack."

"But nothing has happened at the Montezuma."

"That's what I told her. But she said people were still scared, and so was she. I sent wires out, but it won't be easy getting a new nurse for the hotel, let alone one that can care for the consumptives staying there. Not when they hear about these wolf attacks." Doc gazed down at the floor.

"*Sí, sí.*" Valdes scratched his forehead

absently. "What we do not want is for people to panic. If word gets out the bodies had —" Valdes saw the look on Doc's face. "Do not tell me you told someone."

"I had to." He pulled a tobacco pouch and paper from his pocket.

"Who?"

"Mrs. Harvey."

"*Dios mio.* Why did you have to tell her?"

"Because I'm the hotel doctor, and she asked me," he said, trying to roll a cigarette in his shaking hands. "I had to tell her. You know that."

Of course, Valdes knew. Sally Harvey was the wife of Fred Harvey. And just about everybody west of the Mississippi had heard of him. He had a string of restaurants called Harvey Houses along the Atchison, Topeka and Santa Fe rail line. Fred Harvey also managed a handful of big hotels for the railroad. One of them was the Montezuma, and it was said to be the biggest. Mr. Harvey and the railroad had a lot invested in the Montezuma. Just like they had in the first Montezuma Hotel, and it was still a topic of discussion, burning down like it did over a year ago. Valdes remembered it well. That fire turned the whole sky orange. And now, with so much at risk on the new Montezuma, word was Mr. Harvey had come down with a bad case of nerves. Doc had heard it was so bad, Mr. Harvey's own doctor had advised him to take a long ocean voyage. The timing could not have been worse. Promoting the new hotel was paramount. With Mr. Harvey away, Mrs. Harvey had brought their five children to stay there for the summer to do the promoting for him. So if Mrs. Harvey asked a question, it was pretty much the same as if Mr. Harvey was asking.

"All right, then," Valdes said. "What did you say to her?"

Doc struck a Lucifer and lit his sad-looking cigarette. "I told her they were wolf attacks, just like what we've been saying. And then she looked me in the eye and said she could tell there was something I wasn't telling her." He shrugged. "That's when I told her about the blood."

"And what did she say?"

"She was worried, but not for herself. Said it was for her children and the hotel guests and employees. She wanted to know what steps you were taking, and I told her about the patrols and the wolf traps. She also asked if I knew what the cause of this was."

"And?"

"I told her the truth. I don't know."

"And she is not scared?"

26

"If she is, she's hiding it. She said she had to do what she thought best, and if she took the children and left the Montezuma, it could ruin everything. She decided staying inside at night was probably the best protection. That's what everybody there has been doing, she said, guests and employees alike."

"Good. That is very good," Valdes said.

"Believe me, Mrs. Harvey doesn't want word of this getting out any more than we do."

Chapter Four

"We need your help, Hattie," the bearded man said.

"It's an unusual case," the clean-shaven man added.

Hattie Lawton showed the two Pinkerton brothers into the parlor of her modest row house off Union Square in the city of Baltimore. They had sent word they wanted to see her and arrived promptly at six o'clock on this hot July evening. Crossing the room to the settee, the taller, clean-shaven brother brushed his head against the pull-chain pendant hanging from the chandelier. The light from the shaded gas flame illuminated the parlor with a pleasant glow.

Hattie asked if they cared for something to drink. The bearded one said water, the other, whiskey.

William had a full beard but no moustache, like his father. His younger brother, Robert, favored his mother's looks. Both men, though, were as astute and strong-willed as their late father, Allan Pinkerton, who had created the Pinkerton Detective Agency.

Hattie had worked as a detective for Mr. Pinkerton for nearly twenty years, until her son, Tim, took ill. The last time she had seen the brothers was at Tim's funeral almost a year ago. They had been most solicitous about her welfare, and she was grateful they had come, as the distance was far for them to travel. Robert ran the New York office of the agency while William had taken charge of the Chicago branch. And now they were here again, but this time asking for her help. An unusual case, Robert had said. The prospect of returning to detective work was more than tempting. After her son, it was what she loved most. But it had been almost three years since her last case. And the Pinkerton brothers knew that.

She sat on an upholstered parlor chair across from them.

"We received a letter," William said. "From Sally Harvey, the wife of Fred Harvey."

"*The* Fred Harvey?" Hattie asked.

"The Harvey House man himself," Robert said.

"Both he and his wife were good friends

of our father," William said. "Mrs. Harvey has requested our services."

"And where is Mr. Harvey?"

"A sea voyage," William said. "Doctor's orders."

"I'm listening." Hattie pushed a loose strand of her long, dark-auburn hair behind her ear.

"Something is happening around the town of Las Vegas in New Mexico Territory. Not far from Mr. Harvey's hotel."

"The Montezuma," Robert said.

"I read it burned down," Hattie said.

"But they rebuilt it." William set down his glass. "Guaranteed not to burn down. Had its opening just a few months ago."

"A palace, they say," Robert said. "Rooms for three hundred guests. The crown jewel of Mr. Harvey's hotel empire, with every amenity, even the telephone."

William put his hands together. "Some of those guests are there for the salubrious climate the territory affords for those suffering from consumption."

Hattie cast her eyes down.

"My apologies," William said. "It was not my intention to upset you."

She glanced at the framed photograph of her son that stood on the sideboard. The hurt of loss remained. She thanked William and asked him to go on.

"Mrs. Harvey is concerned because people have turned up dead," William said.

Robert cleared his throat. "Three now."

"Consumption patients often die," Hattie said.

"But they weren't consumptives," Robert said.

"And they died of unnatural causes," William said.

"Unnatural?"

"The three men were all found with their throats torn out."

"Sounds like some animal to me," Hattie said. "Maybe a wolf or a mountain lion. Perhaps what Mrs. Harvey needs isn't a detective but a hunter who's a good shot."

"You might think that," William said, "except all the blood was drained from each of the bodies."

Hattie leaned forward. "All the blood?"

William nodded.

"Not natural," Robert said. "That bit of information has been kept quiet."

"But how many people do know about it?" Hattie asked.

"Only the doctor and the deputy," William said.

"The deputy?"

"The sheriff is away in Cincinnati. There

are other deputies, but just the one the sheriff left in charge knows about this. And Mrs. Harvey, of course."

"How did she find out?"

"The doctor for the hotel told her."

"Is the doctor married?" Hattie asked.

"A widower," William said.

"Any children?"

"A married daughter. She and her husband live in California."

"And the deputy?"

"A wife and four children."

Hattie gave the brothers a look. "And he hasn't told them?"

William picked up his glass. "Our understanding is they have been out of town for several weeks and know nothing of this situation."

"How many people live in the town?" Hattie asked.

"Around two thousand."

"I'm surprised the deputy and the doctor and Mrs. Harvey have been able to keep this blood business quiet," she said. "Does this town have a newspaper?"

"Two," William said. "The *Las Vegas Optic* and the *Daily Gazette.*"

"And what do they say about these deaths?"

"They are calling them wolf attacks," Rob-

32

ert said.

"It seems some animal carcasses have been found in the surrounding countryside, as well," William said.

"All with their necks torn out," Robert added. "Hunters that found them believe they must have bled out from being clawed up and all."

"But it's those people turning up dead that has Mrs. Harvey concerned," William said. "You can appreciate why she chose to send us a letter and not a telegram."

"Tell me about the three victims," Hattie said.

"Mrs. Harvey didn't include those particulars."

"I see."

"Mrs. Harvey feels that if this thing gets any worse, it will scare away the hotel guests. She says the Montezuma has had enough bad publicity what with the fire."

"Is Mrs. Harvey currently at the hotel?"

William nodded. "She and her children are spending the remainder of the summer there."

"Prove to folks the hotel is safe to stay in," Robert said.

Hattie frowned. "She's aware of these killings and still wants to stay?"

"She insists," William said.

"That is devotion," Hattie said, but she could not help wondering about the strange business of the bodies drained of blood.

"I should tell you," William said, "we have no other operatives available at this time to assist you with this case, should you accept. But we hope to have one soon."

"Perhaps two weeks." Robert drained his glass. "Maybe longer."

"The guests at the hotel are, for the most part, of the wealthy class." William spread his hands. "That includes the consumptives staying there, as well. Mrs. Harvey also mentioned the nurse caring for them recently left. A new nurse has yet to be found to take her place."

Now Hattie understood why they came to her. It made sense. "You want me to pose as a nurse?"

"Yes. I do not wish to appear indelicate, Hattie, but you have the experience, as you cared for your son."

"You are not indelicate. Go on."

"The consumptives would be your main responsibility. You would be working with the doctor. His name is Burwell. You wouldn't arouse suspicion. You could move freely. Should anything happen at the hotel, your instincts, your skills would be invaluable."

Robert nodded. "Father always said women were the best operatives. He also said you were the best he'd ever seen. The most driven."

She recalled it a bit differently but said nothing. In truth, it was she who told Mr. Pinkerton that women made the best operatives. Men were too easily manipulated and distracted, which made them dangerous. Women were much smarter in that regard, more refined and more heedful. Women had a keen eye for detail, and that made them excellent observers.

William leaned forward. "Will you take this assignment?"

CHAPTER FIVE

Before she departed for New Mexico Territory the next day, Hattie needed to visit her son's grave. Rising early that morning, she went to Green Mount Cemetery. Tim's headstone was made of white marble. His epitaph read: A FINE SON TAKEN TOO SOON.

"I won't be by to see you for a while," she said and placed a small bouquet of flowers in front of the headstone. "The Pinkerton brothers have asked me to work on a case. A very strange one from the sound of it. I look forward to telling you about it."

She missed Tim so. His smile. His laughter. She loved the gleam in his eyes when she told him about cases she worked on and about playing parts, like a fortune-teller, a silk purchaser, a con-woman, and other roles in the service of Mr. Pinkerton, in order to apprehend criminals and wrongdoers. Those exciting exploits made Tim want to join the Pinkertons.

But the one story she had not — could not — tell her son was when he asked about his father, for the truth was laced with shame.

"I wish I'd told you," she whispered. "I should have told you. Before —"

A gentle breeze rustled the leaves of a nearby maple tree.

"You weren't an orphan of the war between the North and the South. I knew who your father was."

She took a deep breath. The long-held words flowed out.

"After the South took up arms against the North," she began, "President Lincoln ordered Mr. Pinkerton to gather information about the Confederate operations. Mr. Pinkerton sent Timothy Webster and me to Richmond, Virginia, the new capital of the Confederacy. Timothy was a fine detective and had a wife and family. We posed as a wealthy married couple. Ingratiating ourselves into Richmond society, we soon heard all about Confederate plans and strategies. We relayed them back to Mr. Pinkerton by a special courier who carried our messages in the hollowed out handle of a riding crop.

"Some months later we were found out, charged as spies, and thrown into Castle

37

Godwin, a hellhole prison. I was sentenced to one-year imprisonment, but they decided to make an example of Timothy. They hanged him in the early hours of April 29, 1862. A Richmond newspaper reported that it was a glorious spring morning.

"Until that day, I had refused to give up hope, for I was carrying Timothy's child. You, my son. You see, Timothy was devoted to his wife and family, but he and I had fallen in love. And . . . and I never told Timothy about you. It would have only made things more difficult.

"You were born in that terrible place. I named you Augustus, after my father, and gave you the middle name Timothy. Why I always called you Tim.

"On my release, I carried you out of there and was escorted to the Union lines. Mr. Pinkerton was understandably surprised to see me with a baby in my arms. To avoid the scandal the truth would have created, I said that another female prisoner in the cell next to mine had given birth to the child, and she'd died shortly thereafter. I told Mr. Pinkerton I'd promised the poor woman I'd care for her child, and that I told the prison commandant I would not break my promise to a dying woman. I said the child's mother had named him."

She wiped her eyes and smiled.

"You had your father's eyes and curly hair. And a strong temperament, a trait I know you inherited from both of us.

"I raised you by myself the first year. After that, I told Mr. Pinkerton I was ready to resume my duties with the agency. I engaged a nurse to care for you while I was away on assignments.

"And then, on a summer day not long after your nineteenth birthday, a dry cough commenced deep in your lungs. Fevers followed. You started losing weight and spitting up blood. Consumption, the doctor said. There was no cure. I took leave from the agency to care for you.

"Some doctors were convinced the smoke and soot of large cities, like Baltimore where we were living, were the cause of the illness. They said go to the dry outdoors of Florida or Colorado or the New Mexico Territory.

"Then word came about Doctor Edward Trudeau's sanatorium in the Adirondack Mountains. It was just a few small cottages he built for consumptive patients. Red cottages he called them.

"When we got there, he assured us that this disease could be stopped. Said he was proof, having contracted the malady a decade before but regained his health after devising his own cure. He started you on a regimen of exercise and a healthy diet of beef, fresh vegetables, and fruits. I did my best seeing to your comfort and assisting with nursing duties. Scrubbing your room each day, changing your bed sheets, treating your fevers. And we took daily walks. Short ones at first.

"Do you remember a snowfall one day that precluded our walk? You called me over to the window. Near the trees, two wolves cavorted in the snow in the early light. Neither of us had ever seen such a thing. You said it was like they were dancing. Those wolves soon ran off, and you wanted to go out and see where they'd been. I couldn't recall the last time I had seen you so excited. You marveled at all the paw prints in the snow.

"You did so well for a time, then everything changed. One afternoon you looked at me and . . . and your voice was so small. You said to me, 'You miss it, don't you?' I didn't know what you were talking about. And you said, 'The pursuit. You need it. Like the air in your lungs, the blood in your veins.' I told you all I needed was for you to get better.

"Then you took a breath and said, 'Remember what you told me your mother said? Some are born to do great things, and . . . and some to undertake unsavory tasks. Promise me, after I'm . . .' "

She placed her hand on the headstone.

"Those were the last words you ever spoke. I've never forgotten them. My tears fell on your sweet face. I asked God to take you into the comfort and care of His arms."

Reaching down, she touched her son's name.

"I can't say when I'll be back, Tim, but I'm certain you approve of my going. There are unsavory tasks to undertake."

CHAPTER SIX

Hattie departed that afternoon from the Baltimore train depot. Strapped to her leg above her knee was her Forehand and Wadsworth "Swamp Angel" revolver. The .41-caliber, five-shot revolver had been a gift from Mr. Pinkerton.

Inside her scuffed brown travel bag she carried a coat, two gray cotton dresses for her nursing duties, and two other dresses for wearing into town and Sunday services. Keeping the proper appearance was crucial for "Sarah Andrews," the name she'd chosen for her cover. Widowed with no children, Sarah Andrews had worked as a nurse for eighteen years, the last three with patients suffering from consumption. The Pinkerton brothers had approved of her name and background.

Also in her bag was a telegram she had received from Doctor Burwell in Las Vegas. She had sent him a telegram shortly after her meeting with the Pinkerton brothers. It read: *Understand you have need for nurse. Have experience caring for consumptives. Worked with Dr. Ed. Trudeau at his red cottages sanatorium in New York. Will leave immediately on your acceptance.*

His brief response had arrived that morning: *Come at once.*

If Doctor Burwell had already hired a nurse, Hattie told the Pinkerton brothers, she was prepared to journey west, register at the Montezuma Hotel as a guest and begin her investigation.

Hattie was also aware the brothers had sent Mrs. Harvey a telegram stating simply: *All is well.* It was how they let her know they had accepted the case. That was Pinkerton procedure.

For Hattie, though, the most important aspect of this operation was that no one — not Doctor Burwell, not the deputy, not even Sally Harvey — knew her true identity. That, too, was Pinkerton procedure. The reason, as Hattie and other operatives with the agency knew well, was because no one could keep a secret.

Sitting in a seat in the rear of the passenger car, Hattie opened an envelope the brothers had given her. It held a single handwritten page containing all the information they had about her destination. She was headed to a place eighteen hundred miles away and about six thousand five hundred feet above sea level. The air was dry and pure there, the climate comfortable. The Montezuma Hotel was famous for its hot springs and their curative effects for asthma, paralysis, St. Vitus dance, nervous afflictions, strictures, old sores, ulcers, ague, and skin and blood diseases. Only cases of cancer, heart disease, and consumption were not, as yet, effectively cured. As for Las Vegas, the report said it was a small Mexican town "until the railroad arrived."

At the bottom of the page was a message written in a different hand that looked very much to her like Robert Pinkerton's. "Be aware," it read, "former New Mexico territorial governor Lew Wallace claims all calculations based on experience elsewhere fail in New Mexico."

Hattie smiled. The challenge was clear. She slipped the report into her bag. The details were few, but it felt good being out again, on a case.

She perused the other passengers, catching bits of conversation. A young couple was on their honeymoon. A salesman sat hunched over his valise, pencil in hand, doing some figuring. Two little girls and their grandmother were on their way to visit cousins in Columbus, Ohio. The girls wore crimson-colored bows in their hair.

The train stopped to take on water at a station in West Virginia. A roadhouse stood close by. The proprietress, a large woman wearing a stained apron, waved a ladle at the passengers, inviting them to come and eat. Roadhouse food usually consisted of meat stew and bread. Hungry, Hattie made her way down the aisle, as did some of the other passengers. She passed the grandmother and her granddaughters, who were enjoying sandwiches they had brought with them. Hattie smiled as she noticed a book lying between the girls. *Grimm's Fairy Tales.* The faded cover illustration was still recognizable. Little Red Riding Hood, holding her basket, looking at the Big Bad Wolf disguised as Red's grandmother sitting up in bed, his sharp teeth bared in a horrid grin.

Two things astonished Hattie as she stepped off the train to stretch her legs when they reached Kansas City. The first was the train depot, a massive building with great stone towers, rows of arched windows across its two stories, topped with a steeply pitched roof adorned with great gabled dormers. She heard someone say it reminded them of the insane asylum back home.

The other startling thing was the summer heat. Over one hundred degrees, a woman complained. And the humidity was thick and stifling. Baltimore was hot and muggy in the summer, too, but nothing like this. The air here was dead still. Even the thin funnels of black smoke from the riverboats on the Missouri River hung motionless against the cloudless sky.

"Get your fans! Only a nickel!" a boy wearing a cap shouted, hawking paper fans.

She purchased one and opened it. It read: "Compliments of Hornbeck's Funeral Parlor."

Inside the depot, water was available. She took a cup and sat down on a bench. A headline on a discarded newspaper caught her attention:

STILL UNSOLVED
A Year to the Day Since the Grisly Murder

The story stated that a young woman had been found dead near the railroad depot, and no leads were forthcoming.

Hattie wanted to know more. She spotted

46

a depot baggage handler wearing a dark coat and black bowtie. He stood off by himself in a nearby corner. Sweat ringed his white collar. He took a drink from the cup he held in his hand.

"Excuse me," Hattie said.

"Yes, ma'am," he said. "We have plenty of free water right over there. Help yourself."

"Thank you, I did, but I have a question. This story in the paper, about the murder. Were you here then? Do you know what happened?"

He hesitated. "Very unpleasant, ma'am. Not an appropriate story, if you get my meaning."

"It's all right. I'm a nurse and can assure you, I've seen dead bodies before."

"Begging your pardon, but I don't know if you've seen anything like this."

"I've seen quite a bit," she said, using her fan to try to cool her face. The heat was just as suffocating inside the depot.

He pulled a pocket watch from his coat and checked it. "Next train's not due for another half an hour yet." He drew his lips tight. "Well, it was a terrible thing, ma'am. Something like that stays with you."

He said a young woman started coming around the depot some nights. She claimed she was waiting for a friend who was com-

47

ing in. About this same time, people began getting robbed.

He took a drink from his cup. "It always seemed to happen whenever she came around."

"What did she look like?"

"Kind of plain looking. She had a job."

"Oh?"

"Worked at Crocker's Print Shop in town. You wouldn't think she was a thief, but she must have tried stealing money from the wrong person."

"You mean whomever killed her."

He nodded gravely. "But there was something strange about it."

"Strange how?"

"When the police came out, the only wounds they found on her were two little holes, right here." He pointed to the side of his neck.

"But that doesn't make any sense. A wound like that wouldn't kill someone."

"That's what I thought."

"What did the police say?"

"They didn't know what killed her, either." The baggage handler walked to the window and pointed out, past where Hattie's train waited for an open spot amid the long coach yard where passenger cars waited for repairs.

"She was found right over there," he said, "behind a stack of rail ties. The station agent had us move those ties out of there fast after the murder. He didn't want folks coming around gawking."

Hattie wondered how thorough an investigation the Kansas City police had conducted. In her experience, few large city police forces, town marshals, or county sheriffs paid much attention to details. They often trampled the scene of a crime, missing or destroying valuable clues.

"How long was the woman out there?" she asked.

"As I recall, they figured maybe two, three days. The wind sort of blew this direction, and that's when somebody got a whiff of that dead smell."

"There must have been some animals gathering around over there. Crows maybe, or dogs. Someone had to notice."

"That was another strange thing."

"What do you mean?"

"Nothing went near her. No dogs or nothing. Yard crews find dead animals from time to time by the tracks, maybe starved or got run over. But that woman, except for those two holes, there wasn't a mark on her. It got me wondering if the dogs and all stayed away because they were scared of something."

Hattie knew there had to be an explanation. Something the baggage handler was unaware of. An injection, perhaps, say of a poison. That might explain the marks on her neck. And a poison might explain the animals staying away. Whoever had killed her may have administered some kind of agent that gave off a scent of some kind.

"There was a rumor going around," the handler said, interrupting her thoughts. "I gave it no credence, you understand. I think someone started it to stir things up."

"What was this rumor?"

He looked around and lowered his voice. "The woman's body had no blood in it."

Hattie kept her surprise to herself. "Well, that would be very strange."

"The way I see it, something like that you'd expect the newspapers to print. Saw nary a word. Of course, the papers in this town aren't worth a tinker's damn, you ask me." His face turned red. "Sorry ma'am. Didn't mean to curse like that. But I put no store in such wild tales."

"Board!" the conductor called from the train.

"That's my train," she said.

Boarding the train she felt a trickle of

sweat make its way down her back. She fanned herself, wishing something could relieve this awful heat.

CHAPTER SEVEN

More than a week had passed since the creature feasted. Craving the nourishment of blood, it could wait no longer. It needed to feed damn quick, and the thought of consuming animal blood was repellent. The creature's hunger had grown into a ravenous need that only human blood could sate.

In the light of the half moon it moved, keeping low, using the cover of trees and bushes as it made its way down the gentle slope, away from the bright lights of the hotel and the people there, all gathered together. It had to find proper prey. Apart. Exposed. Unguarded. Deserving.

Light shone at the livery stable. A short, muscled man slid open the double doors at one end of the long breezeway. He led a bay horse inside.

Drawing closer, the creature heard the sounds of a commotion. The horse snorted. Something was wrong. Yes, this was proper prey. The creature ran its long tongue over its teeth and broke into a run.

Snorting grew louder. The creature sensed the horse's distress.

"Whoa now!" it heard the short man shout.

Coming around a stand of trees, the creature saw into the long breezeway clearly. The short man, his sleeves rolled up, strained to hold the reins of the horse fighting him, trying to pull away, fear white around the animal's eyes. More sounds alerted the creature, the snorting and neighing of other horses in their stalls. More than a dozen stalls lined each side of the breezeway.

"What the hell is wrong with you, horse?" the short man shouted.

The creature charged.

Rearing back, head twisting, the horse jerked the reins from the short man's hands and bolted away.

The creature heard the other horses paw and kick and scream in panic at their confinement.

The short man cursed, staring at his injured palms. The leather reins had sliced them open like a knife blade.

Blood dripped from the short man's hands.

The creature knocked the short man to the ground. Pinned him there. Baring its teeth, the creature sank two fangs into the prey's throat. The prey screamed. Blood gushed into the creature's mouth. Sweet. Warm. The prey's scream turned into a wet gurgle as he tried to fight, legs kicking. The creature felt the prey's fist strike its head. It clamped its jaws tighter to hold the prey down but careful not to rip apart the flesh.

Not yet.

Screams of the horses grew louder. Trying to quiet the horses, to calm them, the creature dragged its prey out of the livery. The prey went still. Blood flowed. Life giving. The creature lapped the blood.

"Somebody get that horse!" a voice called out.

Men were coming. The creature heard the rush of their feet.

Hurry! Drink!

"What's going on in there, Zach? You all right?"

The men were almost here.

No more time! No time!

"Zach!"

The creature took another deep swallow of the still-flowing blood, and with its jaws still clamped around the prey's neck, raised its head and looked toward the direction of the voice.

A big man with a long face and close-cropped white hair stood stone still at the opposite end of the breezeway, his mouth hanging open.

"God have mercy," the big man whispered.

Ripping the flesh from the prey's throat, the creature turned and ran into the darkness. It made for the stand of trees and, willing the change, in that very instant, the creature's shape shifted, becoming much smaller, more agile. Spreading its black wings, it flew up over the tops of the trees, disappearing into the darkness, leaving no trail to follow.

CHAPTER EIGHT

Hattie woke the morning of the sixth day of her travels to a wondrous sight. The conductor told her they were called the Sangre de Cristo Mountains.

"It means Blood of Christ in English," he said. "And when you see them at sunset, you'll understand why those Spanish named them such."

After the monotony of the flatlands of Kansas, the red mountains proved a tonic to Hattie. And she would reach her destination in a few hours, a town sitting at the foot of those beautiful mountains.

"Fifth killing! Get your paper here!" shouted the boy in a squeaky voice.

Hattie could not see the young hawker as she stepped off the train at the Las Vegas depot, for the platform was crowded with people anxious to board. She thought it a grim greeting, as it meant two more killings here since she'd left Baltimore almost a week ago. She reminded herself that no case was ever easy.

"A mad dog is on the loose," a man said.

"I heard it was a wolf," someone answered.

"Scandalous is what it is."

Her bag in hand, Hattie stood on her toes to try to see past the heads and hats of the crowd when a harried-looking conductor appeared.

"Please," she said, "can you tell me how I can get to the Montezuma Hotel?"

He pointed but kept moving. "Spur line. End of the platform. Train'll be along shortly."

Hattie turned and found herself face to face with a haughty-looking older woman in a feathered hat.

"If you're stopping here," she said to Hattie, "I urge you to get back on the train. This is no place for a decent woman, or anyone else."

Hattie asked her what had happened.

"Haven't you heard? A man was killed here last night," she said. "A horrid thing."

"I meant where did this happen?" Hattie asked. "Was it in the town?"

"At the hotel."

"Which hotel?"

"The Montezuma."

57

A man wearing a frock coat and tall hat came up beside the woman.

"Thank heavens you're back, Hiram," the woman said with relief. "Tell me you have our tickets."

"Of course, Mother," he said.

"I was just telling this good woman she should leave immediately."

Hattie looked at Hiram. "She said a man was killed at the Montezuma Hotel."

"Yes," he said. "A stable man at the livery. Ghastly."

"Mark my words, dear," the old woman said to Hattie. "No one is safe around here. This place is cursed."

A conductor announced the train for Trinidad, La Junta, Dodge City, and other points east was ready to board.

"At last," the woman said as she moved toward the passenger car. "We're going back to Philadelphia where it's civilized."

The spur line train arrived fifteen minutes later. Boarding a passenger car, Hattie asked the conductor how far it was to the Montezuma Hotel.

"Six miles, ma'am," he said.

The car was less than half full. Talk of this latest wolf attack drifted through the car, and Hattie could not help noticing the

58

young woman wearing a blue dress, sitting in front of her with her two children and her husband, checking nervously out the windows. Hattie, however, paid the talk no mind. Until she spoke to Doctor Burwell, the deputy, and maybe even some witnesses, if any, it was all speculation and rumor.

The spur line travelled through the middle of the town, following a river called the Gallinas. That was Spanish for chickens, a plump, pink-cheeked man in a bowler hat sitting across the aisle said. He was on his way to the Montezuma to avail himself of the hot springs.

"Those springs have worked wonders for my lumbago," he said. "Came here the first time five years ago. Been coming every year since. Made me feel like I was a young man again." He flicked ashes off his cigar.

"Look! They have telephone lines here just like home," the boy exclaimed.

"Those aren't telephone lines," his father said. "It's the telegraph."

"I hate to contradict you, sir," the pink-cheeked man said, "but your boy is correct. Las Vegas is the first town in the territory to have them. You can see the poles there along the river. They run all the way up the Montezuma."

Hattie remembered the Pinkerton broth-

59

ers telling her about the telephone service. But the information they had given in their report regarding Las Vegas had been sketchy at best. She counted several church steeples and numerous shops, like a grocery, tobacconist, and hat maker on this side of the river. Many houses built in the popular Queen Anne style — with their pitched roofs, sharp gables, long porches, and tall chimneys — lined the streets.

But across the river she saw squat brown buildings with flat rooftops and short chimneys. Some had words painted on them she did not recognize. Cantina. La Fonda. Yet, a handful of places further away amid the low dwellings stood three stories high. They had rows of tall windows, and words painted on the sides in English in bold letters too big to miss. One proclaimed: CHAS. ILFELD DRY GOODS.

"You're wondering about the town," the pink-cheeked man said.

"I am," Hattie said.

"This New Mexico is a peculiar territory, I'll give you that," he said. "You see, when the railroad came, they laid their tracks and built the depot on this side of the river. But the town sat over there on the other side of the Gallinas. But the railroad wasn't worried.

"Being situated on the Santa Fe Trail, Las Vegas has been a stopping place for traders and merchants for many a year. And the railroad brought a lot more folks a lot quicker from the East, and some, well, they didn't like what they saw across the river. My wife, rest her soul, said it looked like a bunch of hovels dropped on cow paths passing for streets. She wasn't far wrong." He snorted. "Those folks who decided to stay built their own town here on this side. Homes, churches, and shops like they knew back East. Called it New Town, and the Mexican side over there, that's Old Town."

"But that big dry goods store is over on that side," Hattie said. "And other places, too."

"My father used to say business is where you find it. This is a good town." He lowered his voice. "But it'll be better when they get this wolf business settled."

Once past the town, she saw timbered mountains, as well as scattered swaths of verdant green grasses.

The two children in front of her stood at the window, enticed by what they saw.

"What are those?" the boy asked pointing at the twisted gray trees scattered on the hillsides.

"Those are called cedars," the pink-cheeked man replied. "And you see those thick silvery colored bushes? They call them rabbit bushes."

"Why do they call them that?" the boy asked.

"Rabbits hide under them in the daytime so hawks can't get them. And in the fall, those rabbit bushes get a bright golden blossom all over them."

"Do they really?" asked the little girl.

"Indeed they do. When the Spanish came up from Mexico, they thought gold grew wild here."

The pink-cheeked man gave a knowing smile to the children's father and others sitting nearby. Hattie enjoyed the man's little fib and smiled at the wide-eyed expressions on the children's faces. Their mother, however, continued to fidget.

The train pushed slowly into the mountains. Tall pine trees overtook the cedars. Hattie found the scent in the air as sublime as it was cool and refreshing.

Rounding a bend, she heard a gasp behind her and, looking out the window, saw the reason for it.

Across the way, a most daunting and unexpected sight rose like some great stone castle from a fairy tale she recalled hearing as a child. The Montezuma Hotel stood upon a hillock. Mountains and canyons surrounded it on three sides. A great five-story tower capped by a grand bell-shaped turret rose majestically above the hotel at one end. The sun caught the turret's silvery color, dazzling to the eye. Extending away from the tower was a long façade three stories tall lined with the windows of the guest rooms with a smaller tower fixed to the other end of the façade. A covered porch ran the entire length of the first floor and appeared to extend on around the main tower. The red sandstone walls gleamed. So breathtaking, it was almost too much to try to take in all at once.

"Magnificent," someone said as the train came to a stop at the hotel depot.

"I had no idea."

"I see the telephone lines. But what about the electricity?"

"Comes from a pump house down by the river here, I believe," Hattie heard the pink-cheeked man say. "You get outside you'll see the chimney down the way. Can't miss it. It's a hundred feet tall."

A line of carriages waited to take guests to the hotel. The conductor announced that guests' luggage would follow shortly. Handlers began unloading trunks and bags onto wagon beds.

Hattie stepped into the aisle. The woman in the blue dress appeared more nervous than ever.

"Come along, darling," her husband said.

The woman sighed. "All right, children. Take my hands, and do not let go."

CHAPTER NINE

"Welcome to the Montezuma Hotel," the driver with the big shoulders and arms like anvils said to Hattie. Taking hold of her hand, he helped her into the carriage. His palm felt rough and callused, his grip firm. Deep creases lined his long face, and most of his close-cropped hair was white. He wore a crisp white shirt and black bowtie. All the drivers did.

"I can put your bag in the back here if you'd like, ma'am," he said.

"Thank you, I'll hold on to it."

Hattie raised her hand to shield her eyes, for the sun was quite bright. Now she wished she had brought a hat.

Other carriages had already left the depot. Hattie saw they followed a wide path along the edge of the flat open grounds that were covered in bluegrass toward the hotel, better than a hundred yards away. In the center of the grounds a fancy fountain balanced on a mound of black rocks sprayed water high into the air. Scattered along the pathway were pergolas and, underneath them, benches. A fenced square lay ahead. Inside it were ponies and lambs and baby goats, like a little zoo for children. But, aside from the line of carriages and these animals, the grounds were deserted.

As the driver adjusted his hat and climbed into the driver's seat, he said, "The Montezuma is America's great resort for health, pleasure, and rest. Our hot springs are famous. Cure most everything. There's near forty springs situated around the grounds. We also have a bathhouse, if you prefer, over yonder there."

He pointed at the red stone building far off to the left on a rise halfway between the depot and the hotel.

"Did I mention that Kit Carson himself came here to avail himself of the springs many years ago?"

"You didn't, but that's interesting," Hattie said.

He grunted and looked back over his shoulder. "I hope I'm not boring you, ma'am."

She shook her head.

He snapped the reins. The sorrel mare nickered, and the carriage clattered across the wooden bridge over the river and onto the pathway leading to the flat bluegrass-covered grounds.

"This area here is what we call the terrace," the driver said. "Nice for taking walks in the cool of the day. The hotel wants guests to know what amenities are available, and they feel this little ride we have to take is as good a time as any to tell you about them. Of course, any other day there'd be guests out here taking those walks, enjoying themselves, playing croquet or what have you."

Hattie noted that he had pronounced the *t* in croquet.

"But this wolf business has . . ." He paused. "Well, folks don't want to wander too far from the hotel. Speaking of which, the hotel also wishes to apologize for any inconvenience you may have had when you arrived in town."

"I appreciate that," Hattie said. "There were a lot of people at the depot anxious to leave."

"This wolf business has created a lot of trouble."

"I'm sorry I wasn't here when it happened."

"Ma'am?"

"I'm the new nurse for the hotel. Sarah

Andrews."

"Oh, for the lungers."

"If you're referring to the consumptives, yes."

"Yes, ma'am, but you ought to know the ones come here call themselves lungers. They even formed a club. Call it the Lungers Club."

"Did they?"

"Started a few years back. But I'm glad to know you, ma'am. Name's Marmaduke Pennick. But call me Duke. Everybody does."

"Thank you. I was about to say I might have been able to offer help to the injured man."

"I can tell you for certain, ma'am, Zach Barrow was well past needing a nurse."

"Could you tell me what happened to Mr. Barrow?"

"Tell you? I was the one saw it. Happened up at the livery there." He jutted his chin at the long building closest to the hotel. A cupola sat atop the roof. "I was going in last night to see things were in order before closing up. One of the horses come running out like the place was on fire. I ran inside, and there's the biggest wolf I've ever seen. It had Zach down just outside the other end of the livery." He shook his head. "Wolf was at his neck."

"It must have been a terrible shock."

"Yes, ma'am. This wolf, it raised its head and looked right at me. Something about its eyes stopped me cold. I thought it was going to come at me when, all of sudden, it ran off. The horses in the stalls were scared real bad, pawing and kicking. That's when I got my voice and gave a holler. The other stable men came running. But Zach was dead as could be. And that wolf? I hope I never see it again."

"So Mr. Barrow was alone?" Hattie asked as they followed the pathway around the water fountain. Mist from the spray brushed her face.

Duke nodded. "Since you're working here, I'll tell you something. With all that's going on, I carry this, in case." He reached down and brought up a Bowie knife. The vicious-looking clip-point blade was over a foot long and a good two inches wide at the base. "That wolf comes at me, I'll make him sorry he tried."

"I believe you would."

"Carried this during the war." He set the knife back down. "It saved my life on more than one occasion."

Hattie knew that many Union and Con-federate soldiers had carried Bowie knives.

So had Missouri bushwhackers and Kansas jayhawkers. Something about Duke Pennick's temperament told Hattie he had likely worn the gray.

He went on. "The hotel, they say they don't want us carrying weapons. No guns or nothing. But I don't care. I figure I can always get another job. But if I'm dead, I can't get another life."

She could not argue with that. "You mentioned something about the eyes of the wolf."

"Red. Like burning coals. I know it makes no sense, but I know what I saw. And that wolf was all black. Black like I've never seen. Don't misunderstand, there's black wolves around here, but not like this one. It was like something come out of hell. Big, too. Big as a man."

His exaggeration was understandable. Red eyes. Big as a man. Hattie felt certain Duke had been startled by what he had seen. And frightened.

"We sent word to the jail," Duke was saying. "A deputy come up. Talking to everybody in sight."

"Where's the body now?"

"Doc Burwell's I reckon. Deputy took it down on the spur train early this morning. Put it in the baggage car. I helped load it.

Some of the guests leaving the hotel didn't like the idea of riding on a train carrying a dead body. Made them uneasy, they said." He snorted. "What did they think Zach was going to do? Rise up like Lazarus and come in and have a little talk with them?"

They started up a gentle slope. The hotel tower loomed above them.

Hattie saw a man standing out on the covered observation deck of the turret. He wore dark glasses. He did not look down.

Duke pulled around into the circular drive at the entrance of the hotel. An impatient looking bunch waited, more guests wanting to depart the resort.

"You'll want to see Mr. Kenton. He's the manager," Duke said as he helped her from the carriage.

Hattie thanked him and glanced up at the observation deck. The man was gone.

CHAPTER TEN

"The Montezuma Hotel welcomes you," the doorman said, greeting Hattie.

From what she observed once inside the busy lobby, half of the people at the front desk wanted to register while the other half clamored to leave.

"Mr. Harvey is going to hear about this!" one man exclaimed.

"How much longer must we wait for our room?" another complained.

The two men working at the front desk did their best to remain composed. Both wore stiff collars and buttoned coats. One had lacquered his hair into place. Using his thumb, he wiped the sheen from his forehead.

Uniformed boys carried luggage for guests departing out of the lobby and then brought the bags belonging to the new guests in.

"The boy will show you to your room," one of the deskman said and handed the room key to the boy.

Pushing a luggage trolley laden with bags, the boy told the guests to follow him.

Deciding to let the crowd thin out, Hattie acquainted herself with the lobby. The polished wood of the floor, pillars, and ceiling shone under the warm glow of the electric lights of the chandeliers and table lamps. Across the lobby from the front desk a massive stone fireplace with intricate carvings dominated the room. A large Persian rug with an ornate design spread across the wooden floor. Plush leather chairs and a settee were strategically placed. Nearby was a grand piano. One wide staircase led to the upper floors. A large window of stained glass faced the landing. Another staircase went down. Both staircases were carpeted in burgundy red. Hattie noticed a printed sign by the stairs going down. It read: We Regret the Bowling Alley Remains Closed.

A bowling alley? The Montezuma was filled with surprises.

A ratcheting sound drew Hattie's attention to the opening of the wrought iron door of the birdcage elevator standing next to the down staircase. Several guests stepped out of the elevator.

"I do wish they'd get that bowling alley finished," one of the guests said. "I was so looking forward to a few games of tenpins."

"If they complete their repairs before we must depart, I would be happy to join you," another said.

"Splendid! You know, we have a bowling alley not far from us in Chicago, but I understand the one here is the only one west of the Mississippi River."

A short hallway on the other side of the front desk led the way to the dining room, but the doors were closed. In an alcove nearby were two wall telephones. Holding the receiver to his ear, a man in a wrinkled suit spoke into the transmitter wanting to know about the next train leaving the Las Vegas depot heading east. A woman lifted the receiver of the other telephone and turned the crank. "Hello?" Hattie heard her say. "Are you there, operator?"

Seeing a lull in the activity in the lobby, Hattie crossed to the front desk. "Could you tell me where I'd find Mr. Kenton?"

"That would be me," sighed the man with the lacquered hair as he finished making a note in the ledger. "How may I help you?"

She no sooner introduced herself as the new nurse than a woman wearing a flowered bonnet butted in, demanding to know when the spur train would be leaving.

"In about an hour, ma'am," Kenton said.

"Carriages will be along to take you down to the depot right outside."

Kenton turned back to Hattie. "I'm sorry. You said your name was Miss Andrews?"

"Sarah Andrews," Hattie said.

"Yes, we heard a new nurse was coming. I'm Millard Kenton. Glad to have you."

"Thank you. Could you tell me, is Doctor Burwell here today?"

"He's due day after tomorrow, I believe. He comes twice a week to check on the lungers. However, you can take the train into town. He doesn't live far from the depot, if you don't mind a little walk."

"That's fine."

"The clerk at the depot can direct you. But let's get you to your room. Service!"

A uniformed boy with a cowlick that refused to obey appeared at the desk.

"Show Miss Andrews to the nurse's quarters," Kenton said, handing him the room key.

The boy offered to take her bag, and she relented. Following the boy, she commented that she was fascinated by the electric lights. He led her past the stairs and elevator and into a reading room off the lobby.

"Let me show you how they work," he said, indicating a square gold plate affixed to the wall by the doorway. There were two buttons, one white and the other black.

"Push the black one," he said.

She did and the lights went off. Trying the white one, the lights came back on.

"That is astonishing," she said.

"The white button is mother of pearl. The black one, I think, is onyx," the boy said.

He led her down a long hallway with guest rooms on each side. From what she could tell, the hotel was constructed in a rough L-shape.

"Looks like I chose a busy day to arrive," Hattie said.

"Yes, ma'am, but this is something else again." He lowered his voice. "Some hotel workers have quit — a few desk clerks, maids, even a couple of bellmen — and we've had forty-four guests leave early, and more this morning on account of that killing at the livery last night. And I heard there's been twenty-seven cancellations."

"That is unfortunate."

"One of the other service boys told me. He picks up the telegrams from the Western Union office."

They entered a vestibule at the end of the hallway where an elegant winding stairway stood. Hattie stopped for a moment to have a look. It rose up three flights.

"They polish the handrails every morning." The boy grinned. "Sure would like to ride down on that railing. Bet it would be fast as lightning."

Turning into another hallway, they stopped at the first door.

"Here it is, Miss Andrews," the boy said and slid the key into the knob.

Going inside, the lights of the hanging chandelier brightened, surprising Hattie. She had not expected to see the glowing flame of gaslights.

"I thought the entire hotel had electric lights," she said.

"Only part of it. The lobby and the reading rooms on the first floor have electric lights. But the dining room has electric lights and gas lights."

"Both electric and gas?"

"That's right. All the rest of the hotel uses gas. The kitchen, the hallways, the guest rooms, the tower, the observation deck." The boy placed her bag on the bed and lowered his voice. "What I heard was they were going to put electric lights every place like they had in the first Montezuma Hotel. But when they were building the hotel, somebody decided it was too unreliable. Electricity, I mean."

"I don't understand."

"Me either. I guess they didn't want to

take the chance this one might burn down, too, on account of electricity. The gas valve for your room is here by the door. The nurse's station, too. The pilot stays lit, so it comes on right away."

It seemed very odd to her that the Pinkerton brothers had not told her about this. They had indicated the hotel was powered solely by electricity. Had they not known? Their father had prided himself on being thorough.

The boy threw open the velvet drapes covering the double windows, revealing an oval courtyard. Hattie spotted a couple of pergolas with vines of purple flowers draped over them, as well. The room had a large bed with an exquisitely carved headboard. All the furnishings were elegant: the desk and chair, dresser, vanity, the leather covered easy chair.

"But no need to worry about a fire in this one," the boy continued. "There's fire plugs and hose reels in every hallway. The plug and reel for this hallway are right across the hall from you. So's the nurse's station. Your room key opens it."

Hattie reached inside her bag, took out a coin, and offered it to him.

The boy smiled but refused. "We both work here. The hotel pays us."

He handed her the key and left. Hattie opened the closet and found several gray dresses hanging there. A couple of full white-bib aprons, each one pressed and folded, sat on a shelf, along with a couple of starched white hats. They would all identify her as the nurse. There was also a simple straw hat with a wide brim. She hoped it would fit, for the sun in this place was quite bright. She tried it on, relieved that it fit well enough.

Across the hall, a sign hung over the door: Nurse's Station. Stepping inside, she turned the gas valve to light the room. Two beds made up with sheets and blankets, a wash-basin, an examination table, and a desk and chair greeted her. In the top drawer of the desk she found a journal kept by the previous nurse. She had logged daily entries showing patients seen, care given, and the like. Hattie decided she'd study that more thoroughly later. Items in the medicine cabinet included bottles of chloroform, diluted carbolic acid, laudanum, and liniment, as well as a sewing kit for catgut sutures, a stethoscope, and towels. While the consumptives were her main responsibility, she knew she would be expected to treat cuts and most aches and pains that might come along while she was here. Her time

79

with her son at the sanatorium in the Adirondacks had prepared her for all those instances.

Two windows faced the mountains in the distance. Between them stood a door. Opening it, she realized this was the side of the hotel with the long veranda she had seen when Duke brought her up from the depot. Several empty chairs were placed on the veranda by the door, a good idea for anyone who might need to wait for her. From here, Hattie could see down to the terrace and the spur depot. Looking across to the right was the livery stable, its double doors wide open.

She had an investigation to make.

Before she reached the open doors of the livery, Hattie could smell the fresh hay. Inside, horse stalls lined both sides of the place, twenty on each side.

"Hello?" she called out.

No one answered.

"Is anyone here?"

Silence greeted her again. The quiet seemed almost eerie. Apprehensive, she began checking each stall by sight. Fresh hay covered the stall floors. A horse snorted. Several horses remained in their stalls.

Duke had said he heard the horses panic. The closer she got to the other end of the breezeway, the more gouges she found in the wood of the stalls. They were all over the inside of them, every wall. Deep gouges. Long scrapes. Like the horses had tried to kick their way out.

She peered down, searching the breezeway. The ground was hard packed. Then she saw the fresh dirt. Using her hands, Hattie began brushing it away, revealing a wide circle of dried blood, soaked into the hard, brown earth. The stablemen probably threw the dirt down to cover it up. Who could blame them?

At the breezeway opening, boot prints and hoofprints were in evidence. But not the prints she wanted to find. Duke said he saw a large, black wolf run away. Maybe it made for that stand of trees.

Wait! There! Outside the livery. A print. Two more here, making for those trees. She followed them maybe ten feet, and then they just stopped, like the wolf had disappeared.

Hattie stepped back and peered down at the few tracks still there. Good God, they were big. Could it be possible? Maybe Duke had not exaggerated as much as she thought —

"Ma'am?"

Startled, she turned and saw Duke, coming out of the livery. "You're here," she said.

"Only because my horse threw a shoe. But you ought not to be here without one of us stablemen around. Wouldn't want you getting hurt."

"After what you said happened here last night, I got curious. Did you see these tracks?"

"What tracks?" He came over, his eyes searching where she pointed. "Look at that. Just like I said. A wolf." He squatted down and placed his hand flat on the ground next to the print. "Every wolf track I ever seen before was no bigger than my hand. And this one, it's better than twice that size. I told you it was big."

Hattie looked about, taking in the scene of the killing.

"Hope I haven't scared you none, ma'am," Duke said, brushing the dirt from his hands.

She gave him a faint smile. "No. I was thinking we don't have anything like this happen back in Baltimore."

"Well, I never been north of the Mason-Dixon line myself. But there was a fellow I knew down Texas way some years back. Heard he killed a bear and was in the midst of skinning it. Had blood all over his clothes when a pack of wolves came on him. They smelled that blood. This fellow killed three of them before the rest got him." Duke blew out a long breath. "Zach Barrow wasn't skinning any critter. He was doing his job. And he didn't bother nobody, either. Good with horses, he was. Wouldn't have hired him if he wasn't."

"I believe you."

Duke shooed a fly away from his face. "Tell you something else. Wolves only do three things. They hunt, eat, and, begging your pardon, ma'am, make baby wolves. When they hunt, they hunt in packs. But this one last night was alone. And from what I could see, he didn't look like he was starved none, either. Just plain vicious. Mean."

The train whistle blew twice. She turned toward the sound.

"You looking to go back to town?" Duke asked.

"I was hoping to see Doctor Burwell."

"Let's get you to the depot, then. I got another horse already hitched up."

CHAPTER ELEVEN

It was the first good news Deputy Valdes had had in weeks. Sitting at the sheriff's desk in the jail office, he read the telegram again to make certain of it. The sheriff was leaving Ohio today with his prisoner and expected to be back in Las Vegas in four days.

¡Bueno! He smiled and placed the telegram in the top drawer of the desk. Inside was a long spear-point knife the sheriff had taken from a big Jicarilla Apache that Valdes had helped him capture a few years ago. That Indian had been stealing horses and cattle from ranchers all over the county. The sheriff kept the knife, saying it could come in handy because you never know when you might need a little extra help with some belligerent lawbreaker.

The jailhouse door opened. Five grim-faced men entered, spoiling Valdes's good spirits. There was Mr. Otero, the round-faced president of the San Miguel National Bank of Las Vegas in his coat and striped trousers, the dry goods store owner, Charles Ilfeld, and a few other business owners.

"What can I do for you, gentlemen?" Valdes asked.

"We wish to talk to you, deputy," Ilfeld said in his heavy German accent, "about these wolf attacks. They're bad for business, bad for all of us."

"We've made a decision," Otero said, just before he wiped his nose with a handkerchief. "We talked to many of the other business owners, and we all agree this is best for the town."

"And what is that?" Valdes said.

"Go right up Tilden Street," the clerk at the Las Vegas train depot told Hattie. "You won't have any trouble finding it."

It did not take long before Hattie saw the sign posted in the front yard.

Nathan Burwell, M.D.
Consulting Physician at the Hot Springs
Chronic Diseases a Specialty
Coroner

The Queen Anne–style house was painted a soft yellow. A picket fence surrounded it.

A man with graying side-whiskers swept the front porch with a well-worn broom.

"Doctor Burwell?"

"I am."

"I have your telegram here." She took the folded paper from the pocket of her dress and opened it. "I'm Sarah Andrews."

"Wonderful! The new nurse," he said and invited her inside.

"Thank you, Doctor."

"Call me Doc. Most everybody does."

They sat in the front parlor. The furnishings were worn, but comfortable. He brought her a cup of tea.

"I'm pleased you're here, Miss Andrews," he said as he sat down across from her. "But you should know, things have changed."

"What do you mean?"

"All but three of the consumptives at the hotel have left. We had about twenty. It's these wolf attacks. People are scared."

"Yes, I saw the headline when I arrived," she said. "I can't say that I blame them. To be honest with you, it scares me, too. People getting their throats torn out."

"Well," he said slowly, "I thought you might say that. Tell you the truth, I half expected you would decide to leave."

"Oh, no. You misunderstand. I'm here and ready to care for the patients who remain."

He sat back in his chair, surprised. "That is a relief."

"Good. When I accept a job, I see it through." She took a sip of her tea. "If you would, please tell me about those patients still here."

"Gladly. One is a man from down Texas way. Morgan Quince is his name. Then there's a fellow from Pennsylvania, I believe he said. Ash Prescott. He came here in late May, not long after the hotel reopened. The other is Mrs. Florence Shaw. She hails from Chicago. She is . . . well, I think she came here in the hopes of feeling a little better before she dies. She knows her time is short."

"I can appreciate that."

"There's a journal the former nurse at the hotel kept. It's probably in the desk in the nurse's station. Have you had chance to look in there yet?"

Briefly, she said, but promised she would acquaint herself with it thoroughly.

"I've been going up about every other day to look in at the consumptives, check their vitals. The hotel has been very good about seeing to their comfort, getting them out in the fresh air. Mrs. Shaw, she's about sixty years old and in a wheelchair, but there's always a bellman to push her around outside for a bit. And Mr. Quince gets out some. Wish I could say the same for Mr. Prescott."

"Oh?"

"Sadly, he seems to have little interest in improving his condition. Mr. Quince, though, is another matter. His condition fluctuates, improving for a few days or a week." The doctor drew his lips tight. "This consumption is a strange malady. I've seen people come here facing death's door. Some die, some recover, and I can't tell you the why of it."

Hattie thought of her son and nodded, for she did not know the answer to that either.

Then she said, "I'll introduce myself to each of them shortly."

"That's fine. You should also know the hotel keeps local venison, beef, and buffalo meat on hand. Oranges and limes are shipped in almost daily. Mr. Harvey's orders. He insists the meals be of the finest quality for all the guests, but he's well aware the consumptives need fresh food, and he's seeing that they have it. As you know, the appetite goes, the wasting follows."

Hattie knew that well enough.

"And the oranges and limes also help keep the scurvy away," the doctor added.

"Yes, very important. What I am concerned about are these attacks. What else can you tell me?"

"Folks are jumpy. I'm surprised somebody hasn't been shot by accident. Patrols are out at night, but they can't watch around the whole town. A couple of men here tried tracking this wolf, but they lost the trail. Like it up and disappeared, they said."

Just like she had found at the livery stable.

"I heard about Mr. Barrow at the hotel," she said. "Someone said his body was brought here."

"Wyman's Mortuary already came and got him. He's got a brother in Tennessee. Leaving out on the train today. Mrs. Harvey . . . she's staying at the hotel, you know . . . she said her husband would pay all the expenses. Casket, travel, everything."

Hattie had hoped to take a look at the body. Maybe see something that could help with her investigation. It was too late now.

"There were other killings the newspaper said." She set her tea cup on the table.

"Four of them," Doc said. "First one was a man by the name of Terrell. Another man claimed he was cheating at cards. Terrell called him a liar. A deputy was in the saloon having his supper at the time and hauled them both over to the jail before any shooting commenced. This Terrell was new in town, so the sheriff told him to get and not come back. He was found later that night, face down in the river."

"Was he a card cheat?"

"Who knows?"

"What about the man who accused him?"

"He didn't kill Terrell, if that's what you're thinking."

"You sound certain of that."

Doc chuckled. "He called the sheriff a nasty name. Sheriff kept him in jail all night."

"Doc!" It was a loud voice coming from the back end of the house. "Are you here?"

Hattie heard an accent in the voice. Spanish.

"In the parlor," Burwell called out. He looked at Hattie. "Better see what this is about."

They moved toward the hallway.

"Do you know what the idiot town fathers have done?" the voice continued. "They are offering a thousand-dollar reward for this wolf. They sent it out over the wire yesterday but tell me about it now. This town will be —"

Hattie and Burwell stepped into the hallway, interrupting a man. She saw he was about thirty. He had a heavy moustache and wore a dark suit and a gun belt. She also noticed he had a scar across his chin. An old scar.

"Forgive me," he said, removing his hat and trying to hide his embarrassment. "I did not know you had a guest."

"This is Sarah Andrews," Doc said. "The new nurse at the Montezuma. And this is Deputy Valdes."

"Antonio Valdes," he said to Hattie with a nod.

"It's a pleasure to meet you, deputy," she said. "The doctor was telling me about my duties at the hotel, and of the recent unfortunate incidents here."

Hattie noticed Valdes stiffen. He shifted his gaze to Doc and did not look too pleased with him.

"The newspaper can tell you all about those incidents," Valdes said. "If the doctor is finished telling you your duties, I have important matters to discuss with him. *Por favor.* Please."

"Perhaps I could be of help in some way," she said. "I know —"

"I do not wish to be rude," he said, cutting her off, an edge in his voice, "but this is a matter for the law. You have your job to do. Allow me to do mine."

"All right, deputy. Doctor, thank you for your hospitality. I'll be going."

"I'll see you at the hotel day after tomorrow then."

"No," she said. "I'm afraid you'll have to find another nurse."

"But — but you said you were staying," the doctor sputtered.

"I can't now."

"I don't understand."

"You've had a vicious killing at the hotel. If I'm going to work there, I should know what is going on."

"Who are you to make demands?" Valdes said.

"All right," Doc said, raising his hand. "Let's calm down. I was just telling her about the other victims is all. Besides, she's *here,* and I need her. And I'm certain Mrs. Harvey'll be glad, too. Shows everything at the hotel is running smooth."

Valdes glared at her, but Hattie was careful not to return the glare. She had made her point, but, more importantly, she wanted information.

They went back into the parlor. Hattie and Doc sat down. His hands shaking, Doc yanked out paper and a tobacco pouch and started rolling a cigarette. Valdes did not take a chair, choosing instead to stand in the hall doorway.

After lighting the cigarette, Doc seemed calmer and explained that the second victim was a whiskey drummer. His body was found in back of the Plaza Hotel, where he had taken a room. "Jess Culpepper was next. He was killed in town, too. Folks around here called him Shakespeare."

"Oh?"

"He tended to make up his own poetry."

"I see. So he was a performer?"

Doc looked over at Valdes, who snorted. "Let us say no one is sorry he is gone."

"The fourth one was some drifter," Doc said. "Didn't know his name. Those fellows I told you about who went tracking the wolf, they found the drifter."

"Where?"

"The road that goes out from town to the hotel." He looked over at Valdes. "You said you found him lying in a shallow gully."

Valdes nodded.

"And then Zach Barrow last night at the Montezuma."

"When did the other killings happen?"

"Let's see. That Terrell fellow was about four weeks ago. Right after the sheriff left for Ohio, wasn't it?"

"*Sí.*" Valdes crossed his arms. "July the sixth."

"That's right," Doc said. "We had a big celebration on the Fourth of July. The whole town was on the plaza that night. Fireworks

93

and bonfires. Went till all hours."

"Doctor," Valdes said sharply. *"Por favor."*

"Sorry," he said and drew deeply on his cigarette. "The drummer, he was five days after that. July eleven. I remember it was the same day Mrs. Hopkins had her baby. Jess Culpepper was a couple days later. Then the drifter I'm guessing was maybe a week later. That's when we found him anyway. And Zach Barrow was last night, making it, let me see, better than two weeks between him and the drifter."

The killings all sounded random to Hattie. Not much to go on yet. She recalled some of the things Duke had told her.

"It's strange," she said.

"What is?" Doc asked.

"I don't know a lot about wolves," she said, "but they hunt for their food, don't they?"

"They do," Valdes said.

"Tell her about the animals," Doc said.

Valdes shot him a hard look. Then he said almost everything from rabbits to deer had been found, even other wolves. "Every one of them had their throats torn out."

"Maybe some of those wolves were fighting over food with this wolf," she said.

"Maybe," Valdes said. "But these other animals do not kill like this one does. And

94

this wolf does not kill to eat its prey. The others do."

"These men who were killed. Do you think they provoked this wolf somehow, to make it attack?"

"No way to tell," Doc said.

"Did any of them have blood on them for any reason before the attacks? I'm told the scent of blood attracts wolves."

"No blood," Valdes said evenly.

She waited a moment. "Were there any other injuries?"

"They were attacked," Valdes said. "That is enough."

Hattie recognized the expression on Doc's face. It was the kind she had seen people get when they had something to hide.

"Doctor Burwell?" she said.

He glanced at Valdes. "Maybe we should tell her."

Valdes turned his face away, then looked back at Doc, angry. "You are a fool."

"Well, it might be best, considering." Doc took a nervous pull on the cigarette.

"Tell me what?" Hattie was pretty certain where this was headed, but she had to play her part.

Valdes gave her a steely look. "You do not say a word about this to anyone. Do you understand?"

She nodded.

"I want to hear you say the words."

"I understand, deputy. Everything will be kept between us."

He muttered something she did not catch, then shrugged at Doc. "Go on. You tell her."

Doc stubbed out his cigarette. "Except for Zach Barrow, in each of these wolf attacks, the bodies were completely drained of blood."

"What? But how can that be?"

"We don't know," Doc said.

"What about Mr. Barrow?"

"Deputy Valdes thinks the wolf got scared off when the stable men showed up."

"It was the only thing that made sense," Valdes said.

"And there was no blood found in the other attacks?" she said.

"Some. Not much," Valdes said.

"Plain confounding." Doc scratched the back of his neck.

Hattie shifted her gaze from him to Valdes.

"Now you understand why this cannot get out," Valdes said.

She did. But an odd coincidence nagged at her. It was the story the baggage handler had told her in Kansas City about the dead woman found a year ago there. He said she had two holes in her neck. He also told her there was a rumor that she had no blood left in her body. And that made all the difference, for a rumor was not a fact.

CHAPTER TWELVE

Father John Lanigan sat slouched in a chair in the parlor of his small rectory. His head throbbed, like a blacksmith hammering on an anvil. But today felt no different than any other day since the archbishop of Santa Fe had assigned him here to this parish some ten months ago. Our Lady of Sorrows was his first parish as a pastor. As far as Father Lanigan was concerned, God was punishing him, and for no good reason. It was not fair.

He had said Mass earlier that morning. The daily Mass. He was certain he had. If he had not been at the church, someone surely would have come looking for him. He rubbed his eyes and looked at the clock on the wall. It was past noon! He had been passed out for hours. God, how his head pounded.

He rubbed his face with both hands and glanced up. The rafters supporting the roof were still those ugly tree trunks.

Rousing himself out from his chair, he glanced down and saw the buttons of his cassock were undone down to his belly. When did he do that? After buttoning up, he was tempted to reach into his pocket for the whiskey flask but told himself he should not have any more to drink. Not yet. Try to resist for a while. Maybe for an hour. That would be good. His legs felt unsteady. All right then, half an hour.

The loud ringing of the telephone assaulted his ears, making his head throb all the more. How he hated that sound. But it had to ring loudly so he could hear it if he was outside.

Stumbling to the cramped kitchen where the contraption hung on the wall, he snatched the receiver from its hook and held it to his ear.

"Father Lanigan," he snapped into the receiver.

The voice at the other end belonged to Mr. Kenton, the manager out at the Montezuma Hotel. He asked Lanigan if he was coming out that day. Several guests were leaving soon and wanted him to hear their confessions before they departed. "We hope you're feeling better, Father. It's been five days since you were here."

"Tell them I'll be there."

"And one of our other guests has requested a visit from you, as well. Quite adamant that you come."

Even before Kenton said the guest's name, Lanigan knew whom he was talking about. As the pastor of Our Lady of Sorrows, he was the only priest for a good thirty miles, and it was part of his duties to come to the hotel or anywhere else in this parish if someone was ill. Or requested the sacraments. Or expected his help.

Replacing the receiver on the hook, he realized his palm was sweating and his hand shook. It was because of that hotel guest, the one Kenton mentioned. All right. No more waiting. He pulled the flask from his pocket and took a drink. The warmth spread through his body, calming his nerves a bit. He was about to take another pull when a knock at the front door made him wince. What now? Then he remembered it was Thursday. Every Thursday, Teresa Analla brought him the altar linens after she had washed and ironed them. It would not do to greet her with whiskey on his breath.

"Just a moment," he called out.

He hurried to his bedroom where a basin stood on his dresser and splashed water on his ruddy face and slicked back his ginger-colored hair. Then he took a peppermint from the dish he kept next to the basin and put it in his mouth to cover his whiskey breath.

"I'm coming," he said, heading for the front door. But when he opened it, it was not Teresa but her mother who stood there holding a large basket of clean laundry in front of her.

"Mrs. Lucero," he said. "Where's Teresa?"

"Resting at home." She handed him the folded altar linens from the top of the basket.

"Is she not feeling well?" He took a couple of coins from the plate of loose coins on the side table next to the door. Holding them out to her, he tried to keep his hand steady.

She took them, and he saw her eyes well with tears.

Fighting the desire to reach inside his pocket for the flask, he invited her inside and regretted it immediately. His head pounded. They sat in the parlor. He asked her if she wanted some water. She wiped her eyes and shook her head.

"Do you want to tell me what's troubling you?" he asked, hoping she would decline.

"It is her husband again. He came home this morning." She held back her tears. "I was not there. I had gone to a neighbor's house. To get eggs. When I came back, Teresa, she was on her bed, crying. I asked her what happened. She say he came in, she asked him where he had been, and he hit her. She showed me her face. He hit her here." She pointed to her cheek. "It is very bad, very swollen."

"I'm so sorry," he whispered.

"I tell her go to the sheriff, but she refuses." A determined look came over the woman's face. "I know where he has been, *Padre*. The smell was still in the house. It was the perfume water from the whores he beds. It was not the first time. He is not a man. He is an animal."

"Do you want me to come talk to her?"

"She will only tell you what she tells me, that she loves him. I pray every day, 'Please, God, open her eyes and make her see.' But it is as my mother used to tell me. *Dios consiente, mas no siempre.*"

"And what does that mean?"

"God consents, but not always."

Father Lanigan knew there was much truth in that saying.

"Can I tell you something, *Padre*?"

"Of course." His mouth felt so dry.

She leaned in close and lowered her voice. "Sometimes I wish her husband was dead."

"Wishing evil on someone is a grave sin," he said.

"I know it is wrong, but I cannot help it. It is because I love my daughter." She drew her lips tight. "I have a gun now."

He watched as she reached inside the basket and took a small, short-barreled revolver from under the clean clothes.

"Where did you get that?"

"A friend. He say I need it, in case the wolf comes around. Or other bad things."

He shook his head. "You should let the law take care of this."

"The law says they can only do something if my Teresa tells them to, but she will not. I must protect her. I should go. *Gracias,* for listening to me."

At the door, he told her he would pray for her and her daughter.

"I love my Teresa, *Padre.* I have felt so helpless, so weak. But I will not be weak anymore."

After she left, he leaned back against the closed door and yanked the whiskey flask from his pocket. Putting it to his mouth, he took a long pull. It did nothing to relieve his pain. Nothing did. But it was all he knew to do to live in this uncivilized place. And to live with himself.

Ordained less than a year ago at age

twenty-nine, he was certain he had made the right choice, dedicating his life to God. He was also certain that God, as well as the archbishop in Baltimore, had great plans for him. Say, pastor of a fine, beautiful church in a prominent town. The archbishop and Lanigan's mother were brother and sister, after all.

He was stunned when informed his uncle had decided to send him to the Archdiocese of Santa Fe. Lanigan did not even know where that was. Priests were needed there, he was told.

Assigned as pastor of Our Lady of Sorrows parish in Las Vegas, he found misery. The rectory looked like a pile of crumbling bricks, and, inside it, blankets hung in place of doors. He was given a horse, but no buggy. The stable behind the rectory was, at best, rickety. Across the street from the rectory stood his church with its twin bell towers and pitched roof. But a new bell was needed in one of the towers, and the roof leaked in dozens of places, including right above the altar. Most of the people of his parish spoke Spanish, and Lanigan had little patience for learning it. Why should he? He did not deserve this. Not any of it.

He had spent hours praying, begging God to release him from this purgatory. But God ignored his pleas. Was that fair? Of course not. So, he ignored having repairs done to his church. He took solace in a glass of sacramental wine before sleep. And another when he woke. Two glasses became four. A bottle of Irish whiskey arrived, a thank-you gift for a wedding he had performed. Lanigan preferred it to the grape. He stole money from the collection plate to purchase more whiskey, as well as a flask.

So far, he had not fallen into a stupor saying Mass for a wedding, a baptism, or funeral. And he had not drifted off while hearing confessions, either, or when called to the Montezuma Hotel or the other hotels in town that catered to those wretches suffering from consumption.

But God had abandoned him. That was certain. Nothing was fair. He stared at the flask in his hand. Misery compounded misery. Despair and weakness ruled his life. Weakness corrupted his faith.

And there was still something much worse. Far worse. It waited for him at the Montezuma Hotel.

CHAPTER THIRTEEN

The train whistle shrieked as Hattie came out of Doc's house. She saw the engine smoke billowing up beyond the rooftops.

"You missed your train," Valdes said, getting on his horse.

"Well," Hattie said, "I'll go wait for the next one."

Valdes grunted and rode away.

"Let me take you back to the hotel," she heard Doc say as he came up behind her.

"No, that's too much trouble."

"Train won't be back for two hours," he said. "About the only train that runs on time in the territory."

Riding in Doc's covered buggy, Hattie guessed they had gone about three miles when Doc said this was the place they found the drifter's body. "I remember that dead tree there."

"Could we stop for a minute?"

"What for? There's nothing here."

"I'm part of this now," she said, not unkindly. "I'd like to see it for myself."

Doc sighed and reined in his horse. "Fine."

Hattie climbed down from the buggy. Feeling unsteady, she took hold of the wheel to keep her balance.

"Are you all right, Miss Andrews?" Doc asked.

"I think so. Just dizzy all of a sudden."

"Sit back down. I have some water." He reached underneath the seat and pulled out a canteen. "Just take a few sips."

She put the canteen to her mouth. The water tasted fresh and cool.

"Feeling better?"

She nodded and took another sip.

"This air up here is drier than what you're likely used to," Doc said. "Happens to some folks. Best if you drink a lot of water until you get used to it."

Thanking him, she handed him the canteen and took a few deep breaths. They helped, too.

"You take it easy now," Doc said.

"I will," she said, getting to her feet. "But we're here, and I really want to take a look around."

Near a tall pine tree she found a ring of

rocks. Inside it, the remains of burnt wood and gray ashes from a campfire lay undisturbed.

"The man's coffee pot was still sitting here when we came up," Doc said. "A plate of beans, too. Half eaten."

"Perhaps he heard something. Maybe he pulled his gun. Do you think he shot at it?" Hattie studied the ground, looking for anything that might help. Dried blood, tracks, anything.

"Deputy Valdes thought so. He found the drifter's gun over there. One cartridge spent. We didn't find any blood, if that's what you're looking for." He paused. "I didn't notice this before."

Hattie turned and saw Doc running his hand over an odd bare spot on the trunk of the tall pine. It went almost all the way around the trunk.

"It's like the bark's been rubbed clean off," he said.

"How do you suppose that happened?"

He frowned. "We found the horse on the way back to town. Funny, it didn't occur to me until now."

"What?"

"I thought maybe that drifter had ground tethered his horse, but he must've tied him here. When the wolf came, the horse tried to get away, pulling against the rope. The rope stripped the bark clean off before it came loose. We found the horse later, down by the river. Must've been one scared horse."

Just like the horses in the livery stalls, Hattie thought, running her fingers over the stripped part of the trunk.

"Why do you suppose the wolf didn't go after the horse?" she asked. "You said it killed other animals. Why not this horse, or any of the horses in the hotel livery?"

"Couldn't say."

"Do you remember where the body was when you got here?"

He turned and pointed. "Over there about fifty feet, I guess."

Hattie slowly paced off the distance, not wanting to take the chance of another dizzy spell. She did not see any evidence of blood anywhere. But there appeared to be several partial boot prints, probably those of Doc, the deputy, and the men who found the drifter. Some partial wolf tracks, too, maybe. The rocky ground made any prints hard to read. It was a good thing it had not rained. Suddenly, she saw something else.

"Looks like maybe he was dragged," she said. "The marks in the dirt, from the camp fire over to here."

"We saw them, too. We figured he put up quite a struggle trying to fight off the wolf."

"Are you saying he had other injuries?"

"He had claw marks all over, clothes torn up. Nothing as serious as the neck wound, though. That's what killed him."

"But I heard the wolf is supposed to be as big as a man."

"You've been talking to Duke up at the hotel." Doc grunted. "Maybe the drifter fellow was trying to get away, and that's as far as he got."

Hattie said nothing as she studied the ground. Doc stood by the tree where the horse had been tied. The campfire ring was a few feet away, and the drifter probably close by the fire when the wolf struck. Perhaps the drifter did fire at the wolf. And perhaps they did fight. But maybe he crawled over here trying to get away. Or was he dragged? Zach Barrow had been dragged outside the livery, away from the frightened horses. The drifter's horse was scared, too. The wolf did not attack the drifter's horse or those in the livery stalls. Why not? Why only the men? And why drink all the blood?

"Would you mind my making an observation?" Doc asked as they climbed back into the buggy.

"Not at all," she said.

"I have only known you a few hours, but you are the most inquisitive nurse I have ever met."

She gave him a brief smile. But she was thinking that in her many years of investigation, she had learned that each case required patience, hard work, and good common sense. Thus far, though, little about this case made any sense at all.

CHAPTER FOURTEEN

"You two get in there," Valdes heard Deputy Cuddy say as he pushed Charlie Ross and Phil Larson in through the front door of the big wooden jailhouse. Ross had a black eye and Larson a bloody lip. Their clothes were torn and dirty.

"What is this, Sam?" Valdes said. Sitting behind the sheriff's desk, he cleaned a double-barrel shotgun. Two shotgun shells lay close by.

"I was on my way to deliver the summons to Dave Pickett and found these two fighting in the street in front of Phil's house."

Valdes looked at Larson and asked him what they were fighting about.

Both men spoke fast and at once.

"Simmer down!" Cuddy said, shaking both of them by the shoulder.

"Mr. Larson," Valdes said, "you tell me your side first."

"He's a damn thief!" Larson pointed his

finger at Ross.

"And you're a greedy son of a bitch!" Ross said.

Larson swung at Ross. Ross ducked. Larson hit Cuddy in the face. Ross came up and caught Larson across the chin. Larson fell backward. Valdes drove the butt of the shotgun into the side of Ross's face, dropping him to the floor.

Valdes asked Cuddy if he was all right.

"Damn near busted my nose," the deputy said, his hand over his face.

Valdes snatched the shells from the desktop, loaded them into the open breech of the shotgun, and snapped it shut.

"Get up, you two," he said, leveling the double barrels at Larson and Ross.

The heavy wooden door leading from the jail cells opened, and a surprised Deputy Silva, a broom in his hand, brought the broom up, ready to fight.

"Easy, Cleofas," Valdes said. "Sam, you put Mr. Larson in cell number one. And, Cleofas, you take Mr. Ross here and lock him in cell number three. These two have done enough fighting."

The deputies took hold of the dazed brawlers and pushed them through the doorway to their cells, leaving cell number two empty between them. There were six cells, all on one side of the long room. Small barred windows near the top of the rear of each cell wall permitted the only light.

Valdes approached the cells. "Now, Mr. Larson, you want to tell me what started this."

"Well, first I want to say I'm sorry I hit you, Sam. It wasn't on purpose or nothing."

Sam nodded, wiping his nose.

Larson moved his sore jaw around. "Well," he said, jabbing a finger toward Ross, "he come over to my house last night, saying he wanted to borrow my Sharps rifle. Says he's gonna do some hunting. He's lent me tools before, so I said fine and gave it to him. Then this morning he comes back with a big deer on his buckboard. I ask him what he plans to do with it. He says he's going to collect that reward. I says what reward? He says the one the town merchants is offering on that killer wolf. A thousand dollars."

Valdes whispered an oath.

"So I ask him, 'How you getting that money?' He says he's going to stuff the deer carcass full of strychnine, enough to kill a whole pack of wolves, and stake it out as bait."

"Is that true?" Valdes glanced at Ross.

"So far," Ross said, rubbing the side of his face where Valdes had butted him.

114

"Go on." Valdes looked back at Larson.

"Then I says to him he ought to give me half that reward money."

"The hell I ought to!" Ross said.

"You used my rifle to get the deer!" Larson yelled. "It's only fair!"

"Fair my ass!"

"Shut your mouths!" Valdes shouted.

"I want to press charges," Ross said. "He come at me with a axe."

"That's a lie, and you know it!"

Valdes turned to Cuddy. "Is that true?"

Cuddy shrugged. "I seen a axe lying on the ground."

Valdes gave Larson a sharp look. "What made you go get an axe?"

"I wanted what was mine."

"And what was that?"

"Half that deer."

"See, that don't make no sense," Ross said.

"Mr. Ross, no more!" Valdes looked at Larson. "Why do you think half of the deer belongs to you?"

Larson glanced at Ross. "On account of he wasn't going to share the reward money."

"If I hadn't lent you my rifle, you wouldn't've got the damn deer!"

"Enough!" Valdes said. "You can tell your stories to Judge Baylor this afternoon. He

115

can sort this out."

Ross threw his hands up.

Silva whispered in Valdes's ear.

Valdes sighed. "Looks like you two will be here for a few days."

"What for?" Ross said.

"Because Judge Baylor is out of town."

"This ain't right," Ross said, taking hold of the cell bars.

"Deputy Cuddy, after you write your report, go back and get the Sharps rifle and the axe."

"What do you need my rifle and axe for?" Larson said.

"Evidence in the case." Valdes turned back to Cuddy. "And then you take the deer carcass over to Delmonico's and tell the Hopper brothers to have it butchered."

Ross stamped his foot. "You can't do that!"

"I cannot allow that carcass to stink up the town," Valdes said, heading back into the office, followed by the deputies.

"But I got a wolf to catch!" Ross cried as Cuddy pulled the heavy door closed.

Valdes put his hands on top of the desk. "All this foolishness because of that damn reward."

"What about the charges against those two?" Cuddy asked, jerking his head toward the cells.

Valdes scratched his head. "Start with disturbing the peace." He thought a moment. "Wish I could charge them with being stupid."

Silva chuckled. Cuddy snorted. Valdes joined them. Then he told the deputies he was going to get something to eat.

Stepping outside, the aroma of *frijoles* and *posole* from the cantina across the street was a welcome greeting. A piece of paper was caught against the nearby telephone pole. Valdes picked it up. It read:

REWARD
$1,000
For the Killer Black Wolf
Preferably Dead

"Idiotas," he said, disgusted.

He knew every wolf hunter and tracker and any desperate fool wanting that bounty money was on their way here.

CHAPTER FIFTEEN

"A little warmer today, wouldn't you say, Father?" the driver called Duke asked.

"I suppose," Lanigan said, riding in the carriage along the pathway toward the Montezuma Hotel. The wide brimmed padre hat he wore kept the sun off his thin face. The long black cassock covered the rest of him. His pale Irish skin burned so easily in the sun. On his lap he held a black leather valise tightly.

The valise was a gift from his mother the day he was ordained a priest. She had his initials hand tooled into the leather: *JFL* for John Francis Lanigan. Most priests had some kind of bag. It was a necessity. Inside it he carried the purple stole he wore to hear confessions, holy oils for anointing the sick, and a pyx, the small brass container that held the consecrated pieces of bread for those who were too ill or unable to attend Mass to receive the sacrament of Holy

Communion. There was also a small bottle of holy water wrapped carefully in a towel. He had placed it with the other five bottles in his valise, each of them protected, as well.

Lanigan had started bringing those extra bottles with him to the Montezuma almost four weeks ago. Every time he boarded the train to the hotel he brought them, usually three times a week. Sometimes four.

Except last week. He claimed he was feeling ill and could not come. In truth, Lanigan was scared. The whole business of those other five bottles had become too much for him, in spite of the promise he had made. But now he was too frightened not to come.

His head no longer throbbed. A couple of pulls on the whiskey flask before boarding the spur line had seen to that, followed by a peppermint candy to cover his breath. After all, there were those hotel guests waiting for him, the ones that Mr. Kenton called him about earlier. And that other guest.

Duke swung the carriage around into the circular drive at the entrance of the hotel, and Lanigan was surprised to see a wagon with a four-mule team sitting off the driveway path. Words emblazoned in bold gold leaf lettering on the side panels of the box-shaped wagon proclaimed: E. F. DRUMMOND Photography.

As his carriage pulled to a stop, Lanigan noticed an agile fellow wearing a wide-brimmed straw hat, coat, and striped tie jump down from the photography wagon. The man had a full face that broke into a smile when Mrs. Fred Harvey, Sally to many, came out the front door, greeting him by name. Mrs. Harvey was a small woman but sturdy. She spoke with an accent. Lanigan had heard one of the housekeepers say she came to America when she was a young girl from somewhere over in Europe, a place called Bohemia.

Standing there, Lanigan could not help witness the exchange.

"Mr. Drummond, how good it is to meet you," she said. "My husband told me to expect you. He says your expertise in photography is unmatched."

"Thank you, Mrs. Harvey," he said, tipping his hat. "I hope I can live up to his expectations. I'm honored he chose me to photograph such a grand hotel as the Montezuma."

"Yes," she said, taking his arm and leading him toward the entrance. "Mr. Harvey says he is very anxious to show the hotel is open and thriving."

"Well, I have a good camera, and I guarantee excellent pictures, be it clear or cloudy days."

Kenton, the starchy manager, came out and waved at several stable men coming around from the other side of the hotel.

"Hurry up now," he called to them. "And be very careful with Mr. Drummond's wagon."

"No, please," Drummond said. "Is it possible to keep my rig here? More convenient for me so I can get to my equipment and develop my pictures. The wagon is my dark room."

Kenton appeared flummoxed. "It's most irregular," he said.

"I believe we can make an exception for Mr. Drummond," Mrs. Harvey said. "Perhaps having his office on display here in front of the hotel will be a boon for business, as well."

"As you like, Mrs. Harvey. We must stable the mules in any case."

"Of course," she said and noticed Lanigan. He saw her gray eyes brighten. "Hello, Father. So glad to see you here."

"Mrs. Harvey," he said, allowing them to pass.

Kenton appeared beside him, a piece of paper in his hand. "I took the liberty of writing down the names and room numbers of the guests who requested you come today."

Lanigan took the paper as Kenton hurried inside to catch up with Mrs. Harvey.

Glancing at the paper he saw several names. Three wanted their confessions heard. The fourth, no confession could help. Lanigan needed a drink.

"Good to see you again, Father," the doorman said, holding open the door. "Please, come in."

Lanigan hurried into the reading room on the left side of the lobby. Relieved to find it empty, he opened his flask and took a couple of short pulls. The whiskey burned going down his throat but calmed his nerves. He drew a deep breath and took one more pull from the flask. Now, he was ready.

Sitting at the table in Mrs. Winters's second-floor guest room, Lanigan wiped his hand over his dry lips, unable to concentrate on the sins Mrs. Winters was confessing. She was saying something about having unkind thoughts about a friend who had refused something or other.

"Father?"

Startled, Lanigan sat up straight. "Please go on."

"I was asking you if that was a sin."

"I . . . yes." He did not know what she

had said, but he was not about to admit it. How he wanted a drink. "Do you have any other sins to confess?"

"I believe that's all of them."

"And are you sorry for your sins?"

"I am," she said, holding her spotted hands together in prayer.

He spoke quickly. "Then for your penance say five Our Fathers and five Hail Marys, and humbly ask God for His grace and forgiveness." Making the sign of the cross with his hands, Lanigan blessed the woman in Latin.

"Thank you, Father," she said. "I feel much better about going back home now. You're a good man. I wish you could be on the train with me back to Maryland."

Lanigan said he appreciated that. He did not say how much he truly wished he could be on that train.

Clutching the handrail, Lanigan came down the circular staircase to the first floor, passed by the closed door of the nurse's station, and followed the long hallway toward the guest's room. It was the last room at the end of the hallway on the side of the hotel that faced the woods. He gripped the handle of his black valise tight. Somehow the soft pad of his footfalls on the red carpet sounded like harsh echoes. He was not even aware he was breathing. His mouth felt so dry, but his hands sweated. He wanted to drain the flask in his pocket. He wanted to turn around and run, but knew he could not. More than anything he wished he had never gone to the river the night of the Fourth of July celebration only a month ago . . .

The festivities began late that afternoon on the plaza. Red, white, and blue streamers hung from the balconies of the buildings. People danced and ate and drank. A band from Fort Union played. The celebrating continued into the night with bonfires of piñon wood glowing in the streets and fireworks illuminating the night sky.

Going down to the river for a walk, Lanigan hoped to get away from the raucous cacophony. A half moon hung amid the twinkling stars. The further he got from the center of town, the quieter things became. The steady babble of the river seemed barely a whisper. The air grew still. A strange, unsettling quiet had descended. Wary, he took a tentative step back. A hand covered his mouth. Something sharp pricked at the side of his neck.

"What are you doing out here, Father?" the soft voice of a woman said, close to his ear.

"It's dangerous being out here by yourself, you know."

Lanigan stiffened as the woman inched the tip of a knife blade along his throat.

"Calm down," she said.

He let out a ragged breath.

"Good. Now, real careful, so I don't get agitated, reach in your pocket and give me your money. And don't try acting like you don't got any. I seen that collection plate getting passed around the church."

Lanigan nodded and made a show of slipping his hand into his cassock pocket.

"That's fine," she said.

Her hand slid away from his mouth, and the knife drew from his neck. Holding a few coins in his hand, he turned, the stillness of the night broken by the sound of her excited gasp.

The woman's back was to Lanigan. Her arms hung open. Someone, a man, held her close, one arm wrapped around the small of her back, the other supporting her head. His face lay buried in her neck.

The priest heard a voice command him to wait. He obeyed, too startled to do otherwise.

After a minute, the man let the woman slip through his arms. She fell at his feet, lifeless. On the side of her neck were two small holes.

Father Lanigan stared at the man with the pallid countenance and drawn features. Drops of red blood dripped down his chin. The blood appeared black in the moonlight. Two prominent white fangs, like those of a dog or wolf, withdrew into his dark mouth. The blood on his chin suddenly flowed backward up to his lips. His eyes flashed red.

Unable to make his legs move, Lanigan shut his eyes. How could this be? He was seeing things! A moment passed. A voice spoke low to him, with a trace of a Southern accent, sounding almost friendly.

"I know who you are. You're the priest who comes to the Montezuma Hotel."

Lanigan opened his eyes, his breathing shallow, his heart pounding, and more frightened than he had ever been. The man stood there dressed in black clothes, a white shirt, and string tie. He could have been on his way to church.

Stepping casually over the dead body of the woman, the man in black raised his head and sniffed the air. "I can smell the whiskey on you."

Lanigan shook his head. "You . . . you killed that woman."

"I saved your life."

Glancing down at the woman's body, at her knife nearby, the blade glinting in the moonlight, Lanigan knew he spoke the truth.

"I have heard your parish is quite poor," the

pallid man said. "A bell in one of the church towers is cracked. The roof leaks and needs repairing. Very costly."

Lanigan stammered a yes.

"And you have a great thirst." The corner of his mouth curled up in a smile. "So do I."

Lanigan fumbled for the flask in his pocket. Pulling it out, he dropped it.

"I can help you," the man said, retrieving the flask. "All the money you need is yours, if you help me. You could get that new bell for the tower. Fix the church roof. Put doors in the rectory." He held the flask out to Lanigan and shook it, the contents making a sloshing sound. "Purchase more courage, if you like."

How did he know about all that? Wiping his hand on his cassock, Lanigan accepted the flask but did not take a drink. Best to try to keep his wits about him.

"Will you help me, Father?"

Wary, Lanigan asked, "How . . . how can I help you?"

"It's a simple matter," the man said, his voice calm. "You come to the Montezuma several times a week."

"I do."

"I'm a guest there."

"All right."

"Bring me blood."

Lanigan blinked. "Did you say blood?"

127

"Look at that whore, Father. She was going to rob and kill you. I gave you your life. You can give me mine."

"What are you talking about?"

"I need blood. To drink. Any blood will do."

"Why? What . . . what for?"

"To live."

Lanigan stepped back. "You stay away from me."

"You must help me," the pallid man said, coming toward him.

"You're insane."

"No, Father. I am cursed."

Lanigan did not see the man's hand thrust out, but suddenly it had him by the throat, its grip as strong as iron and cold as river water.

"Look at me," the man said.

His eyes closed, Lanigan struggled.

"Look at me, Father!" the man demanded.

Lanigan opened his eyes. The man's face was close to his. Something drew Lanigan to his eyes. Something mystifying, unnatural. He could not look away. And he saw it. A river of blood roiled and churned deep in the man's eyes. Paralyzed with fright, Lanigan struggled to look away and then saw something far worse. Flashes of death. Horrid. Vile. Bodies drained of blood, their necks torn and gaping, rose to the surface of that river of blood.

"You see what I am," Lanigan heard the man

say, and he listened to the man tell how he came to be this unholy thing. This creature. Depraved, horrifying, yet mesmerizing.

"I can give you all the money you need," the pallid man said, taking his hand away from the priest's neck. "If you will help me."

Gulping air, Lanigan nodded.

"Good." He motioned at the whore. "Put her in the river."

"But . . . but she is a child of God. She deserves to —"

Lanigan saw the flash of anger in the man's eyes as he whispered, "Join me, or join her."

Almost before he realized it, Lanigan was rolling the whore's body into the river. He tried not to look at the red, swollen bite marks in her neck. Thankfully, the swift current carried the body away.

"We have a bargain, Father," the pallid man said. "Money for blood."

Standing at the guest room door at the end of the hallway, Lanigan heard the familiar voice before he knocked.

"Come in, Father."

He turned the knob and entered. The curtains were drawn, the room dark. He shut the door behind him. A sharp scratching sound alerted him, and he saw the flame of the Lucifer lighting the candle on the table. A soft yellow glow filled the room.

A pallid but veiny hand brought the burning Lucifer up to the face of the creature. Breath from its mouth blew out the small flame. A wisp of smoke drifted up.

The creature wore a dark suit. The collar of its white shirt was unbuttoned. It sat in the chair next to the table.

Going to the other side of the table, Lanigan opened his valise, took out the first bottle and unwrapped it, revealing the dark crimson blood it contained.

"Rabbit blood," he said holding it out to the creature. "It's all I could get."

"It'll have to do, for now," the creature said and drank it down.

Lanigan tried not to listen to the gulping sounds the creature made as he pulled the towels from the other four bottles and placed them on the table.

The creature grabbed the second bottle and drank half before pulling the bottle away from its mouth.

Raising one eyebrow at Lanigan, it said, "You were supposed to be here days ago."

"I was sick." Lanigan kept his eyes averted and tried to sound convincing.

The creature drained the rest of the bottle and reached for the third one. "You were drunk. We made a bargain. I give you money. You bring me animal blood."

"And I did. I can't help it if I get sick."

"Lying is a sin," the creature said and consumed the blood in one gulp. "Because of you, I had to feed on that man at the hotel livery last night."

The creature took a fresh bottle and drank the crimson liquid down.

Lanigan wrapped the empty bottles in the towels. He did not watch the creature drink but almost dropped a bottle when the creature said maybe he did not need Lanigan anymore.

"What?"

"There are others here at the hotel who might be better suited to help me. One of the baggage handlers. They come here almost every day."

Lanigan stopped himself from grabbing for the flask in his pocket. This was no time to demonstrate his weakness to the creature. But he needed the money the creature gave him so he could buy whiskey. More than ever he needed it!

Think, he told himself. *Think! What to do?*

The creature took the last bottle in its hand but did not drink it. "Yes. One of the baggage handlers."

"But, I . . . I can do it," Lanigan stammered.

"You failed to bring me blood when I sent word for you to come. That was our agreement."

"And I told you I was sick. That's why I couldn't get here sooner."

Lanigan saw the creature's eyes flash red, and in an instant it was on its feet, its powerful pale hand gripping Lanigan's throat. The creature threw him across the room. His head struck the heavy dresser on the other side of the bed.

"Don't lie to me, priest," the creature hissed, inches from his face. "I can smell the fear, like I can smell the whiskey on you. You drink up all the money I give you. You know how I know? There's no new bell at your church. The roof still leaks when it rains. You're a scared, miserable man."

Lanigan got to his feet, relieved his head was not bleeding. Seeing blood, the creature would have surely killed him to feast on it.

Bringing the last bottle to its mouth, the creature drained it, then threw the bottle at Lanigan.

"Animal blood," it said, its mouth curling in disgust. "Like drinking mule piss."

It reached into its pocket and tossed a few twenty-dollar gold coins on the table.

Lanigan stared at them.

"You see, I keep my promise," the creature

said. "Take them. Get out."

Desperate, Lanigan saw no other way. He spoke, his voice shaking. "I can tell you where to get human blood."

"I don't need your help for that."

"But I can make it easier for you."

The creature studied him. "Human blood."

"Just like you want," Lanigan said, picking up the coins.

"Go on."

"There's a man in town. He beats his wife."

CHAPTER SIXTEEN

The spray of the fountain felt cool and refreshing on Hattie's face. She saw no other movement on the manicured green of the terrace below the hotel as Doc drove his buggy along the pathway. She also noticed the animals in the miniature zoo were being removed by the stable men who were hauling them up to the livery in wagons. This wolf business was taking its toll. Along the veranda only a few chairs and rockers were occupied.

"I see Mr. Harvey got his photographer," Doc said, pulling his buggy around to the front of the hotel.

Hattie could not miss the wagon with E.F. DRUMMOND painted on the side panel sitting off the pathway. Doc explained that Mr. Harvey had devised a campaign to advertise the new Montezuma Hotel. "He told me about it before he left for London. Souvenir mailing cards, he calls them. He says they'll be a big seller. Bigger than penny postcards."

Hattie frowned. "What does Mr. Harvey have in mind?"

"He wants to put photographs of the Montezuma on postcards and sell them at the train depots and his restaurants and hotels. Folks'll buy them, he says. Some to mail and some to keep as souvenirs."

"What do you think?"

"I say if Mr. Harvey thinks it'll make money, it will. That man has a golden touch."

As she stepped out of the buggy, Doc reminded her to be careful and drink more water. "You don't want to risk a fainting spell."

At the front desk, Hattie asked if anyone was in need of medical assistance and if there were any messages for her. None of either, she was told. "But one of the consumptives, Mrs. Shaw, has been asking for you. She's in the reading room there. I believe she's by herself."

The clock on the wall said it was a quarter to four, and Hattie wondered if it was possible to get something to eat. She had not eaten since breakfast on the train this morning. That had probably contributed to her dizzy spell, too. The desk clerk told her the dining room was closed now in preparation for supper, but he would see if the kitchen could put something together for her.

She thanked him and headed for the reading room, its glass doors open.

Sitting by a large window was a wheelchair, facing the tall windows. The top of Mrs. Shaw's head appeared above the back of the chair, her salt and pepper hair pulled into a bun. Hattie walked softly across the ornate rug covering the floor so as not to awaken the woman in the event she was taking a nap.

"Are you Miss Andrews?" came a voice from the wheelchair.

Hattie smiled as she realized her reflection showed in the window. Stepping around in front of the window, she faced Mrs. Shaw. Hattie guessed she weighed maybe ninety pounds. Her cheeks were sunken, and dark circles surrounded her eyes, giving her an almost skeletal appearance. She also wore bifocals, and a green linen dress with a gold brooch pinned at the neck. A red and black blanket covered her legs. She held a book in her hands. Placing a bookmark inside, she closed the volume and set it on the side table beside a glass holding a cherry-colored liquid. In spite of the wasting effects of her consumption, Hattie could tell the woman was intent on holding onto as much dignity as she could muster.

"It's a pleasure to make your acquaintance, Mrs. Shaw."

"All mine," she said, and Hattie thought she saw Mrs. Shaw's eyes brighten. "I figured it was you. You've got a lighter step than the bellmen around here, and you're not dressed like a Harvey girl. But you're not dressed like a nurse, either."

"No, but —"

"Don't mind me," she said, cutting Hattie off with a wave of her hand. She removed her bifocals. "Let me have a good look at you. You're older than that other nurse was."

"Well," Hattie said, "I'll take that as a compliment."

"Good for you! I'll tell you this much, you're prettier than I was at your age."

"Kind of you to say."

"It's the truth." She began coughing, but it quickly passed. "Being an old woman and time running out for me, I say what's on my mind."

She reached for the glass on the table next to her, brought it to her mouth, and took a few sips.

"Are you feeling better now?" Hattie asked, taking the glass from her hand.

"I'm never going to feel better, but sarsaparilla helps to calm this cough most times. And mind you, it's only sarsaparilla in that glass. That other nurse kept watching to see if I was adding whiskey to it. Been a temperate woman all my life."

"That's good to know."

"Wish I'd known about getting up here in fresh air and sunshine before this damn consumption settled in like a bad tenant. Every breath's a struggle." She coughed again and wiped her mouth with a silk handkerchief she took from under the blanket. Blood stained it. "You've heard of that English poet, Lord Byron? Wrote that poem . . . what's it called? 'She Walks in Beauty'?"

"Yes, I have."

"You know what he said? 'I should like to die of consumption.' " She snorted. "Made it sound like it was some kind of romantic disease. Man was a jackass."

Hattie laughed.

"Good for you!" Mrs. Shaw said. "You've got a sense of humor. That other nurse didn't. And you know something else? You're a lot braver than she was, too."

"Why do you say that?"

"She left, and you're here. Those wolf stories didn't scare you off."

"You're not afraid of the wolf?"

"Why the hell should I be? If it came at me I'd likely have a coughing fit and scare it away."

Mrs. Shaw was not morbidly awaiting death as Doc had insinuated earlier, Hattie thought. More like a firecracker that keeps exploding.

"Would you take me back to my room?" Mrs. Shaw said. "I'd like to lie down for a bit before supper."

"Gladly," Hattie said, thinking perhaps she ought to do the same.

Mrs. Shaw's guest room was on the first floor, not far from Hattie's room. Pushing Mrs. Shaw through the reading room and into the hallway, they passed by the elegant winding staircase. Hattie noticed Mrs. Shaw eyeing it as they went by. The old woman let out a wistful sigh.

"Is everything all right?" Hattie asked.

"I'd give every dollar my late husband left me if I could get out of this wheelchair, climb that staircase, and walk back down without coughing to death. Damn this consumption."

Hattie took the room key from her and unlocked the door. Inside, the drapes were open, and sunlight filtered in through the windows.

Helping her into her bed, Hattie noticed

the framed item hanging on the wall next to it. It was Florence Shaw's gold-colored certificate of membership in the Lungers Club. It read: "Cure our maladies, we tuberculars unite. Coughing and wheezing, we continue the fight. For rest and recuperation, in hot springs we soak. At the Montezuma Hotel, we laugh at jokes. We might be sick and crazy, too, as we form a club with members so few. Some have not as others have wealth, but we bask in a warm sun and return to good health. So join us now if you will and very soon, better you will feel. Lungers ever, retreating never."

"I read that every morning when I get up," Mrs. Shaw said from her bed. "It makes me laugh."

After seeing to Mrs. Shaw's comfort, Hattie headed down the hallway, her hotel key in her hand. She opened the door to the nurse's station to see if anyone might be waiting out on the porch. It was empty. She got a cup from the medicine cabinet, walked to the basin, filled the cup with water from the pitcher, and drank the water down. She opened the desk drawer, took out the nurse's journal, and searched first for the entries about Mrs. Shaw, Mr. Quince, and Mr. Prescott. There were coffee spills on some pages. Hattie guessed the former nurse had tried to blot it up with a towel, smudging the ink in places. Feeling tired, Hattie rubbed her eyes, then took another drink of water.

"Miss Andrews?"

Hattie looked toward the open door. One of the bellmen held a covered tray in his hands, a tall glass of amber liquid to one side.

"I was asked to bring this to you," he said. "Sorry for the delay. The kitchen regrets they could not do better."

"Thank you. Please put it here," she said, closing the journal and indicating the desktop.

He set it down, along with a linen napkin and silver stemware. Hattie noticed the handles of the knife, fork, and spoon were each engraved in a florid script with the word *Montezuma.*

"That's tea in the glass," he said. "If you'd like something else, I'd be happy to fetch it."

"Thank you," she said again. "The tea will be fine."

The bellman left, and Hattie took the cover from the tray. She expected perhaps a bowl of soup. Something simple. On the bone china plate were generous slices of spring lamb with French peas, cream fritters, fresh fruit, and toast with a side dish of red currant jelly. If the kitchen sent this with regret, she could not imagine what they would send otherwise.

She brought a peach slice to her mouth and heard a moan out in the hallway. Stepping out the door, she saw a man dressed in a priest's black cassock. He sat hunched over on the bottom step of the circular staircase. He held his head in his hands, his ginger-colored hair disheveled. Beside him were a black valise and a black hat.

Hurrying to him, she thought she heard him mumble, "What have I done?"

"Are you all right, Father?" she asked.

He glanced up, startled. "No . . . I mean I'm fine. Fine," he said as he tried to stand. Unsteady, he sat back down.

She saw the swelling high on his forehead. "That's quite a bump you have there. Why don't you let me put something on it."

"I don't . . . well . . . I . . ." he stammered as she helped him to his feet. She noticed the initials *JFL* tooled into the top of his bag. He quickly grabbed it and his hat. The sound of bottles rattling inside the bag was unmistakable. Hattie said nothing, helping him into the nurse's station.

At first she thought he might have been

drinking. He would not be the first man of the cloth to imbibe, but Hattie did not smell any liquor on him. Only peppermint. But drinkers sometimes used that to cover the smell of whiskey. Of course, those bottles could well be among the tools of his profession, containing sacred wine and holy water.

She wet a towel and held it on the bump. "Let's see if we can get that swelling down. That bump's about the size of a turkey egg. Did you fall?"

"I . . . did," he said. "I was coming down the stairs too quickly and slipped, and — and hit my head on the banister."

"You must be more careful. Are you a guest here?"

"No. I'm the priest in town. I came to hear the confessions of some guests. They're leaving tomorrow. I look in on the consumptives now and then, too."

"We have something in common." She introduced herself.

"I'm Father John Lanigan," he said. "I . . . I should go. I need to catch the train."

She took the towel from his head. "That swelling is going down, but you'll have the bump for a day or two, I think."

"Yes. Thank you." He picked up his hat and bag.

"Are you certain you're all right? Maybe

you should rest for a bit."

"It's nothing. A lot on my mind is all."

She followed him out and watched him walk down the hallway. He did not stumble or stagger. But she sensed something wasn't right. The priest was a very nervous man.

Back inside the nurse's station, Hattie sat down and ate. Perhaps it was because she was so hungry, but the meal tasted even better than it looked.

She needed to find Mr. Prescott and Mr. Quince, but between the long day, a full stomach, and the lingering effects of the thin air, she felt tired.

As she lay down on the soft feather bed in her room it was hard to believe it was a little past six o'clock. She heard the spur line train whistle blow and glanced out the window. Shadows were stretching across the ground. Beyond the timbered hillside across the way, magnificent white clouds drifted against the blue sky. She unstrapped the Swamp Angel pistol from her leg and placed it on the bedside table. Lying back down, she closed her eyes.

Just for a few minutes, she thought, before sleep quickly overtook her.

Chapter Seventeen

The creature stood naked in the middle of its darkened hotel room. It needed no light to see in the darkness. It glanced at the open pocket watch on the dressing table. The hands read a quarter past ten.

It felt a cool breeze waft through the open window. The curtains fluttered briefly, exposing the twinkling stars in the night sky. It was quiet at this end of the hotel, away from strolling guests, away from everything.

The creature knew that a number of the male guests were likely downstairs in the basement of the hotel, drinking and enjoying their cigars in the bar where Faro, poker, and roulette wheels beckoned. Others might be in the billiard room, cues in hand, wagering on games of Straight Rail.

The rabbit blood the priest had brought had satisfied its thirst, but there was nothing so sweet as the taste of human blood on its tongue. And the priest had given him the

145

name of Emilio Analla and told him where to find the man. Said he would likely be there tonight. From what the priest said about Analla, he was indeed proper prey.

Time to prepare.

Since its Becoming, the creature was well aware of its shape-shifting power. At first, it feared the ability to change its form, fearing it as much as it despised it. But with time and a growing, gnawing hunger — the creature could not help but embrace its nature. There were only a few shapes it could take. Like last night at the hotel livery stable when it was feasting on the prey that had been whipping the horse. And, when all the shouting and uproar approached, it had willed itself into a black bat and flown off over the trees, leaving no trail to follow. A prudent thing. But it preferred the shape of the wolf. As the black wolf, the creature always took its prey down with ease. After all, most prey tried to put up a fight.

In the quiet confines of its room, the creature willed the change. Only a few moments were needed. It felt its heart race. Breathing became shallow and rapid. It dropped down on all fours. Bones grew. Other bones shortened. Tufts of hair appeared, changing into black fur, growing and spreading quickly. Its eyes narrowed and sharpened. The cheekbones disappeared, and the snout grew long. Its ears slid up the sides of its head, growing into pointed triangles. The spine arched, widened, then stretched out long. Its fingers and toes became stunted as sharp claws poked out from the knuckles, growing long and curved and vicious. Its hands and feet became great, savage paws. Every tooth in its mouth sharpened to a wicked point.

The creature drew in a deep breath, filling its lungs with the night air. It detected no human presence. The only animals nearby were in the livery. They were safe this night. Pricking its ears, the creature listened. No crunch of footsteps on the pathways. No voices close by. The night was as still as death.

It slipped through the open curtains and landed on the pathway, only a couple of feet below the window.

Making its way down the hard ground of the slope, it noticed no small animals inside the fenced enclosure, but it caught the scent of the lambs and goats and ponies from the livery. The hotel had moved them. An understandable precaution.

Halfway across the terrace, it stopped suddenly, catching sight of the swaying movement of a lantern light, then voices coming from the hillside over to the right near the river. Hot spring mineral baths bubbled up there. These were guests headed back to the hotel. Two couples, carrying thick white towels, hurried along the pathway. Brave souls to be out at night like this. The creature let out a low growl.

"What was that?" the creature heard one of them say.

"What?" another asked.

"Did you hear something?" said a third.

"No."

"I heard something."

"I told you this was a bad idea."

"Just keep going. And stay on the damn path."

The creature sniffed. Their fear held a strong scent. Unmistakable. Like copper. The same smell as fresh blood.

But these people were not proper prey.

At the river, the creature halted again and listened. Nothing. The train depot stood dark. The animals of the woods had scattered. They always did whenever they sensed the creature nearby.

The creature headed for town, its thirst growing.

Lights in town came into view a mile off. The creature veered away from the river. It knew some of those hunting it had laid their traps and snares near the riverbanks. Traps waited in other places, too — near roads and woods and trails. These town fools baited their traps with animal entrails. And some added poison. But the creature knew well, none of these people understood what had come among them.

Keeping to the edge of Old Town, the creature avoided the saloons, gambling halls, and bordellos entertaining their customers this night, as they did every night. The rowdy sounds of the town's revelers singing songs, firing pistols, and shouting at the moon filled the night air. The priest had said that Emilio Analla's small house stood on a narrow street, just off of Lopez Avenue. "Look for the rickety fence in front."

The creature crouched by a lone cedar tree. A few scattered houses sat along the street. Electric lines stretched from house to house, but only one appeared to have a telephone line. It was not the Analla house. And none showed a light in the window. Except at the Analla house. Though the shutters were closed, a hint of light shone through the cracks.

The half moon hung in the sky. Squat adobe houses threw their shadows across the hard dirt street. A skinny yellow dog loped out from behind a corner. The creature watched, its gaze penetrating the shadows. The dog stopped, turned its head in the direction of the creature, and darted off into the dark, its tail tucked between its legs.

Rising up off its haunches, the creature curled its lips into something resembling a smile.

"Get away, dog!" someone griped. "*¡Vamos!*"

A large, big-bellied man came out of the shadows where the dog had disappeared. He wore a battered hat, wrinkled clothes, and worn brogans. Swaying uneasily, he mumbled something in Spanish, scratched between his legs, and chuckled. He stank of strong liquor and the cheap perfume whores doused themselves with. The sound of loose coins jingled in his pocket. He did not carry a gun.

Emilio Analla was just as the priest had described him. The blood craving grew.

The creature watched the prey try to open the front door to his house. When the door refused to yield, the prey kicked it open.

Inside, a woman shrieked. The prey slammed the door shut behind him.

"*¡Cállate!*" the prey shouted. "Shut your

mouth, woman!"

The creature's ears pricked up, listening. Muffled cries followed. The prey spoke, his voice gruff.

The creature's thirst increased. It started toward the house. Sounds of a woman crying drew it closer. It heard crashing sounds, then the snap of wood breaking.

Another voice cried, "No! No more!"

The prey shouted, "*¡Mi casa!* My house! I do as I please!"

There was the sound of a hard slap. A woman sobbed.

Reaching the front door, the creature halted. It peered through a slender crack in the wood. An old woman in her nightdress picked herself up from the floor. A couple of chairs lay overturned. One was broken. The prey stood in the middle of the room, a wild look in his eyes. Another woman, younger, but the same size as the old woman, curled up in a corner and sobbed. A blanket hung off her shoulders. The prey jerked her up by the arm. She pleaded something in Spanish through her tears. The prey slapped her hard across the face. She twisted away, her lip split open, blood gushing.

Enough! The blood craving struck. The creature reared up and smashed through the door, one hinge pried loose.

The prey turned, a startled expression on his face. The creature slammed into him, sinking its sharp, gleaming fangs deep into his throat. The prey flew backwards, breaking a table in half as he fell and hit the hard floor, too stunned or too frightened to struggle. The creature drank greedily. Human blood! The big-bellied prey lay on his back. Limbs twitching. Dying. Sweet crimson blood flowed into the creature's mouth.

The creature saw the younger woman crumpled in the corner. Eyes closed, blood dripping onto the front of her nightdress. The side of her face was a bright red from the prey's slap. But where was the old woman? Maybe she had run away, maybe to get help. But the creature heard no screams, no frightened shouts. No matter. The creature's tongue lapped at the warm blood, the smell of copper filling the air.

Feasting.

A whisper came from across the room. *"Dios mío."*

The old woman had not fled after all. The creature raised its eyes and saw her standing in a doorway near the fireplace, horror in her eyes, her hand covering her mouth.

The prey's body shook. Taking its eyes from the old woman, the creature clamped its jaws harder on the prey's neck. The death rattle ceased. The creature thought it heard the sound of a gun cocking from where the old woman stood. Raising its eyes it saw the flash from the barrel as the gun fired.

The bullet pierced the creature's rib cage and tumbled over and over as it went around its lungs. The creature had never been shot before! In the next instant, it burst into a pack of scurrying black, ugly rats.

Through a hundred eyes, the creature saw the bullet, clean and bloodless, fall to the rug-covered floor . . . the old woman gasp . . . a smoking short-barreled revolver drop from her hand . . . her knees buckle . . . her body sink to the floor.

The rats climbed over each other, scurrying into place, contorting into a grotesque-looking thing. Their snouts elongated, legs curled, tails twisting and twitching. Its blood surging through its veins, the creature's shape-shifting was almost complete. For a brief moment its eyes flashed red, like the devil himself. The black fur grew and glistened. Again it was the wolf.

Lowering its head, the creature snarled at the old woman. She lay on her back inside the doorway. The creature saw her chest rise and fall. She had fainted. There would be no more surprises from her.

The creature closed its eyes. It felt no pain from the shooting, no shock from the sudden shape-shifting. But there was always the torment. The torment of this living death. Constant. Growing. Consuming. One thought filled its mind. *If only the old woman* had *killed me.*

Its eyes open, the creature saw the prey was dead, the jaw hanging slack, the eyes dim and vacant. The two bite marks in the prey's neck were red and swollen. Something more was necessary with this prey. Like the one it had taken in the livery. Like so many others before. With its jaws around the prey's neck, the creature tore away the flesh, ripping it down to the bone. Blood dripped, forming a small crimson pool on the rug underneath the prey's neck.

Licking blood from its lips, the creature wanted to stop this horror but could not. The hunger would not be denied. The creature, impatient and ravenous, drank those last drops of blood oozing from what remained of the prey's throat.

And those terrible words the creature had heard long ago in a far away place echoed in its head: "blood is life, and life is blood."

But the creature knew too well that blood was its curse. The craving for it, the feasting on it, and the need for it, overwhelmed. The creature tried to resist. So many times it had tried. But the thirst and desire drove it. They were one — thirst and desire. No distinction. No denial. Only need. Vicious need. Feeding the need was the only way to satisfy it. Drinking human blood only made the creature desire it more the next time the craving struck. That next need. That next torment. And it could not leave any prey alive. It must not.

The prey lay drained, bloodless. The creature's thirst and desire were sated. But there was still more to do this night.

Moving away from the town, the creature, its jaws gripping the body of the dead prey by the neck, dragged it over verdant grasses, past thick clumps of silver-colored rabbit bushes, and around needle-sharp yuccas. It stopped and saw the prey had lost one of its brogans. No reason to concern itself about that now.

The creature made its way along the edge of a hillside wood for half a mile before turning toward the river. All the while it kept alert, listening for the sounds and watching for the movements of armed hunters ready to shoot. The creature raised its head and sniffed the air, searching for the smell of fresh animal entrails covering the bitter scent of poisoned carcasses staked to the ground as bait. None of these hunters realized what they hunted was no wolf.

The creature slowed, its eyes detecting disturbed earth and cut branches laid out in a strewn fashion, a telltale sign of a deep hole dug in the ground to try to trap it. The scent of fresh deer entrails and blood rose up from the covered pit. The creature listened for the breathing of some hunter lying in wait. Moments passed. It heard nothing, except the gentle sound of the river flowing not far off.

The body grew heavy, but the creature did not stop to rest. Its task was far more important.

At the banks of the Gallinas River, the creature opened its jaws and dropped the body on the embankment. Thanks to the almost daily thunderstorms over the past couple of months, the river still ran high and fast.

The half moon had risen higher in the night sky, where stars lay scattered in their courses.

The creature remembered a time when it found the stars beautiful. It had not been so long ago. Now, the same stars were ugly pockmarks in the blackness of a long, terrible night.

Rolling the body into the river, the creature watched the current carry it away. The river flowed south for many miles. It passed no other towns, no villages, nothing. More than likely, Emilio Analla's body would never be found. The creature knew that bodies of prey hastily left behind, like that stable man the night before, only increased the panic of the living.

The creature watched from the bank as the body floated swiftly down the river on its long journey to decay. This way was best. Always.

CHAPTER EIGHTEEN

Mrs. Lucero opened her eyes and groaned. Startled, she sat upright, her foot brushing against her revolver. The side of her head throbbed.

¡Madre de Dios! The beast! Those rats! Where were they? And Teresa? Where was . . . ? There, in the corner. Dried blood stained the front of her nightdress. She was not moving. Groggy, Mrs. Lucero went to her, praying to God that her daughter was still alive.

"Teresa? Teresa!"

Moving her head, her daughter moaned.

Thanking God, Mrs. Lucero glanced about the room, fearful of what she might see. A deathly quiet enveloped the house. Blood splattered the floor by the broken table. But the unholy beast had vanished. Her daughter's *bastardo* husband was gone, too.

Mrs. Lucero made her way to the front

door. It hung crooked from a lone hinge. In the half moonlight, the street, even the town, seemed to lie in an eerie silence. There was no time to lose.

"Get up, Teresa," she said. "We must pack our things."

With a small leather pouch clutched in her hand, Mrs. Lucero sat with her daughter on a bench at the train depot. Teresa dozed, resting her head on her mother's shoulder. She wore her shawl pulled down over her face. The clock on the far wall read a quarter to seven. They had been at the depot for hours.

A green carpetbag lay at Mrs. Lucero's feet. Next to Teresa was a smaller bag. Those two bags held most of their meager belongings. The pouch in Mrs. Lucero's hands contained two train tickets she had purchased that morning, and seventeen dollars — money Teresa had made from washing clothes, money they had managed to hide from Teresa's cheating, gambling husband.

The station agent approached, adjusting his hat. Mrs. Lucero looked up at him, a hopeful expression on her face.

"Train's on time, ma'am," the agent said. "We got no word to the contrary, as yet."

She nodded her thanks.

A few minutes had passed when the sound of heavy boots approached. Snapping her head toward the sound, she saw a black figure, and raised her hand to shield her eyes. The morning sun glinted off something bright and shiny.

"Forgive me, *Senora* Lucero, I did not mean to startle you," Deputy Cleofus Silva said, stepping around in front of her, blocking the sun from catching the silver badge on his black coat.

"*Gracias,*" she said, straightening the black *rebozo* covering her head.

"I am surprised to find you here," Silva said.

"We . . . My daughter and I, we are going away."

"Away?"

"*Sí.* To my sister's. She lives in Las Cruces."

"Deputy Valdes asked me to go by your house this morning."

Mrs. Lucero tightened the grip on her pouch. "And why did he want you to do that?"

"To see if Teresa's husband was home. He wanted me to bring him to the jail. To have a talk with him about Teresa."

She sat straighter and raised her chin.

160

"Her husband is gone."

"You had trouble at your house last night. A broken door, a broken table. What happened?"

"Her husband came home, drunk, as usual, stinking of whiskey and *putanas.*"

"That is unfortunate," the deputy said, sounding like he meant it. "I also found blood on the rug and walls."

"The blood is my daughter's." She patted Teresa to wake her.

Teresa sat up, her shawl falling away from her face. One eye was black, her cheek and lip swollen.

Silva grimaced.

"What is it?" Teresa asked. "Is the train here?"

"Not yet," Mrs. Lucero said, then turned back to Silva. "Her husband did this to her. All because she asked him where he had been."

Teresa laid her head back on her mother's shoulder.

"I'm sorry, *senora,*" Silva said.

Mrs. Lucero continued. "I got my gun. I was going to shoot him."

"Did you shoot him?" he asked.

"No."

"One of your neighbors told me she thought she heard a shot coming from your

161

house last night."

She shook her head. "I hear shots in town almost every night."

"Where is the gun?"

"My daughter's husband must have taken it."

"Why do you think he has it?"

"Because he came at me when I told him to get out. I tried to shoot, but the gun, it . . . how do you say?"

"Misfired?"

"*Sí.* And he came at me and hit me, here," she said, touching her fingers to the side of her head. "He knocked me down. When I woke up, he was gone. So was my gun."

"Do you know where he might have gone?"

"To hell, I hope."

Silva ran his hand over his heavy moustache. "When do you think you and your daughter will be coming back to town?"

She glanced at Teresa. "Perhaps a couple of weeks. Perhaps a month. *¿Quien sabe?*"

A train whistle shrieked. A plume of white smoke rose in the distance from the oncoming steam engine.

"We must go now," Mrs. Lucero said, helping her daughter up.

Silva carried their bags to the train and helped them on board. Mrs. Lucero thanked him. He looked like he wanted to ask her something else but must have changed his mind. Relieved, she watched him walk away.

After getting her daughter settled, Mrs. Lucero sat next to her. The only other passenger was a man in a bowler hat at the opposite end of the car, reading a newspaper, his back to them.

The train whistle blew, and the car lurched forward. Teresa began to cry. Giving her a handkerchief, her mother comforted her.

The train tracks ran alongside the river. After about a half mile, Mrs. Lucero reached into her carpetbag and pulled out a canvas sack tied with a strip of rawhide. Inside was her revolver. In her haste to gather their belongings and get away, she had forgotten to get the bullet. The one she had fired at the devil. But the deputy had not mentioned it. He must not have found it and did not know about it. So, it did not matter. After she got Teresa out of that house, she was not going to go back inside to try to find it. And if someone should come one day and ask her about it, she would tell them it must have belonged to that *bastardo* husband. Who was to say it did not? And the gun. She just wanted it gone. It would only raise questions she could not answer. Would not answer. She could not tell the truth about what had happened inside the house, what she saw. The wolf. The rats. *El Diablo*. Not ever. None of it. Who would believe her? All that mattered, what was truly important now, was that Teresa's no good husband would never hit her again. Never.

The other passenger appeared to be sleeping; his head slumped forward, lolling gently. *Bueno*. She lowered the window, glanced about to see if the conductor was coming, then threw the sack out and watched it splash into the river below. Making the sign of the cross, she blessed herself, closed the window, and sat back down.

"It will be better now," she said to her daughter. "We will never come back here. This place, it is cursed."

CHAPTER NINETEEN

The creature had gotten back into its room just before sunrise. After pulling the curtains closed, it washed its face in the water basin, then put on fresh clothes. It pulled down the bed covers and rumpled the sheets. Taking the pillow in its hands, it brought up a bit of blood into its mouth, then coughed it onto the pillow.

It sat down and waited. Soon, a gentle knock sounded at the door. The creature listened as the footsteps went away. It opened the door and found a covered tray waiting. It placed the tray on the table and lifted the cover. Poached eggs, bacon slices, and a piece of toast sat on the plate. The creature recalled a time when it savored such a breakfast, but no more. Even the smell of food was repulsive.

The creature wrapped the food in the napkin and slipped it into its coat pocket. Opening the door, it placed the tray with the empty plate on the floor and walked down the hallway.

Outside, the hotel provided shade from the sun as the creature made its way around to the kitchen veranda. The windows there were clouded over with steam, the dishwashers already busy scrubbing the breakfast dishes. Several large wooden barrels sat nearby. After a quick glance about to see if anyone was around, the creature took out the napkin and tossed the food into the barrel they used for scraps. It dropped the napkin on the veranda and started back to its room. The creature smiled. Every morning and every evening it took its meals in its room. The hotel was happy to oblige. After all, the creature was a long-term guest.

Hattie woke. Her head felt clear, and that was a relief. Out the window, the sun was well up over the mountain ridge to the east. The sky shone as brilliant a blue as she had ever seen.

She realized she had fallen asleep wearing her clothes from the previous day. She put on the room light, walked to the dressing table, filled the basin, and rinsed her face.

There was still the nurse's journal to read. She also needed to see Mr. Prescott and Mr. Quince today. And continue her investigation. She changed from her wrinkled dress into one of the gray cotton nurse's dresses and then strapped her Swamp Angel pistol back on her leg. Taking a white bib nurse's apron from the closet shelf, she put it on. After running a brush through her hair, she pulled the dark-red tresses into a bun at her nape and secured it with a long hairpin. She put one of the nurse's hats on her head, looked in the mirror, and thought she indeed looked the part of a nurse.

Odd sounds came from the hallway. Then mumbled voices.

Hattie carefully opened the door, surprising two workmen, one on a wooden ladder, the other holding the ladder to steady it.

"Very sorry to have disturbed you," the man holding the ladder said in a German accent. He smelled of tobacco and had bushy eyebrows. "We should not be long, *fräulein.*"

The other worker tinkered with the chandelier hanging from the ceiling. Glancing down the hallway, she noticed all the other chandeliers were dark.

"Is something wrong with the lights?" she asked.

The German spoke to the other worker in Italian, who said something back to him in Italian. The German turned to Hattie.

167

"No worry," he said. "Only cleaning and adjustments."

"I need to go to the nurse's station." She pointed at the door across the hall. "Should I wait until you're finished?"

"No. Go, please. We finish soon. *Ja.* Get lights back on."

Stepping inside the nurse's station she closed the door and turned the gas valve. Light filled the office. The journal was on the desk where she had left it. In spite of the coffee-stained pages, she found the entries she was looking for, though some of the ink had become smudged, making the handwriting in places illegible. She did her best to make sense of it.

"Mrs. Shaw sometimes on her feet, but only for short while," Hattie read aloud in a soft voice. "Is difficult most days."

Reading that last line Hattie could not help but smile.

"Shaw's cough worsening. More blood, sputum . . . night sweats, feverish last three days . . . Dr. Burwell examination June 28: Lung capacity sixty percent . . . July 7: no change . . . pallid. Fever continues. Appetite lessening.

"Mr. A. Prescott obstinate; refuses any exercise. But went out on veranda twice in one week. A miracle! Informed by housekeepers they have found blood on pillow and sheets. Some mornings find bed not slept in. Odor of liquor in room . . . instructed housekeepers to leave room windows open daily. Appetite fluctuates. Refuses fruit, vegetables. Fever two days. Cold compresses applied. Lung capacity fifty percent. Prescott refused examination July 1. Refused July 8. Claimed exhaustion, needed sleep. . . . sat on veranda for ten minutes today.

"M. Quince prefers walks in early morning, evenings. Often goes by himself. Appetite appears good: beef, fruits most days. Complains of occasional night sweats. Blood on sheets sporadic. June 24: bad day; weak, pale, agitated. July 5, improved. Dr. Burwell examination July 7: lung capacity seventy percent. Pallid, agitated."

A gentle knock at the door made her look up. It opened. The workmen and their ladder were gone. A plump-looking woman wearing a blue dress and a stylish hat with a blue feather looked in.

"You must be our new nurse," she said with a smile. She had pleasant gray eyes and spoke with a slight European accent Hattie could not place. "I'm Sally Harvey."

"A pleasure to meet you, Mrs. Harvey," Hattie said, getting up from the desk.

169

"I wanted to welcome you and ask if you have everything you are needing."

"I think so. I was just preparing to make my morning rounds."

"That is good then. So you have not met our tubercular guests?"

"Only one yesterday. Mrs. Shaw."

"Yes, Mrs. Shaw." Her smile began to fade. "You will notice all the tuberculars have rooms on the first floor. Mr. Harvey thought it would be easier for them."

"I'm certain it has."

"We have not half our rooms filled. Many cancellations." An uneasy expression crossed her face. "It is unfortunate, this . . . wolf."

"I gather much is being done to try to stop it."

"Do you think so?"

To Hattie it sounded less like a question and more like a plea. The Montezuma had only been open for a few months, and all of this turmoil was obviously not helping business. Yet somehow Hattie could not help feel there was more to Mrs. Harvey's disquiet. Of course, Hattie was aware that Mrs. Harvey knew about the bodies drained of blood in these attacks. It was why Mrs. Harvey had contacted the Pinkerton brothers, and why Hattie was here now. Hattie wished she could give Mrs. Harvey some encouragement, some hope. But she could not. It was a necessary part of her job. And, at least at this moment, one of those unsavory tasks she had to perform.

"I'm sure everyone is doing all they can," Hattie said. "Doctor Burwell tells me you have your children here with you. I hope they are enjoying themselves."

"They are, yes," Mrs. Harvey said, her face brightening. "They are going on a burro ride while I must go to town on business. Our livery man, Duke, is taking them."

"Duke is a good man."

Mrs. Harvey smiled again. "Well, I must get to the train."

Valdes walked around the shambles that was the front room of the Analla house. Deputy Silva had not exaggerated. Blood on the rug. Blood spots splattered on the walls. Overturned furniture. Broken front door.

They would have to bring Emilio Analla in now. Mrs. Lucero had made the complaint, at least as far as Valdes was concerned.

Curious neighbors were trying to watch him through the open door.

"Did you see anything last night? Hear anything?" he asked them.

They said no, nothing they had not heard before.

"I thought I heard a shot," one woman said. "But maybe not."

Valdes asked the men if any of them could repair the door. "So no one will be tempted to steal everything."

One man said he would.

Back inside the house, Valdes took another look around. In the bedroom the bed was unmade and drawers left open. Mrs. Lucero and her daughter must have been in a big hurry to leave. A pile of clothes lay in the corner by a straw mattress in another room. In the kitchen, a cooking pot hung in the cold fireplace, the smell of burned frijoles hung in the air. He walked back to the front room. Disgusted, he kicked aside part of the broken table and glimpsed something strange on the rug amid the pieces of wood. He squatted down and picked up a spent bullet. It was a .22 caliber. Not a mark on it.

Silva had told him Mrs. Lucero said her gun had misfired. She had also said Emilio had taken her gun. But Silva had not asked her what kind of gun she had. Nothing to be done about that now. Valdes looked around at the walls for any bullet holes, up at the beams and *vigas* in the ceiling. No bullet holes anywhere he could find. Had Mrs. Lucero lied? But why would she? He slipped the bullet into his trouser pocket. Something about this did not feel right.

Outside, the neighbors had gone back to their homes, but a few watched out their windows. His dun horse, tied to a post, nickered.

Maybe Emilio had left footprints. His head down, Valdes began searching for signs. The ground was hard but better to look everywhere than to miss something important. He made his way around to the back of the house. A lot of small footprints in the ground here, women's shoes, like where a line had been strung to let clothes dry. He moved away from the house, heading where tufts of grasses sprouted up. It was probably a waste of — no! There. Part of a track. A wolf print. And it was big. Other marks, too, like something had been dragged along. Another track! Still more. The signs headed toward the mountains.

Valdes ran back to the house, got on his horse, and followed the tracks and drag marks. Glancing back now and then, he saw no one followed. It was not long before he found a brogan by a rabbit bush. Worn and scuffed, it had a hole in the sole. Very likely Emilio's brogan.

The signs led to the banks of the Gallinas River, amid the green pines, cottonwoods, and red branch dogwood bushes. The wolf had dragged Emilio almost a mile away from town and then cut over to the river. Why all that way? Had the damn wolf sniffed out the traps and stayed clear of them? Could it be that smart? But what had it done with Emilio's body? The wolf tracks and drag marks went up the river but no further. Had it dropped the body in the river? But that made no sense. And where had the wolf gone then?

Riding along the river for almost a mile Valdes searched both sides of the embankment for signs. He found nothing. The tracks stopped. The wolf vanished. But how could that be? *No fue posible.*

And why drag Emilio Analla to the river? Did it attack him? It must have. And what about Mrs. Lucero and her daughter? Did they see the attack? Valdes had found no blood outside the house. And in all those other attacks, there was always blood somewhere. The attack must have happened inside the Analla house. There was blood there. But Mrs. Lucero told Deputy Silva the blood was her daughter's. If the blood was not Teresa's, why would Mrs. Lucero lie?

174

Valdes took the bullet out of his pocket and held it in the palm of his hand.

None of this made any sense. *Esto era una loco.*

CHAPTER TWENTY

Hattie found Mrs. Shaw in her room. She was in her wheelchair, staring out the window.

Hattie asked her what she'd had for breakfast.

"A little fruit," Mrs. Shaw said weakly. "Didn't feel much like eating. I think they took the tray. I left it by the door."

She clutched something in her hand that hung from a simple gold chain around her neck.

Hattie felt her forehead. The woman was running a fever. She wetted one of the cloths sitting next to the water basin and placed it on Mrs. Shaw's forehead.

"You keep this cold compress there," she said. "It'll help bring your fever down."

Mrs. Shaw sighed. "Maybe." The corners of her eyes drooped, and her hand tightened around whatever it was she was holding.

Concerned, Hattie asked her what was in

her hand.

Mrs. Shaw half smiled and opened her hand, revealing a small gold heart-shaped locket. "From my husband. The first gift he ever gave me. I told him I'd never take it off."

She opened it and held it up for Hattie to see. Each side held a small daguerreotype portrait. One displayed a handsome man with a chin curtain beard. The other showed a young woman, a benign smile on her face.

"That's my husband, Gerald," she said. "He had beautiful brown eyes. And that's me. A long time ago."

"You made a very handsome couple." Glancing over at the bed, Hattie noticed the bloodstains on the pillowcase.

"Happens most nights," Mrs. Shaw said and coughed. "A housekeeper will be here soon to change the bed sheets."

"I'll come by later to check on you."

"I expect I'll be here."

Going to the lobby, Hattie made her way to Kenton at the front desk. She asked if he had seen Morgan Quince or Ash Prescott this morning. "I knocked on their doors, but neither of them answered."

"I haven't seen Mr. Quince yet." Kenton turned to the desk clerk, who was placing notes into mail slots behind the desk, and asked if he had seen Quince.

"I'm afraid not. But he often takes a walk around the grounds in the mornings."

"Perhaps he's not returned," Kenton said. "As for Mr. Prescott, you'll likely find him downstairs in the bar."

She gave him a questioning look. "The bar?"

"That's where the poker tables are."

Passing the sign stating the bowling alley was closed, Hattie walked down the stairs to the basement. She did not want to wait for the elevator. It was on the third floor. She could hear the sound of voices up the open elevator shaft urging others to hurry along.

The basement was quiet. The first room to the right at the bottom of the stairs was the bar. The beveled glass doors were closed. Across from it was the Curiosity Shop. Its windows were dark. A sign pointed down a side hallway to the barbershop. Further down the main hallway was the entrance to the billiard room. At the end of the short hallway was the bowling alley. Another sign there, larger than the one upstairs, said the alley was closed, with the hotel's regrets.

Hattie tried the bar door, and it opened into as plush a room as she had seen at the hotel. Hand carved panels lined the walls. A small terra-cotta fireplace stood near the long, ornate mahogany bar. Polished cuspidors were placed every few feet along its foot rail. She counted three Faro tables and five poker tables, each covered in green felt. The chairs at the tables were upholstered in rich leather. And the smell of cigar smoke hung thick in the air.

The barman, wiping a glass with a towel, recognized her nurse's outfit and cocked his head in the direction of the only other person in the place, a pallid-looking gentleman seated at the poker table in the far corner.

Hattie approached his table. He did not look up from his game of solitaire. His face was drawn, his hair long and straight and in need of washing. Closer now, Hattie saw the cuffs of his coat were beginning to fray, and his tie looked more like an old shoelace. A glass of whiskey sat within arm's reach.

"I'm looking for Mr. Ash Prescott," she said.

"And I am looking for a black seven."

"Mr. Prescott, I'm Sarah Andrews, the new nurse. I'd like to talk to you for a moment."

"I gathered as much." He glanced up. "Sit, if you wish."

She sat down opposite him. The barman asked her if he could bring her anything. "Water, sarsaparilla?"

She smiled. "Thank you, no."

"Tell me," Prescott said, continuing to play his game, "why did you take this job?"

"I needed the work, and I want to help."

"The first is understandable, the latter is noble. Good for you. It's been a pleasure making your acquaintance."

Hattie agreed with the former nurse's judgment. Prescott was a mulish man. She waited. He did not look up from his cards.

"You're still here," Prescott finally said.

"Yes. In order for me to do my job, it would help to know how long you've had your symptoms."

"When did I become a lunger, you ask. I was a student at Western University of Pennsylvania. In Pittsburgh. Do you know it?"

She shook her head. "I'm not familiar with it, no."

"It burned down. Twice. That should have told me something. The first time it burned down was in 1845, and then again four years later. Bad luck, wouldn't you say?"

"Unfortunate."

"That was the very word the vice-chancellor used to describe my tenure there.

My studies were better suited to gambling and drinking instead of the course of study I had been pursuing, whatever that was, when the coughing started. I began raising blood, the night sweats came, and worse. That was, nine years ago. I concluded it best to live my life to the fullest that I possibly could. That meant more drinking and gambling, and a few other entertainments. But then things change, as things often do."

"What changed for you, Mr. Prescott?"

He gave her a crooked smile. "See this glass of fine, expensive whiskey? I order one every morning when I come in here. I never drink it, though. I keep it close by to remind me of better days. Better times."

A deep, wet coughing overtook him.

"Water!" Hattie called to the barman.

Prescott pulled out a handkerchief and covered his mouth. The attack passed, and Hattie saw blood dripping from his mouth. Taking the water from the barman, she went around to Prescott. He pushed the glass away as he wiped off his mouth.

"This damnable disease plays with you like a cat plays with a mouse," he said. "It grabs you and lets you go, and grabs you again instead of killing you outright."

"The last time Doctor Burwell examined you he indicated that you have lost almost half of your lung capacity."

"Do you know how long that gives me?"

"Not exactly. It may be a couple of years. Or a couple of weeks."

"Perhaps I shall avail myself of the gambling establishments over in town later. You see, there are fewer card players frequenting the Montezuma at the moment, and as my room and restaurant bills are coming due shortly, I need to ply my trade, which is poker, in order to pay those bills."

"Mr. Prescott," she said gently, "I need you to understand how important getting outside in fresh air is for you, that you must eat and —"

"And I shall," he said, cutting her off, "for I know the town of Las Vegas is filled with opportunity on a nightly basis."

"That may be true, but leaving this dark room and getting some exercise would do you more good."

"I am exercising," he said, making a show of placing a black jack on a red queen.

He was determined to be obstinate, Hattie decided. There was little more she could do for him at the moment. "Doctor Burwell will be here tomorrow. I know he'll want to see you."

"And I shall be right here."

CHAPTER TWENTY-ONE

Turning his buggy onto Tilden Street, Doctor Burwell was astonished to see Mrs. Harvey sitting in a covered carriage outside his house. He opened his pocket watch. Nearly a quarter past ten.

"Mrs. Harvey, this is an unexpected surprise," he said, coming to a halt in front of her carriage. He could tell from the markings it was a Hutchinson carriage she had rented at the railroad depot. The driver, smoking a corncob pipe, tipped his hat at him.

"I am sorry to come like this," she said. "But I only now could come. I need to see you, if now is good time."

Doc thought she seemed a bit anxious.

"No bother at all," he said, reaching for his Gladstone bag, beside him on the seat.

"That is good," she said as her driver helped her down.

Inside the house, Doc offered her tea. She

thanked him and asked instead for water. They sat inside his front parlor.

"I have concern, Doctor," she said. "This wolf killing at the hotel livery of poor Mr. Barrow the other night. Tell me, please, what you have found out."

Doc told her that the man's throat was torn out, like all the others.

"Yes, yes, but Mr. Barrow's blood, was it all gone?"

"No. It was not. We believe the wolf got scared off. It was seen by one of the other liverymen. He said it ran when it saw him."

She set her glass on the table, reached into her bag, her hand trembling, took out a handkerchief, and put it to her mouth.

"What's troubling you, Mrs. Harvey?"

"I am hoping I am wrong."

"Wrong? What about?"

"What I told you before, about having no worries about these wolf attacks." She lowered the handkerchief. "I am worried more now than ever."

She appeared genuinely frightened.

"I can appreciate that, Mrs. Harvey," he said, his tone soothing. "It's terrible, I know, but —"

"No. It is more than that. More than that."

"I don't understand."

"Have you . . . have you ever heard of *nosferatu?*"

He leaned forward. "Forgive me, what was that word you said?"

"Nosferatu."

Puzzled, he shook his head.

"It is vampire. Maybe you know of vampire?"

He spread his hands apart. "I'm sorry. I don't know that one either."

"In my country, every one knows about vampire. Every peasant boy and girl knows."

"All right."

"Vampire is the living dead."

He sat back in his chair and wondered what in the hell she was talking about.

She said, "A vampire lives to drink blood. It must have blood."

"Mrs. Harvey —"

"Please to listen," she said sharply, then brought her hand up as if in apology. "Vampires drink blood of men, women, and child. Vampires are real."

"Mrs. Harvey, please. This is —"

"You must believe me, Doctor. In my country, parents warn the children not to go out at night. That is when the vampire hunts. But it can also be out during part of the day. It needs human blood."

"I am listening to you. But bear with me.

185

Why must this . . . vampire have blood?"

"To live. It is an evil thing."

"And you said mothers and fathers tell their children —"

"Yes."

"— not to go out after dark."

"Yes!"

"Because a vampire will get them. Is that what you're saying?"

"This is right!"

Sweet Lord above, he thought and spoke gently. "Mrs. Harvey, please hear me out. What you're saying sounds like the boogeyman to me."

She frowned. "Boo? Boogerman?"

"No. Boogeyman. It's a monster, a phantom. Like your vampire, I think. Parents here tell their children stories about it to scare them into behaving, doing what they're told."

"No," she said, shaking her head. "Vampire is no story. Vampire is real." She paused a moment, like she was considering what she was about to say. "I think vampire, maybe, is here. Now. It drinks blood, but it can make other vampires if it wishes."

Doc stared at her. "Mrs. Harvey, what does this vampire . . . what does it look like?"

"Anyone. It used to be human. It still

looks human. But it can change."

He put his hands together, believing full well he needed to be very careful with what he said. "Have you ever seen one of these vampires?"

She raised her head. "No. I have not. And if I had, I might not be here now. Vampires are real. They are."

The sharp ring of the telephone echoed down the hallway. Doc excused himself to answer it. A neighbor of a young couple was calling to let Doc know the couple's boy had cut his foot, and they were on their way to his house. "I think he might be needing some suturing," the neighbor said.

Doc went back to the parlor. "Mrs. Harvey, there's a boy coming in I'll need to tend to. I'm sorry. But, I promise I will pass along your concerns to Deputy Valdes."

She stood up, an almost embarrassed look on her face, Doc thought.

"I understand, Doctor," she said quietly. "I was only wanting to help. I must sound, how you say, silly."

"Mrs. Harvey . . ." he said, then paused. He wanted to tell her he believed her, but her story was too fantastic. "I know how difficult this must be for you. And I have no doubt you are trying to help. But, believe me, we are doing all we can."

"Maybe you are right," she said with a wan smile and left.

Doc rolled himself a cigarette. The whole town was having a conniption fit over these attacks, there were bodies drained of blood for no good reason he could see, and Mrs. Harvey was bringing him fairy tales.

CHAPTER TWENTY-TWO

Hattie asked the hotel doorman if Mr. Quince had passed by.

"He went out earlier," the doorman said. "Likes to take a walk around the terrace. Hasn't come back, that I know of."

Never having seen Quince herself, she asked what he looked like. The doorman described him as well dressed, for a fellow from Texas. "He was wearing a dark suit and cowboy boots. Fancy ones, too. Shiny. Got a moustache. And a fine felt hat with a curled brim."

Hattie thanked him and turned to go.

"Oh," the doorman said, "and he's wearing tinted glasses."

Outside, Hattie heard a noise and noticed that the door at the back end of the box-shaped wagon belonging to E. F. Drummond was open. Climbing backwards down the wagon steps was a spry gentleman wearing a straw hat. On his shoulder he carried a wooden tripod with a bellows camera fixed to it.

Hattie headed for the terrace to look for Quince. Taking the path down the slope, a strange feeling began nagging at her.

On the croquet court she found a few guests playing a match. The men were dressed in vests and colored cravats, and the women in long, flounced dresses.

One of the gentlemen knocked his red ball through a wicket with his mallet and said, "Good morning, nurse. No injuries here."

"That's very good," Hattie said.

"There haven't been any more wolf attacks, have there?" one of the women asked, her voice timorous.

"Not that I've heard," Hattie said.

"Good," another gentleman said. "Because I didn't come here to spend two weeks indoors. Could just as well have done that back home."

Hattie described Quince and asked if they had seen him pass by.

"There was a man sitting under the pergola down there," the other woman said. "It might have been him."

"How long ago was that?"

"An hour ago, at least."

Wondering if he might have gone to town, Hattie walked to the hotel train depot. None of the waiting carriage drivers or baggage handlers there recalled seeing him. Light-headedness came over her again, as swift and unexpected as it had yesterday. Getting to a bench she sat down and asked for some water. A baggage handler brought it to her in a silver cup.

"Nice and cool for you, ma'am," he said.

She took a few sips and lowered her head. After a bit, the water revived her spirits. But she had been unable to shake that strange feeling, only it had grown worse. She glanced about but saw nothing out of the ordinary.

Ready to continue her search for Quince, she made her way to the bathhouse on the far side of the terrace. The attendants thought maybe they had seen a fellow who looked like him pass by.

"He might have been on his way to the springs," an attendant said.

She followed the path to the hot spring baths along the hillside past the bathhouse. The few guests enjoying the springs said they had not seen anyone for better than an hour. Going up to the livery, she was told no guest named Quince had requested a horse or a buggy.

Frustrated, she headed back to the hotel. The day had warmed quickly, and she could feel trickles of perspiration running down her back. And that strange, uncomfortable feeling still nagged at her.

"Has Mr. Quince returned yet?" she asked the doorman.

"I saw him out on the veranda just a little bit ago."

Few guests were enjoying the long veranda. Hattie recognized the woman from the train, the fretting one, and her husband and two children. The woman seemed less anxious now, playing a game of gin rummy with her little boy and little girl, while her husband was engaged in a discussion about politics with another guest, a tall man with a full beard.

That strange feeling kept at her, like she was being watched. And now it was making the hairs on the back of her neck stand up. She stopped and looked about. There were guests milling around, the coming and going of a few carriages, and baggage handlers loading and unloading luggage. Everything appeared settled — nothing of a suspicious nature.

The last few people near the end of the veranda were an elderly man asleep in a rocking chair and two women, each reading a book.

Where was Mr. Quince?

"I understand you've been looking for me."

She turned, startled.

The man she saw was dressed just as the doorman had said. He was also wearing a pair of fine gloves, possessed a hint of color in his cheeks, and a charming grin, the kind that would make some women nervous, should he direct it their way.

"I'm Morgan Quince."

She noted the Texas accent and introduced herself.

"It's getting warmer," he said. "Perhaps we could go inside."

"Yes," she said. "And maybe something cold to drink in the dining room would help us both."

He seemed hesitant but agreed.

Once inside, Quince removed his hat and tinted glasses.

Whatever color Hattie thought she had seen in his face had vanished, if it had been there at all, and was replaced by a wan pallor.

Quince suddenly turned his head away and coughed, covering his mouth.

Passing the front desk, Kenton saw them.

"Mr. Quince," he said, "do you wish to have Father Lanigan come by to see you today?"

"No need," Quince said. "We spoke yesterday."

"You saw Father Lanigan?" Hattie asked, as they turned toward the dining room hallway.

"Yes. He's a good man. I find he often brings comfort when he comes by."

Hattie had not taken a close look at the dining room since she arrived. She stepped through the open double doors, onto the polished floor, and was immediately surprised at how immense it was. Great golden chandeliers hung from the ceiling. Tall windows, each with squares of blue, yellow and gold stained glass at the top of each pane, ran along three of the walls. Two walls of windows looked out on the timbered mountains that stood behind the hotel. The windows of the third wall, on the left side of the dining room, faced the same courtyard Hattie could see from her room, where two pergolas stood with great bunches of purple blooms climbing up and covering the lattice work. And in the middle of that third wall stood an elaborate sideboard, a good fifteen feet wide.

White linen covered every table. Although less than half the tables were occupied, there were easily enough of them to accommodate the full hotel guest capacity of three hundred. Harvey girls in their black dresses and clean white bib aprons moved about the tables, taking orders and delivering plates of food. They came and went through two doors connected with the kitchen.

Hattie and Quince followed one of the Harvey girls to a table near the middle of the dining room. Hattie noticed that the massive sideboard opposite it featured a huge stained glass panel across the top and a large oblong mirror set into the woodwork. A good portion of the dining room was reflected in that mirror.

"Would it cause any trouble if we sat over there?" Quince asked, indicating a table in a corner back by the entryway.

"As you like, sir," the Harvey girl said.

Following her to the table, Quince said to Hattie, "Hope you don't mind. I just don't much like looking in a mirror, seeing myself wasting away."

Hattie understood that fine.

They sat down, and the Harvey girl handed them breakfast menus. She said they were just in time, as the kitchen would shortly begin preparing for the mid-day meals. She asked if they would care for something to drink. Hattie ordered a glass of iced tea with a slice of lemon.

"And for you, sir?"

Quince coughed twice and asked for iced tea with a lemon slice, as well.

The menu offered Little Thin Orange Pancakes, Rice Griddle Cakes, French Pancakes filled with Cottage Cheese, and something called Huevos Rancheros. There were side dishes of fresh fruit cups, toast and marmalade, and sour milk biscuits. It all looked very tempting to Hattie.

"Have you eaten yet?" she asked Quince.

"I've not much of an appetite," he said, wiping his brow with a handkerchief.

"But you must eat, to keep up your strength for those morning walks you take."

"I had a good meal last night."

Hattie ordered toast. She had not had any breakfast yet, and toast was her usual morning meal.

She then noticed Quince's eyes. They were a dark brown. Almost black.

"I saw you were wearing gloves outside," she said.

He laid his gray gloves on the table. His hands were as pale as his face.

"That's true," he said. "Since this consumption got hold of me, sometimes I feel cold, and other times it's like I'm burning up with fever. I try to be ready for either one."

"Doctor Burwell told me that you have

periods of improvement, followed by a relapse, and then improvement again."

He chuckled. "Some days are better than others, I reckon. Never feels like I'm going to be rid of this. The sawbones in Fort Worth didn't know what to do at first."

"Is that where you're from?"

"It is." He brought his handkerchief to his mouth and waited. No cough came.

The iced teas arrived. Hattie took a sip from her glass.

"Do you have family there in Fort Worth?" she asked.

"Not any more. My wife and child are both dead."

"I'm sorry. I didn't know."

"Been a while since they've been gone. A long while, it feels like."

Thinking of her son, Tim, Hattie felt a pang in her own heart.

"But, I like this place here," Quince went on, indicating the hotel. "I think it suits me."

"When were you diagnosed?"

"About a year ago. It was while I was in Europe."

"You went to Europe?"

"I went there after my wife and my boy passed."

"I seem to be saying all the wrong things."

"No need to fret over it. Thinking of them

reminds me of a happier time."

The Harvey girl set the plate of toast down in front of Hattie along with the small dish of marmalade on the side.

"Would you care for anything else at the moment?" the Harvey girl asked.

Hattie shook her head. "Thank you."

The Harvey girl left, and Hattie asked Quince if he was sure he would not like some of her toast. Ignoring her question, he pointed toward the nearby window. "See that purple wisteria out there growing over the pergola? Caroline loved them."

"Was she your wife?"

He smiled. "I planted some for her on the west veranda of the house. My father's house. He left it to me. The west veranda had been Caroline's favorite place. She enjoyed sitting out there on an old settee in the evening, watching the purple blossoms against the setting sun. They had grown up around the white columns and hung down the edge of the veranda ceiling. I'd join her there, often with a drink in my hand. I was partial to bourbon whiskey then, though any distilled refreshment would do. Caroline said I'd stay there all night if she'd let me." He seemed lost in some distant memory and then asked, "How long have you been a nurse?"

"A while," Hattie said. "Eighteen years."

He considered her a moment. "You must be good at it."

"Kind of you to say. You said earlier that you feel like you're never going to get better. But you can. I've seen patients do it."

Casting his eyes down, Hattie thought he seemed sad somehow. Like he did not believe it. Or maybe he chose not to believe it.

"Those walks you're taking every day are very helpful," she said.

"I can't stay out too long anymore. This altitude, I think. It saps my strength. I ought to go rest now for a bit."

They got up to leave, and she noticed he had not touched his iced tea.

"Guess I wasn't very thirsty after all," he said.

As they stepped into the dining room hallway, a group of people facing the lobby blocked the way.

"We're almost ready," a voice called out from the lobby.

Hattie looked in the direction of the voice and saw Drummond, the photographer, holding up a small tray by a handle in one hand while he looked through the back of the bellows camera set up on the tripod.

"You'll see a bright flash," Drummond

said. "Don't be afraid."

"Maybe we can get around them," Quince said, pointing the way.

"Don't move," Drummond said.

Stopping, Hattie said to Quince, "We better wait." She heard the pop of a small explosion at the same instant a white flash blinded her for a few moments.

"Very good," Drummond said.

Some of the people gasped; others let out a chuckle of relief.

Hattie glanced about and realized Quince had vanished.

"Here I am," he said.

She turned and saw him coming back out of the dining room, his hat and gloves in his hands.

"Almost left these behind," he said.

That was odd. Hattie felt certain he had his hat and gloves with him when they'd stood up to leave.

CHAPTER TWENTY-THREE

Deputy Sam Cuddy sat on his horse near the town train depot and barely touched his nose. It still hurt like hell. He had to breathe through his mouth, his nose being so swollen and purple now, thanks to that dumb bastard Phil Larson hitting him in the face during the fracas at the jail yesterday. The only good thing about it, if he cared to call it good, was that Larson and the other stubborn jackass, Charlie Ross, were still sitting behind bars in the jail. All on account of them being greedy, hoping to catch the damn wolf.

Cuddy was all but certain that same greed had driven these particular men he watched get off the train that had just pulled into the depot. It was the fifth train today, and here it was, middle of the afternoon. He saw plain enough that some of the passengers were meeting friends or family members at the depot. But it was the others, the wolf hunters, that concerned him. They called themselves "wolfers." Some were dressed in coats and string ties, others in long corduroy dusters. And there were one or two who looked like they'd just crawled out of a cave. A few held slim leather rifle cases under their arms. Others carried packs slung over one shoulder. Some appeared to size up their competition, while others paid no mind to those around them. They were the professional wolfers, and they had a look about them, a way of carrying themselves. Some of the others had been lured here by the promise of money. They had guns with them but little idea as to how to go about hunting the wolf. Cuddy could tell.

He also figured they must have boarded trains from Texas to Wyoming. Hell, all across the territory, too.

While they were making their rounds earlier, Cuddy and Silva had seen others ride into town on horseback or driving wagons. Hard to miss them, loaded down with gear in the hopes of killing the wolf and collecting the reward. By Cuddy's estimate, around sixty had shown up so far. Of course, many of the hotel proprietors and boardinghouse owners were overjoyed, as rooms in their establishments were getting rented out. Every general merchandise store, grocer, cigar seller, and livery was thriving.

Cuddy caught sight of a reporter from the *Daily Gazette,* white skimmer on his head, pen in one hand and paper in the other, asking his questions and jotting down the answers.

"I'll catch it all right," Cuddy heard one of the wolfers say. "You're looking at the best tracker this side of the Rockies."

"For a thousand dollars, I'll bring in that bastard, and that's a promise," boasted another.

It was a damn circus as far as Cuddy was concerned. He was only here now keeping watch because Valdes said he wanted to know how many wolf hunters were coming in. "And make certain they see your badge," Valdes had told him. The wiry-haired deputy had taken a rag and put a good shine on his deputy sheriff badge before pinning it to his coat.

Cuddy spied a fellow on a gray horse coming around the other side of the depot. Barrel-chested and in need of a shave, the man wore a buckskin shirt, dirty pants, and a slouch hat. His spurs had big rowels, the Mexican kind. The pistol at his side was pearl handled. He carried a Sharps rifle in a scabbard tied to his saddle.

Cuddy snorted. Another damn wolfer. Probably going to ask if there was a good hotel in town. Many of them had already.

"I'm looking for the sheriff," the man said to Cuddy.

"He's not here. Something I can help you with?"

"Can you tell me where I'd find him?"

"Somewhere between here and Ohio, I expect."

"Ohio, you say."

"Bringing in a prisoner. County business."

"Who's in charge while he's away, then?"

"That'd be Deputy Valdes."

"And where might he be?"

"Likely as not at the jail."

"And where's that?"

Cuddy sniffed. "Go down to the corner there, turn left. That's Douglas Street. Follow that on around to the bridge and cross it. Keep going straight ahead on through the plaza, pass the church, the courthouse, and you'll see a two-story wooden building. Says *Jail*. Can't miss it."

"Much obliged." The man cocked his head back toward the depot. "Lot of people coming in, I see."

Cuddy looked him up and down. Maybe he had been wrong about what brought the fellow here.

"Wolfers." Cuddy leaned over and spit. "They've come here to hunt a wolf. For bounty money."

"You must have a big wolf problem, or a big bounty."

"You could say that."

"Why is it always beans?" the prisoner Phil Larson asked as Valdes removed the empty plate from the open square of the cell bars.

"I'd like to know about that, too," Charlie Ross said, sticking his plate of half-eaten beans through the open square of his cell.

"You do not like beans?" Valdes asked, taking the plate.

"Not for every meal," Larson said.

Valdes walked out and shut the heavy wooden door behind him. He could hear the two prisoners bickering and blaming each other for their troubles when he saw a big man in a buckskin shirt coming in the front door of the jail. The man nearly filled the doorway.

"Are you Deputy Valdes?"

"*Sí.* I am." Valdes set the dirty plates on the sheriff's desk.

The man told him his name was Virgil Thibodaux, and he was a Texas Ranger. He pulled a folded piece of paper from inside his shirt, opened it, and handed it to Valdes.

"I'm looking for this man. Been after him for a while."

Valdes studied the sketch. The drawing showed a man with a haggard face, a moustache, and curly hair.

"I have not seen him," Valdes said and handed the sketch back. "What did he do?"

"Killed the son of a Texas state senator named Wadlow."

"How do you know this is the man?"

"A little whore near the train station in Austin says she heard some hollering, then a splash in the river. A few minutes later" — he pointed at the sketch in his hand — "this man went running by her. Nearly knocked her down. Says she caught his face in the light of a train pulling out of the station. Claims he had blood on him, too. Being a good citizen, and since the senator offered a reward, she came forward. Of course, when I find this murderer, part of that reward'll be mine. Sure could use it, too."

"What makes you think the murderer has come here?"

"It appears he's been traveling by train. Porters and conductors say they think they've seen him. I've been on his trail. Austin, San Antonio, El Paso, and on up through New Mexico Territory."

206

"Do you know why he killed the senator's son?"

"More than likely it was a robbery gone bad, but I figure the senator's son must've put up a hell of a fight. Found about fifty in silver on him. And this." Thibodaux took a stickpin from his shirt pocket and held it out for Valdes to see. It had a gold oval surrounded by precious stones. The letters *GCW* were engraved on it. "Those are the son's initials. His father identified it. Said he had it made for him some years ago. A good thing, too."

"Why is that?"

"The body was found better than a week later downriver about twelve, fifteen miles. Some bad storms had come through. Body got tangled in some trees and all torn up. Face, limbs, everything. Bad. If it wasn't for that stickpin I doubt we'd of ever found out who it was."

"I hope you find your man," Valdes said. "You are welcome to check the hotels, saloons, anyplace you need. If we can be of any help, let me know."

"I'm obliged to you," Thibodaux said, slipping the stickpin back inside his pocket. "And can you recommend a good hotel?"

"Probably the St. Nicholas and the Plaza hotels are about the best in town. Three dollars a day."

"Not ticky, are they?"

Valdes chuckled. "No."

Deputy Silva came through the door. "There's a lot of people in town anxious to collect that reward and —" He stopped at seeing the big man and stepped aside to let him pass.

"Who was that?" Silva asked once Thibodaux was gone.

"Texas Ranger," Valdes said.

"What's he doing here?"

"He is after a reward, too."

CHAPTER TWENTY-FOUR

Inside the nurse's station, Hattie took a piece of paper from the desk drawer to make notes for her field report to the Pinkerton brothers. She wrote down what she knew so far about the strange case of bodies drained of blood.

Terrell/Gambler/Card cheat?/Found at river/night July 6

Unknown/Whiskey drummer/Rear of Plaza Hotel/found morning July 11

Shakespeare Jess Culpepper/Scoundrel?/Alleyway/night July 14

Unknown/Drifter/In gully/night July 21 or 22, or week later?

Zach Barrow/Liveryman/At Mont. Hotel livery/night August 5

She studied the page. All men. No women. All killings believed happened at night. Dates and locations seemed random, and it appeared that none of the victims knew each other. Except for the manner in which they were killed, nothing connected them. Yet.

When he saw the line of wagons waiting and all the horses hitched to the rails in front of Ilfeld's Dry Goods Store on the plaza, Father Lanigan was pleased. A crowd of customers inside meant confusion and clerks busy writing up sales. It also meant opportunity.

Peering through the tall show windows of French plate glass Ilfeld had installed with some fanfare not long ago, Lanigan saw wolf hunters crowded the place. Stepping inside, he was nearly deafened by the din of customers clamoring for ropes, wolf traps, ammunition, blankets, canteens, and other truck.

Lanigan made his way to the side counter where Charles Ilfeld stocked medicinal items like chloroform, laudanum, bandages, needles, and the like. Lanigan was not interested in any of those, however.

Ilfeld, his hair slicked over his balding pate, and wearing a bow tie and red sleeve garters, was assisting a man in a fur cap. Ilfeld signaled Lanigan to wait. A few moments later Ilfeld finished with the Fur Cap and greeted Lanigan.

"Very busy today, I see," Lanigan said.

"It is," the German merchant said, "but I am not complaining. How can I help you, Father?"

"I need a bottle of strychnine."

A passing wolf hunter snapped his head toward them.

"I'm sorry, we have none," Ilfeld said, a bit loudly.

The hunter moved on.

Disappointed, Lanigan asked him if any was coming in soon.

"You have a vermin problem, Father?" Ilfeld asked low, keeping a watchful eye on the customers so they did not overhear.

Lanigan nodded.

Ilfeld tapped his fingers twice on the countertop. "Here, under the counter. A shipment arrived an hour ago. You're lucky I still have some bottles left. Keeping them on hand for those of us who live here."

"You're a shrewd man," Lanigan said.

A clerk at the gun racks called out, "Mr. Ilfeld, please!" and waved him over.

"I hold a bottle for you. You will excuse me, Father." Ilfeld scurried over to the other side of the store.

Lanigan watched and waited. Hunters passed by, some stopping to consider the contents of the shelves before they moved on. A few customers left the store, their arms laden with purchases. Many congregated over by the canned goods, calling for air tights of beans, tomatoes, peaches, and Arbuckle's coffee. No one appeared to pay any attention to Lanigan.

He slipped around behind the counter, where he saw the small bottles, right where Ilfeld had said they were. Each one was labeled with skull and crossbones and the words POISON and STRYCHNINE in bold red letters. He glanced around the store, bent down, and snatched one of the bottles. He then slid it inside the pocket of his cassock. He started for the door, his hand gripping the stolen bottle inside his pocket. He made himself slow down so as not to draw attention. His eyes straight ahead, he passed the counters displaying women's hats and shoes. His heart pounded. A drop of sweat dripped down his temple. He could see the street outside through the windows. Wagons were moving away. Other men were preparing to enter. He put his hand out, reaching for the door.

"Father!" Ilfeld called out. "Stop!"

Lanigan's breath caught in his throat. Someone must have seen him! He wanted to run, but his shoes felt as though they were nailed to the floor. He squeezed his eyes shut and drew his lips tight. A thief. He would be arrested.

"Father?" he heard Ilfeld say.

Lanigan opened his eyes. Ilfeld wore a grim expression on his face.

"I'm sorry," Ilfeld said in a low tone. "I should have done this before." He held out his hand to Lanigan. "Thank you for coming in."

Lanigan blinked. He let go of the bottle in his pocket, took Ilfeld's hand, and felt a familiar shape. Another bottle of strychnine!

"I'll add it to your bill," Ilfeld said, smiled, and went back to his customers.

Lanigan stood for a moment, dumbfounded and ashamed. Turning, he left the store and hurried back to the rectory. Once inside, he closed up the windows, locked the door, sat in the dark, and drank his whiskey. He told himself the whiskey would take away the pain of his guilt and shame. But he knew that was a lie. So he drank more to try to obliterate that lie. His sins. His weakness. Hours passed. The only sound he heard was the ticking of the clock on the wall. And it came to him that God had not abandoned him as he had thought, but he had abandoned God. His soul ached. Tears ran down his face. He brought the whiskey bottle to his mouth.

CHAPTER TWENTY-FIVE

Late that afternoon, Hattie entered her notes in the nurse's journal. She had taken Mrs. Shaw for a walk around the courtyard oval, Mrs. Shaw's appetite was improved, and she had come to the conclusion she was "too ornery to die." Mr. Prescott refused to yield his seat at the poker table in the bar. And Hattie wrote about the conversation she'd had with Mr. Quince.

She also made entries about a splinter she removed from a little girl's finger, and a sprained ankle suffered by a guest while playing croquet. He had caught his foot in a wicket while attempting to show off for a young woman.

Glancing up from her notes, Hattie saw a reddish hue on the walls of the nurse's station. She looked out the window. The sky had changed to a bright red as the sun was setting. The hotel tower faced west, and as she had not been up there as yet, she decided this would be a good time to see the tower. And perhaps it would help her clear her head some about the strange deaths, consider the case, and perhaps find some clue that evaded her.

To reach the tower's fifth floor meant climbing five flights of stairs or riding the elevator to the third floor where the stairway led up the additional two flights to the observation deck. Hattie decided to ride the elevator. It could hold three people comfortably. When she came into the lobby, three guests were getting on the elevator. They told her there was room, and she joined them on the snug ride up.

A few guests waited as the elevator came to a stop on the third floor. As Hattie and the others on the elevator started for the stairs, she allowed them to go first. Two workmen were coming out of a storage room opposite the top of the staircase as Hattie reached the observation deck. She recognized them as the workers who were outside her room earlier that morning, repairing the hallway chandelier. The one with the bushy eyebrows smiled at her.

"Guten abend, fräulein," he said.

His Italian partner nodded at her.

"You have come to see the setting sun, *ja?*" the German said.

"Yes, I'm looking forward to it. Are you fixing lights up here, too?"

"*Nien.* We finished here tonight." The German wiped his hands on a greasy rag and then closed the door. "Part of deck floor needed sanding before we put coat of linseed oil on it later. Sun very bright. Warp wood, but we fix."

He motioned to his partner to follow him, and they headed down the stairs.

Hattie entered the round room. Immense bay windows allowed nearly unobstructed views. Outside the windows a covered balcony curved around the deck with a carved railing and balustrades painted white.

She had seen sunsets before, but this one startled her. The sun had by now dipped behind the mountain horizon, leaving the shortening red sky turning gold in its wake.

Other guests were there. All seemed as taken as she with the beauty of the sky.

Hattie lingered as the day surrendered to the purpling twilight.

"A pretty sight, isn't it?"

She realized Quince was standing beside her. His face was quite pale, and he was wearing his dark glasses.

"When I was over in Europe I saw churches with many a stained glass window.

Works of art, I suppose. Not one of them could match a sunset here."

A moment passed and she said, "It was you I saw."

He looked at her.

"When I arrived," she went on, "you were standing on the balcony by the railing."

"More than likely," he said. "I come up here every day. I'd stay all night if I could. This is where I find contentment." He removed his dark glasses. "Beautiful and sad at the same time, watching the day trying to hold on and the night coming for it. Kind of like life."

Hattie could understand his feeling of melancholy. Consumptives knew what was coming. The trick was in fighting it and pursuing the cure.

"Well, I ought to be going," Quince said.

"May I ask where?"

"To take a walk. I'm feeling up to it again now."

"That's splendid." She had considered she might take one on her own, but she said, "May I walk with you? I could use a walk myself."

He seemed surprised. "I would like that."

"But we should stay close to the hotel."

Hattie saw the quizzical look on his face. "Because of the wolf," she said. "We shouldn't get too far away."

"I'm not afraid."

"You might be the only one. Almost everyone around here seems scared to death."

"I stopped being afraid of death a long time ago."

He sounded as though he meant it.

"Nurse Andrews?"

She turned and saw one of the bellmen standing there. "Yes?"

He begged pardon for the interruption, then told her Mr. Kenton had sent him to find her. "Said it was important."

"Of course," she said and looked at Quince. "Perhaps we can take that walk another time."

"It would be my pleasure."

"Let us through, please," the bellman said, leading Hattie through the crowd in the hallway outside the hotel bar.

"Terrible thing," she heard one of the men say.

"Yes, but how long must we wait out here?" another complained.

The bellman opened the door. Inside, cigar smoke hung in the air. Hattie saw Kenton by the back poker table with several other bellmen. They were wrapping a body in a blanket.

"Mr. Prescott is dead," Kenton said.

"I am sorry," Hattie said. "What happened?"

"One of the other players at the table said Mr. Prescott laid down a winning hand and started laughing. It was a big pot, he said. As Mr. Prescott reached across the table to gather up his winnings, his laughing turned to coughing, and it wouldn't stop. He was all hunched forward, and the next thing anyone knew, Mr. Prescott was face down on the table."

"You sent for me, Mr. Kenton?" asked Duke. He saw Hattie and touched the brim of his hat. "Miss Andrews."

"Do you have a wagon?"

"Brought it over to the side entrance, like you asked."

Hattie had not realized the basement area had doors leading to outside stairways.

Kenton instructed Duke to take Prescott's body to the hotel icehouse. "First thing in the morning, put it on the train. I've already alerted Wyman's Mortuary. He'll have someone at the depot there to pick it up."

"I'll see to it," Duke said.

"And Miss Andrews," Kenton said, "would you please let Doctor Burwell know the body will arrive tomorrow? For his coroner's report."

"Right away," she said.

Kenton started for the door. Hattie heard him mumble, "What else can go wrong?"

E. F. Drummond sat inside his wagon near the hotel entrance and stared at the silvery image on the glass plate. It was one of the more than two dozen pictures he had taken today at the Montezuma. He was quite pleased with the results thus far. He had images of the hotel, taken from the terrace, images of carriages arriving at the front entrance. He had images taken from the tower observation deck and along the crowded veranda; images at the mineral baths on the hillside and the fireplace in the lobby, of the reading rooms, a guest suite, and many others.

But this one perplexed him. It showed a group of guests standing in front of the entryway to the dining room. On the far left side of the image stood a comely woman. From the apron and cap she wore, he surmised she was an employee of the hotel, likely a nurse. That was why Drummond remembered her, for she stood out from the guests standing there.

Her head was turned to her left. She appeared to be looking at nothing. An empty space.

Drummond could have sworn he had seen a man standing next to her, just before he had taken the picture. A tall, pale man with a dark moustache.

It was getting late. Nearly midnight. Drummond rubbed his eyes. Still, this was very strange indeed. Had he imagined the man standing next to the nurse? He must have, for the man was obviously not there now.

CHAPTER TWENTY-SIX

Hattie woke and sat upright in the darkness of her room. The soft ticking of the clock broke the quiet. A thin slice of moonlight showed along the outer edge of the curtains.

But something was not right. Looking over at the table, the clock read a little past two. Did the curtains move? Of course not. How could they? She had not left the window open.

"There it goes!" someone shouted outside.

"It's heading around to the front of the hotel!"

A gunshot echoed!

"Don't fire unless you got a good target, damn it!"

That last shout sounded like Duke.

Hattie threw off the covers and put on the light. Quickly dressing in her nurse's clothes, she slipped her Swamp Angel pistol inside the apron pocket.

Rushing out the door, she encountered

several male guests in the hallway, some wearing long nightshirts, others in shirts and trousers.

"I heard shots!"

"Me, too!"

"Nurse, what's going on here?"

"I don't know," Hattie called back to them. "But stay in your rooms!"

Reaching the lobby, she saw Kenton and a bellman at the front doors.

"What is it?" she asked.

"We can't tell," Kenton said.

"Who's out there now?"

Two more shots fired.

"Good God," Kenton said.

"Tell me who's out there," Hattie said.

"Duke and some of the livery men," Kenton said. "They've been patrolling the grounds at night."

"I demand to know what all this is about!" someone shouted.

Hattie saw a bearded guest coming down the staircase. He was waving a silver-topped cane.

Kenton went to him. "Please, sir, everything will be fine. No need to concern yourself."

Another shot cracked.

"No need for concern?" the bearded man shouted. "You've got bandits shooting all over the place!"

Watching through the front door windows, Hattie saw that the moonlight cast a soft hue on the circular driveway and grounds. There were more shouts, getting closer.

Reaching down, Hattie slid her hand inside the apron pocket and took hold of her pistol.

"Shoot it!" someone outside cried.

A shot sounded close by.

"You missed, goddamn it!"

Hattie glimpsed a large black figure rush past the far side of the driveway.

"Did you see that?" the bellman asked Hattie, his voice shaking.

"I saw something," she said.

A couple of men with rifles ran past, chasing the shape.

More guests came into the lobby. Kenton did his best to calm them.

"Have you told the sheriff?" one asked.

"What is going on?"

Another shot cracked.

"Someone get me a gun!"

"Ladies and gentlemen, please, go back to your rooms," Kenton said.

Hattie heard more shouts further away. She wanted to see if she could help, but with the men shooting, she thought better of it. One of them might take a shot at her.

Grumbling, the crowd in the lobby started back to their rooms.

A few moments passed.

"Think they got it?" the bellman wondered aloud.

Hattie heard Mrs. Harvey's voice. "What is this, Mr. Kenton?"

Hattie glanced back. Mrs. Harvey was wearing a dressing gown.

"I'm not certain, Mrs. Harvey. The men saw something out there in the dark."

"This is terrible," she said, clutching her hands.

A shout came from outside. "Open the door!"

Hattie saw them coming up from the driveway slope. Three men. Two held rifles and were holding up the third man between them, his arms over their shoulders.

The bellman pushed open the door. In the light thrown from the lobby, Hattie recognized Duke as the man the other two were helping. He had a bad scrape on the side of his face, as if he had taken a fall.

"Put him over here on the settee," she said. "Does he have any other injuries? Bleeding? Broken bones?"

"Don't think so," one of the men said.

"Was it the wolf?" Kenton asked.

"Can't say for sure," the other man said.

"Did you kill whatever it was?" Mrs. Harvey asked.

"No, ma'am," Duke groaned as they got him to the settee.

"Careful with him," Hattie said.

His face was pained as he sat down, his arm across his stomach, holding his left side.

"Let me see," Hattie said, taking Duke's hand away. His shirt was torn, and the exposed skin was very red. She gently touched the spot, and he winced. If it were a broken rib he would have likely pulled away. "It's probably a bad bruise. There's not much we can do but let it heal."

"Tell us what happened," Mrs. Harvey said.

Duke said he was coming up on the nurse's station when he heard a noise. "I didn't see the lights on there and wondered if maybe somebody was hurt and needing help. That's when I saw it."

"The wolf?" Kenton asked.

"I think so. It was big, but it ran off and disappeared into the shadows. I gave a holler and took after it. Things happened fast after that. We got a few shots off, but it was so quick. I almost had it, too."

"How did you get injured?" Hattie asked.

"I chased it past the dining room and down the driveway, toward the terrace.

That's when I saw it coming right back at me, and I fired. I don't know how I missed, but I must have. It was near on me, so I swung at it with the barrel of the gun, and it turned sudden like." He indicated the other two men. "Maybe it saw you boys running down to me. All I know is, it must have run into me and spun me around. Next thing I knew, they were carrying me through the door."

"Thank God you're not any worse," Kenton said.

"Yes," Mrs. Harvey said. "Thank God."

Hattie asked the other men to bring Duke to the nurse's station. "I want to clean up that scrape."

"This is not good," she heard Mrs. Harvey say as they left the lobby. "I wish help would come."

I'm trying, Mrs. Harvey!

Duke sat in a chair in the nurse's station while Hattie dabbed at the ugly scrape on his face with a wet towel.

"I should've pulled my Bowie knife is what I should've done," Duke said. "Cut that beast from gizzard to throat."

"You're lucky you've got no more injuries than you do," Hattie said. "It could have killed you, like the others."

"I'm just angry is all. Missed our chance."

"Did you see where it might have gone?"

He shook his head. "Like I said, it hit me and knocked me cold."

She set the towel aside and examined his scrape. "Not so bad now. But I suspect your side is going to be sore for a few weeks."

"I don't think I broke anything," he said. "Had busted ribs before. This don't feel that bad. When it knocked me down, I think maybe I was more stunned than anything else."

She saw him glance up at her then look away. Something was bothering him.

"Can I tell you something?" he asked, his voice low.

"Of course," Hattie said.

"I didn't want to say anything, you know, in front of the others, but this might sound crazy. And I'm not crazy. I know what I heard."

"I'm listening, Duke."

"When that big wolf was coming at me and I fired, I said I must've missed him, but I'm sure I didn't miss. It was looking right at me, and I know I hit it in the head. And I know that don't make sense because it ought to be dead. But it kept coming, and I swear I heard . . ." He dropped his head.

"Go on," she said gently.

228

He licked his lips, then whispered. "It sounded like . . . like it was laughing at me."

He almost looked scared, and that surprised Hattie more than what he said. She measured her words and said, "You probably thought that's what you heard. It must have been growling."

The look on his face told her he was not convinced, and, yet, she sensed he wanted to be.

"I don't know," he finally said. "Maybe so. Just . . . just don't tell nobody."

"I promise. If you'd like, you can lie down here in one of the beds and rest."

"I've put you to a lot of trouble already."

"No trouble," she said.

"I'd just as soon go."

She helped him to his feet.

"I'll tell you this," he said. "If I ever get another chance, I'm going to kill that big bastard. Pardon my language."

CHAPTER TWENTY-SEVEN

Marta Kolbe got out of her bed shortly before dawn. After a fitful night of sleep, she knew she must go talk to her sister. A stout German woman, Marta pinned her thick blonde hair back into a bun, buttoned up her plain cotton dress, slipped on her work brogans, and opened the door of her bedroom.

Holding a lit candle, as the harsh bright light of the electric bulbs was hard on her eyes this early, she walked down the hallway to the room where her sister Gretl slept. Gretl had come for a visit from the old country, the village of Mittenwald in the Bavarian Alps, where they had both been born and raised. While Gretl said she would stay for only a few weeks, she had remained for five months. Marta would not have objected to this except that her sister complained daily and bitterly about the New Mexico Territory, calling it a coffin for enlightenment. Marta also did not like that Gretl often treated her like a servant.

And, Marta was certain Gretl was stealing money from her.

Marta lived about a quarter mile outside town, where she raised chickens and sold the eggs to the grocers, restaurants, and hotels, including the Montezuma. She did quite well in that regard and kept the money in a covered bowl on a shelf in the kitchen. Her mother had done the same thing in Germany when they were growing up. But Marta was finding the bowl a bit lighter over the last couple of weeks. And, while she had no proof of Gretl's thievery, she did suspect it and for good reason. No one else was around who could have done it. So, last night she told her sister of her suspicions. Gretl had run crying into her room and refused to come out.

Regretting her accusations now, Marta knocked on Gretl's bedroom door.

"Gretl?"

When her sister did not answer, she opened the door and found the bed unmade.

Marta went to the kitchen. Perhaps Gretl was preparing breakfast to try to make some amends. But there were no aromas of sausage and strudel in the air. Her sister was not in the kitchen.

Marta was about to call out her name but instead went to the shelf, took down the covered bowl, and checked the contents. She'd had three hundred dollars in it. Half of it was missing now.

Angry, Marta went through each room in the small Queen Anne style house, searching for her sister.

"Gretl! I will talk with you!" she called out. "Where are you? Come out!"

She went back to her sister's room and looked in the closet. Gretl's clothes were still hanging there. Her hairbrush and scarf and other items were still on the dresser, as well. Gretl had not run away. If she had, at least then Marta would have been rid of her. But where was she? And the one hundred and fifty dollars she had stolen?

Marta blew out the candle and lit the lantern she kept by the back door. It was still dark outside, though the hint of first light was showing in the east. Walking around the house, she did not find her sister on the front porch. Gretl was not at the chicken coops, either, and, thankfully, she had not stolen Marta's horse, for it was still in its corral. That left only the long shed where Marta stored tools and made crates to haul the eggs.

Approaching the shed, she glimpsed something strange strewn across the worn, hard ground. Greenbacks, twenty-dollar gold pieces, some silver coins. They led up to the long shed. Picking up some of them, she realized it was her money. Here was the proof Gretl had stolen it! But what was it doing on the ground?

"Gretl? Are you in there?" she called out, seeing the sliding door was ajar.

A scratching sound came from inside the shed.

"Gretl?"

She heard a flapping noise, and something black flew out the doorway low over her head. Startled, she ducked down and tried to wave it off with one arm. What was that? A bird? A bat maybe?

"Come out!" Marta shouted. "We will talk now!"

No answer.

"Gretl!"

Marta drew her lips into a sharp, thin line. "Then I come in and get you."

She slid the door open further and stepped inside. In the glow of the lantern, she saw it. Marta's scream caught in her throat.

Jumping back outside, she slammed the door and threw the latch to lock it shut.

"Mien Gott," she whispered. Her knees

buckled, and everything went black.

Crossing the lobby, Hattie caught a bright flash in the dining room out of the corner of her eye. Mr. Drummond was already at work this morning taking his photographs.

She was headed for the front doors. Doc Burwell had asked her to assist him with his rounds this morning. She wore a fresh gray dress, apron, and nurse's hat. Her pistol, of course, was strapped to her leg.

A dozen guests had converged on the front desk informing Kenton that they were anxious to leave, cutting their stays short due to last night's incident. She felt sorry for Kenton, and particularly Mrs. Harvey, who was trying her best to help her husband make the Montezuma a success.

Seeing Doc pull around in his buggy, Hattie walked out to meet him. Doc told her he had not been surprised to receive her call last night that Mr. Prescott had died. The man had ignored every warning he had given him.

"Let's see how Mrs. Shaw is doing this morning first," he said, taking his Gladstone bag in hand.

They were nearly to the door when the bellman opened it, and Quince came out, carrying a newspaper under his arm. He wore his coat, hat, gloves, and dark glasses.

"Mr. Quince," Doc said, "how are you feeling this day?"

"Fine, fine," he said. "I've had my morning walk and thought I'd sit in the fresh air for a while. Read the newspaper."

Hattie could not help notice Quince's happy, almost vigorous mood. There even appeared to be a blush to his face. All good signs.

He turned to Hattie. "Good morning, Miss Andrews. Quite a melee around here last night."

"Oh? What happened?" Doc asked.

"All manner of shooting and hollering," Quince said.

"Very early this morning. They thought it was the wolf," Hattie said.

"Good Lord," Doc said. "Was anyone hurt?"

"Not badly. Duke got a nasty scrape and some bruising. Nothing serious."

"I suppose the wolf got away," Doc said.

Hattie's look told him it did.

"They gave that wolf a run, though," Quince said.

"Too bad they didn't get him," Doc said.

"I wish they'd've got him, too. I read that one of the first remedies some early Greek sawbones thought would cure consumption was eating a wolf's liver."

"Hard to believe today," Doc said.

Quince chuckled. "There's a lot of things hard to swallow these days. But, I have to say, if they ever catch that wolf, maybe we could cook the liver and see how it does."

"As you are in such good spirits," Doc said, "this might be a good time to examine you."

"Suits me," Quince said. "But the house-keepers are cleaning my room at the moment."

"Why not the nurse's station?" Hattie said.

"Doctor Burwell!" Kenton stood at the open front door. "I need to speak with you, please."

As Doc went inside, Quince suggested he and Hattie get under some shade. "The sun's feeling a bit brighter."

They walked to the veranda and were no sooner in the shade than Doc came back.

"I'm afraid we'll have to postpone the examination, Mr. Quince," he said.

"Oh? Trouble?"

"Probably nothing, but I should go."

Quince nodded and walked down the half deserted veranda.

Doc motioned to Hattie. "Miss Andrews, I need you to come with me. I may need your help."

"What is it?" she asked as they hurried to his buggy.

"Deputy Valdes rang the hotel. Said I was needed back in town right away. A woman there, Marta Kolbe is her name, says something is wrong with her sister."

"It must be something serious," Hattie said.

"She's got her locked in the shed."

CHAPTER TWENTY-EIGHT

When Hattie and Doc arrived at Marta Kolbe's place, Hattie saw Valdes was already there, talking to Marta on her back porch. The woman possessed a pleasant round face and rosy cheeks. She was whittling on a thick piece of wood about a foot and a half long, concentrating the blade on one end. Marta rubbed her thumb over the sharp point. Not satisfied, she continued at it with her knife, throwing a look toward the long shed.

Valdes did not look pleased to see Hattie, but she didn't care.

"We got here as quick as we could," Doc said, pulling to a stop. "What's all this about?"

"Miss Kolbe has been telling me that she and her sister, Gretl, had an argument last night," Valdes said as Doc and Hattie climbed down from the buggy. He turned to Marta. "Tell them what you told me."

"She steals from me." Marta continued to sharpen her stick. "I know she steals from me. I tell her so. She tells me go to hell, goes to her room, and cries. I go to sleep. I wake early, go look for her. Not in house. In kitchen I find half my money missing. One hundred fifty dollars. She took it."

"How do you know?" Hattie asked.

"She steal before. I thought maybe she was going to train depot, leaving for good. I go outside, find my money on the ground, leading up to the shed. I see the door to the shed is open and hear noise inside. I call her name. Noise stop. I go to shed. Something flew out."

"What was it?"

"Black bat." She ran her thumb over the point on her stick again. "I looked inside shed, saw my sister on the ground. Sitting up. Two holes in her neck."

Hattie said, "Did you say two holes?" She remembered that was what the baggage handler in Kansas City had told her the dead woman near the depot had.

"*Ja*. Here." Using two fingers she indicated a spot on her neck. "Blood was dripping out from holes. She looked at me. I lock door. Then I faint. When I came to, I called jail, said bring help."

"You didn't try to help her?" Doc said.

239

Marta shook her head.

"Why not, for God's sake?"

"Gretl was beyond help."

"That's nonsense. How can you say that?"

"You come see." Setting down her knife, Marta got to her feet and slid that sharpened piece of wood inside the belt she wore around her waist.

She started for the shed, turned back to the porch, and picked up the lantern.

They followed Marta down to the shed. Hattie saw Marta had a mallet stuck inside her belt at her back. *Why would she carry that around?*

Marta struck a Lucifer, lit the lantern, then put her hand on the door latch.

"Do all of you believe in God?" she asked.

Valdes nodded. So did Hattie, though she could not help thinking it was an odd question to ask.

"Yes. Why?" Doc said.

"That may help," Marta said and undid the latch. "It will come from the shadows. Be ready for fight. Do not let it bite you."

Bite? What's in there?

Marta slid the door open. It made a harsh grating sound.

Much of the inside of the shed was in shadows. Hattie counted only a few small windows. Marta held her lantern up with

240

one hand, the other gripping the stake in her belt.

In the lantern light, Hattie caught sight of a hoe and shovel and other tools, as well as rolls of chicken wire. There was a workbench, and a blanket covering the nearby window. She saw other windows were also covered.

"I did not cover the windows," Marta said.

Harnesses and bridles hung from wooden pegs, along with a saddle and other tack. And it was strangely quiet.

Hattie felt her heart pounding. She breathed deeply.

"Gretl?" Doc called out. "I'm Doctor Burwell. Are you hurt? We've come to —"

Behind them, the sharp sound of the door sliding shut made everyone turn.

In the glow of the lantern light, Hattie saw Marta's sister coming at them, arms reaching out. But it was no longer human. It was a thing with fingers like claws and wild, dark hair, its face a pallid gray with eyes nearly black. Shrieking a hideous cry, two white fangs showed inside a blood-red mouth.

Scared, Doc drew back. Hattie reached under her dress for her pistol strapped to her leg. Valdes drew his revolver and fired.

The bullet struck the thing in the chest. A splotch of blood appeared on its torn blouse. It charged him, its shriek growing shriller.

Valdes fired again, hitting it in the stomach.

More blood stained its blouse.

Hattie raised her pistol. The thing slammed into Valdes before she could fire. The deputy and the thing hit the ground. Valdes struck it across the face with the butt of his revolver handle, snapping its head to one side. Shrieking, it grabbed the revolver and jerked it out of his hand.

"Get it off!" he yelled, its teeth snapping at him, its claw-like fingers scratching at his face and arms.

Hattie tried to get in close to put her pistol to the thing's head, but the thing twisted around too fast for her to get at it.

Marta put her lantern on the workbench, and Hattie saw her reaching for something on the wall.

"Help me!" Doc yelled. "Get its legs!"

Hattie shoved her pistol in her apron pocket and grabbed one of the feet as Doc got hold of the other ankle.

Screaming, it let go of Valdes and flipped around. Hattie held on, but Doc lost his grip, and the thing kicked its loose foot, catching Hattie across the face, almost knocking her out. The blow sent her staggering to the shed's wall.

Regaining her senses, Hattie pulled out her pistol, saw the thing rise and backhand Doc hard across the face. He fell to the ground and did not move.

Valdes came up behind it, his revolver in his hand again. He fired at the same instant it turned. The bullet grazed its ear. The thing screamed and leapt on top of him. He stumbled back against the workbench, trying to get hold of the thing's arms.

Hattie cocked her pistol and started across the shed floor, ready to shoot it in the head when she heard Marta scream what sounded like a battle cry.

Marta appeared from the shadows, grabbed the thing by the back of its dirty blouse and yanked it off Valdes. The thing hurtled backwards and slammed into the wall but kept its feet. Baring its fangs and letting loose a hideous shriek, it ran at Marta.

Hattie saw Marta raise the shovel she now held in her hands like a baseball bat. The big German woman swung it hard. The flat of the shovel hit the thing square in the face. Its shrieking stopped. A loud twanging sound echoed inside the shed. Blood burst from the thing's broken nose as its feet flew out from under it. Stunned, it landed hard on its back.

"Kill it!" Valdes shouted. "Kill it!"

Hattie started for it, the red, swollen bite marks evident on its pallid throat.

Marta cried, "Stay back!"

Dropping the shovel, she pulled the sharpened stake and mallet from her belt. Straddling the thing, she put the stake over its heart and, in the same instant, swung the mallet down, driving the stake into the thing's chest.

It let out a sickening wail.

Marta swung the mallet again, driving the stake in deeper. A geyser of blood erupted from its chest, the stake pinning it to the ground.

Hattie stood back and watched, horrified, as Marta, covered in blood, got to her feet.

Its mouth open wide, blood bubbling out, legs kicking, arms flailing, the thing fought to get itself loose.

Marta picked up the shovel and stood behind the thing's head. Holding the shovel handle in both hands, the blade pointed down, she drove it in one swift motion through the thing's neck, severing its head from its body.

Blood gushed from the wound. The thing convulsed, then went still.

"Out," Marta said, sliding the shed door

open enough for them to get through. Hattie and Valdes helped Doc up. She glanced over at Valdes, who was favoring his right hip. "Are you hurt?"

"It is nothing," he replied, a quiver in his voice. "I did not know you had a gun."

She could not tell him she was a Pinkerton detective. "A woman alone needs to be careful these days."

"Well . . . thank you for trying to help me in there. How is your face?"

"It hurts."

Once outside, they leaned Doc against the shed wall. He took paper and his tobacco pouch from his pocket. "Somebody tell me what we just saw in there," he said. His hands shook so much the tobacco refused to stay in the paper.

Hattie glanced down at her own hands. They trembled. She drew them into fists to make them stop.

"El Diablo," Valdes said, concentrating on rolling a cigarette for Doc. "The devil."

"Not devil. Vampire," Marta said, calmly wiping the blood off her face with a rag.

Hattie turned to her. "A what?"

"What we call in old country, *nosferatu.*"

Doc jerked his head up, a surprised expression on his face.

"Are you all right, Doc?" Valdes asked.

"I . . . yes, yes."

"Marta, you need to tell us what we just saw in there," Hattie said.

"As I said. Vampire."

"What is that?"

"Unholy. Not dead, not alive."

"Talk sense," Valdes said.

"I only tell you what I know." She pointed inside the shed. "That is vampire. Gretl was alive before a vampire bite her, then" — she shrugged — "she only seemed to be alive. Vampire drank her blood, but not all of it. If it doesn't drink all her blood, it leaves her between life and death. Then, she must drink blood. I killed her, or she would kill me, and many others."

"Where do we find it, this vampire?" Hattie asked.

"Gone now."

"What did he look like?" Valdes asked.

"I not see it well."

"What did you see?"

"A black bat."

Valdes stared at her. "A *bat*?"

"This is insane," Doc said.

"That is what I saw."

"Everybody simmer down," Hattie said and looked at Marta. "We've never heard of such a thing. Tell us what you know."

Marta glanced from Valdes to Doc before

she spoke. "Vampire is a monster. It must drink blood to stay alive."

Hattie heard Valdes mumble something.

"It can drink animal blood," Marta continued, "but human blood best. Blood gives vampire life, makes it strong. The longer they live, the stronger they become."

"How long was your sister this . . . thing?" Valdes asked.

"A few hours."

"I shot her twice, and she kept coming. How do you explain that?"

"Bullets only make vampire bleed a little. But bullets, they don't stop vampire."

"Do you know where it came from?" Hattie asked. "How it got here?"

Marta shook her head. "I cannot say how. Mama says vampires come somewhere from mountains east of Europe. They exist for a long time. Many centuries. Some vampires live forever, Mama said."

"Imposible," Valdes muttered.

"No. All true. Vampire can see in the dark, can change shape at will."

"Change shape?" Hattie wondered if she had heard Marta correctly.

"Ja. Some can change into mist or vermin, wolf or —"

"Wolf?" Valdes cut in.

"Wolf. *Ja.*"

Valdes looked sick. *"Madre de Dios."*

Doc appeared stricken.

Hattie understood, and she knew Marta did, too, when she saw the realization in her eyes.

"The killer wolf. It is vampire," Marta said.

"What does it look like when it's not some animal?" Doc asked.

"Anyone."

"Anyone!" Valdes spread his hands. "How are we supposed to find this thing?"

Marta shook her head. "Vampire very sly."

Hattie heard Doc groan.

"This is very important, Marta." Hattie indicated the shed. "What you did in there. Is that the only way to stop these things?"

"Wooden stake through heart. Cut off head. That is what Mama said." Marta started for the shed. "I must tend to sister's body. Vampire hates crucifix. Crucifix good. Vampire evil. Crucifix can burn skin of vampire, if it touches it. Crucifix blessed by priest is best. Holy water, same. They won't kill a vampire, but they will keep it away. A new vampire must stay out of the sunlight. That is why Gretl put blankets over the windows. Sunlight burns vampire very bad. But after time, it can go out if it covers skin. Bite marks in neck of person who becomes vampire will heal in a few weeks. And, also, a vampire shows no reflection in mirrors or glass. That is all I remember." Marta walked into the shed.

Hattie stood there, flummoxed. They were looking for a monster they did not know how or where to find. It fed on blood, and changed its shape, and —

A sound drifted out from the shed. It sounded happy.

"Is she humming in there?" Doc asked.

Something occurred to Hattie. She headed for Marta's house, her head down, searching.

"What is she doing now?" she heard Valdes say.

Reaching the back porch of the house, Hattie inspected the ground there.

"I think I found something," she called out and saw Valdes and Doc coming up.

"What is it?" Valdes said.

She pointed. "Do these look like drag marks to you? And, here, what about this?"

"Part of a wolf track," Valdes said.

"I see blood drops here," Doc said.

Hattie was upset with herself. She had not even noticed them when they had arrived, and they had walked all over them.

"Marta said a bat flew out from the shed," she said.

"Maybe it was the wolf first?" Valdes said.

Hattie nodded. "I saw the marks in Marta's sister's throat. I don't believe a bat made those."

Doc shuddered.

"Whatever it was," Hattie continued, "it must have attacked Marta's sister when she came out of the house. These drag marks look like they lead to the shed."

"That helps explain the money Marta found on the ground," Doc said.

A pillar of black smoke rose up behind the shed.

"Something's on fire!" Doc shouted.

Rounding the corner of the shed, they saw Marta standing just beyond the end of the building, backing away from flames and black smoke rising up out of a hole. They ran to her. A putrid stench rose with the smoke that made them cover their noses and mouths.

"Marta!" Doc cried. "What are you doing?"

"Burning the vampire. I douse with kerosene and put in pit where I burn rubbish."

"But she was your sister!"

"*Nien.* No more. Vampire must be burned. Then I put a brick in its mouth, fill the pit with dirt, and cover it with heavy stones. Mama say the brick is needed to keep it from feeding. Heavy stones are the only way to be certain it not get out."

CHAPTER TWENTY-NINE

Hattie sat next to Doc in his buggy. One thought gnawed at her. Some are born to do great things, and some are born to undertake unsavory tasks. It troubled her because this unsavory task frightened and baffled her. How were they to fight something they could not find? Worse, they had no idea who it could be!

They were nearing town. Valdes rode his horse alongside them.

"To kill it we have to catch it," he was saying. "It needs blood. We give it some."

"How do you propose to do that?" Doc asked.

"We get a goat or a sheep and stake it out in a clearing. Pour blood on the ground all around it to draw the thing to it. Then we kill it, like Marta Kolbe said."

"But remember she said it wants human blood," Hattie said.

"And if it can change shape," Doc said,

"what's to keep it from turning into a bat and flying off before we can get to it?"

Valdes said something in Spanish. From the sharp scowl Hattie saw Doc give him, she guessed it might have been swear words. Then Valdes said, "I wish the sheriff would get back."

Hattie said, "That first man with his throat torn out that was found . . . Terrell, wasn't it?"

Valdes nodded. "The gambler."

"He was accused of cheating."

"Sí."

"You said Jess Culpepper was a troublemaker. What happened the night you found him dead?"

"A drunk claimed he hit him and stole his money."

"What are you getting at?" Doc asked her.

"Maybe nothing," she said.

Perhaps the gambler was a cheat, she thought. *Culpepper and Marta's sister were both thieves. But the whiskey drummer and the drifter were strangers around town . . . Marta's sister was bitten and left alive. The woman in Kansas City had two bite marks in her neck, but she was dead, her blood drained. Marta said if a vampire does not drain all the blood, the victim becomes a vampire. Why tear out the throats of some and not oth-*

ers? Why —

"Look at this circus," she heard Valdes say.

Hattie realized they had reached the plaza. Some kind of festivity was underway. A large crowd gathered near the other end of the plaza, near Ilfeld's Dry Goods, with more folks coming in. Some people had pulled their wagons and buggies to a halt and were climbing over the white fence surrounding the plaza. Others sat in the limbs of the few trees, trying to get a better view.

"Hurry!" someone said.

"What is it?" Valdes asked a passerby.

"They caught the killer wolf!"

Hattie and Doc got out of the buggy and hurried toward the crowd while Valdez tied his horse to the fence. Hattie heard a cheer go up.

Hanging by its hind legs from a makeshift tripod was a black wolf. A grinning wolfer stood by the tripod, a rifle in his hand, a yellow bandana around his neck, and a dented hat on his head.

Citizens gawked and congratulated the wolfer.

"One shot, you say!"

"Look at that."

"That's it, all right."

"Don't look so tough now, do you, you mangy critter!"

"What do you think, deputy?"

"I want to see it," Valdes said, going to take a close look at the carcass. Hattie and Doc followed behind him.

"Step back!" someone hollered. "Make way!"

A portly man and another man in a derby hat appeared. Both men beamed.

Hattie asked Doc who they were. He told her the one in the derby was Charles Ilfeld, and the other was Miguel Otero, the president of the bank. "Two of the town fathers who offered the thousand dollar reward."

Hattie got in close and slid the flat of her hand under the front paw of the animal. The width of the paw was only slightly wider than her palm.

"Please keep away there, ma'am," the wolfer told her.

She took a step back, nearly bumping into Otero.

"So, this is the beast that's been causing all this trouble," the bank president said and shook hands with the hunter.

Taking Doc aside, Hattie said, "That can't be the monster."

A hatchet-faced man turned to her. "Here, what was that you said?"

"Nothing at all," Doc said, pulling her away through the crowd.

Valdes soon joined them at Doc's buggy.

"You both know they caught the wrong one," Hattie said.

"Of course, we know. But you'll never convince any of them," Doc said. "And if we told them what we know, what we saw today, God only knows what they'd do."

"Es verdad," Valdes said. "It's the truth."

Another cheer went up from the crowd.

Unsavory tasks indeed, Hattie thought.

"I better get you back to the hotel," Doc said to Hattie.

Riding in his buggy, they drove past Ilfeld's store, then the Plaza Hotel. The crowd around the strung-up wolf had grown. At the corner, Doc reined his horse to the right as Hattie glanced to the left and told him to stop.

"Which church is that?" she asked, looking up at the side of the red stone building with the twin bell towers.

"Our Lady of Sorrows," Doc said. "Catholic church."

She remembered the priest with the bad bump on his head, the one she had helped the day before. "The priest there, his name is Father Lanigan, isn't it?"

"Yes."

"Maybe he can help us."

■ ■ ■ ■

Inside the small stable behind the rectory, Lanigan heard his name called. Peering out through a crack in the closed stable door, he saw Doc Burwell coming around from the front of the rectory.

"Father Lanigan?" Doc said, looking about.

Another voice: "Maybe he's not here."

The nurse from the hotel! There were bloodstains on her apron. Had someone been hurt? Did they need his help? Lanigan hoped not. He had more pressing things to do. Several flies buzzed about.

"Father?" the nurse called out.

Lanigan watched the two of them go around to the back of the rectory. The nurse knocked at the rear door and called his name again.

Doc looked over toward the stable.

Lanigan jerked his head back for fear he might be seen. More flies buzzed around his face. He waved his hand to ward them off. His sorrel gelding in the stall behind him stamped its hooves and snorted.

Lanigan stiffened. *Stop it! Do not make a sound!*

The doctor turned to the nurse. "It

doesn't look like he's here."

"Maybe he's in the stable," the nurse said. "I'll go see."

Lanigan took a couple of steps backward into a dark corner and held his breath. He could see the doctor and nurse through the door crack, getting closer. Closer. Closer. Dropping down, Lanigan turned his back.

Go away go away go away!

The stall door creaked.

No, no, no!

"You are looking for the *padre*?" A Mexican woman asked.

"We are," the nurse said. "He doesn't seem to be here."

"Did you go to the church?"

"He wasn't there. A couple of people inside said they hadn't seen him since he said Mass this morning."

Lanigan heard the stable door close.

"His horse is in the stall," Doc said. "He can't be too far."

Lanigan let out a silent breath.

"Maybe he's on the plaza," the woman said. "You heard the news? They caught the *lobo malo*, the bad wolf."

The voices moved away.

Lanigan put his eye back to the crack in the door. Doc and the nurse — Andrews was her name, he remembered now — were getting into Doc's buggy on the street. The Mexican woman was headed up the street.

The priest took the flask from his cassock, put it to his mouth, and tilted his head back. The whiskey burned, but he needed it. Calm his nerves. Steady his hands.

He went to the small table, got down on his knees, waved off the damn flies, and continued what he had been doing before the doctor and nurse interrupted him. Taking the pan in his hand, he carefully tipped the edge over the bottle he held in his other hand. He let the last crimson drops fall into the bottle, then set the pan down. Picking up the small bottle of strychnine from the table, he placed the lip of the bottle against the top of the blood-filled bottle and poured a thimble-size amount of the poison into it.

When he had finished, he stuck a cork firmly into the top of the blood bottle and placed it next to the other three he had already filled. One more to go.

He took another drink from his flask and licked his lips. "Blessed are the meek for they, for they . . ." He looked at the flask and chuckled. "Shall inherit whiskey."

Two flies landed on his cheek, and he shooed them off. He bumped the wooden crate beside the table with his knee, disturbing dozens more flies. They swarmed up, buzzing and pestering.

He set the flask down and picked up the crate. The contents had begun to stink. He cracked open the door. No one was around. Once outside, he made his way to a stand of trees beyond the rectory. He looked around again. Satisfied no one was watching, he tossed out the carcasses of dead rats and rabbits. After catching them in traps, he had cut them open and drained their blood. They had served their purpose.

Walking back to the stable, he muttered, "Crows have to eat."

"What randy bastard is banging on my door this damn early?" Ranger Virgil Thibodaux heard the woman shout.

Puzzled, he stood in front of the two-story brick establishment. The woman inside had hollered about it being early. Thibodaux did not know exactly what time it was, but he was pretty certain it was around the middle of the day. He had already been to three hotels, five boarding houses, and more than a dozen eating establishments. And, so far, the number of saloons was near equal to the number of brothels, and he was still on the New Town side of Las Vegas.

The door opened, revealing a woman dressed in pantaloons and a bodice that, in

Thibodaux's opinion, was dangerously close to popping open. Only two buttons strained to hold it closed. She had dirty, butter colored hair, most of it bunched over to one side of her head.

"My name's Thibodaux, and I'm —"

"You one of them wolf hunting peckers? You come here and figure you can ride us day and night like we're some kind of damn hobbyhorses or something? My girls need their rest, and so do I."

"I'm a Texas Ranger, and I want —"

"The door to this establishment opens tonight at six. Now git!"

She shoved the door closed, but before it latched, the ranger lifted his boot, kicked it back open, and stepped inside.

"What the hell!" the madam cried and swung at him with her fist.

"You listen here," he said, catching her wrist in his meaty hand. "I don't care one bit about your damn rules. I'm hunting a murderer. Now, you tell me if you've seen this man." Thibodaux let loose of her wrist, reached inside his shirt, and showed her the drawing.

She set her jaw, looked at the sketch, and shook her head.

"What about your prairie doves? One of them might've seen him."

"Every man comes in here has to see me before he can see one of my girls," she said through gritted teeth. "If he was in here, I'd know it. And he wasn't."

He decided to believe her, for the time being anyway.

"Appreciate your help," he said and noticed a cricket crawling its way up some loose strands of her hair and closing in on her ear.

Just before the door slammed shut behind him, he heard the madam say, "Damn Texas mudsill."

CHAPTER THIRTY

Arriving at the Montezuma Hotel, Doc told Hattie he would come back tomorrow to examine Mrs. Shaw and Mr. Quince. His head and back were awfully sore now, he said, and he thought it best to return home to rest.

The doorman stared at her as he opened the door.

Hattie was not unaware of the startled expression on his face when he saw her with blood on her dress and apron, the side of her face red and a little swollen.

She wanted to get to her room and change out of her soiled clothes.

In the lobby, a few curious onlookers watched as Drummond, his tripod and camera in place, prepared to take a photograph of the carved stone fireplace.

She saw Kenton was speaking with Duke at the front desk, and when Kenton saw her, he called her name.

She started toward them. They saw the blood and swelling, too.

"Everything is fine," she assured them, wishing now she had gone around the veranda to the nurse's station.

Kenton told her that Mrs. Shaw had been asking for her. "And a telegram arrived for you."

He took the folded piece of yellow paper from the mail slot box and handed it to her as shouts came from outside.

Through the door windows, Hattie glimpsed something large charging the entrance.

"Look out!" Duke shouted and pushed her behind him.

The onlookers scattered. Drummond grabbed his mounted camera and ran for the fireplace as two cowboys on horseback burst through the doorway.

One wore a stupid grin on his face and held a whiskey bottle in his hand. The other reared his horse back on its hind legs and let out a whoop.

"The killer wolf is dead!" the second cowboy hollered. "Got it hanging up on the plaza in town!"

"You men get out of here!" Kenton shouted.

"It's a great day!" the first cowboy said

and took a swig from his bottle.

"Go on!" Duke yelled, starting toward them. "Out of here!"

The cowboys laughed. The second one doffed his hat with a grand gesture, and they rode out of the lobby, Duke following them to make certain they caused no more commotion.

"My word!" a female guest said and chided Kenton for allowing such a display.

Things quieted down. Hattie passed Drummond, who was setting up his camera again.

He looked at her and said, "That was quite thrilling. I wish I had gotten a picture of it."

The nurse's station was quiet. Inside her room, Hattie opened the telegram. It read: "No plums available. Your Uncle Matthew."

Uncle Matthew was the cover for messages from the Pinkerton brothers. No plums available meant no additional operatives were on the way to help her.

That was frustrating.

She changed into fresh clothes, sat at the small table, and looked over the notes she had written earlier about the killings. Taking a pen from the drawer, she wrote: *Vampire. Evil. Requires blood to live. Can change from a man to an animal. Killing it a grisly matter.*

Crucifix, holy water possibly effective against it. Men have throats torn out. All dead. Women bitten. One dead. One left alive. Why? How to find this monster?

She stared at what she had just written. It still seemed unbelievable, in spite of what she had witnessed earlier.

The vampire could be anyone at all. The only witness, Gretl Kolbe, was dead, killed by her own sister. This bloodsucking monster had the ability to change into animals. The only way to kill it was bloody and horrible. Marta's sister had the strength of three or four people, and she had only been a vampire for a few hours.

How strong was the vampire now? This was like some kind of waking nightmare.

Hattie closed her eyes. The side of her face ached where the thing had kicked her with its foot. That was real enough.

She suddenly remembered Mrs. Shaw wanted to see her. She put away her notes. Stepping out the door, she heard footsteps.

"I thought I better come look for you," a woman said.

Hattie turned. A bellman was pushing Mrs. Shaw in her wheelchair along the hallway.

Thanking the bellman, Hattie took Mrs. Shaw into the nurse's station.

"I thought Doc Burwell was coming by today," Mrs. Shaw said. "I like him. He's — good Lord, what happened to your face?"

"A mishap. It looks worse than it is." Hattie explained that Doc had had an emergency in town and needed Hattie's help. "But he'll be back here in a couple of days. Now, you're looking better."

"Well," she said and coughed, "I think I'd be a lot better if it hadn't been for all that shooting and shouting last night. People are saying it was because of the wolf. I've heard it was caught."

"That's what they're saying."

"Nurse!" a voice cried, followed by the sound of heavy shoes running on the wooden boards of the veranda. "I hope she's in there! Nurse!"

"Sounds like trouble," Mrs. Shaw said.

Out on the veranda, Hattie saw a harried man wearing an apron and houndstooth-patterned black and white trousers helping a similarly dressed man, holding a blood-soaked towel around his hand.

"Thank God," the first man said. "Will here needs help."

"Bring him in and put him in the chair," Hattie said, pointing inside the nurse's station.

The two men were chefs in the hotel

kitchen. Will, the injured man, had been peeling potatoes using a paring knife.

"My own silly fault," Will said. He had a British accent. "I was in a hurry and sliced my hand."

Hattie gently removed the bloody towel and saw the wound just below the thumb. With a wet towel, she wiped away the blood. It was not a deep wound, but more blood flowed out. She told Will to hold the towel against his hand while she placed a square of gauze in a pan of carbolic acid to soak.

"That'll take a few stitches, wouldn't you say?" Mrs. Shaw said.

Hattie glanced over at her. The woman was leaning forward in her wheelchair, watching closely.

"My husband came home with a cut he got fishing one time," Mrs. Shaw said. "Wasn't as bad as this fellow, but he got stitches." She sat back in her chair and coughed.

"Is Will going to be all right?" the chef asked.

"I'd say so," Hattie said.

"If you don't need me, I'll get on back to the kitchen."

Hattie told him to go ahead.

"If you and Will don't mind," Mrs. Shaw

said, "I'll sit here and watch. I'm in no hurry."

Hattie gave her a look. Anyone could be a vampire, Marta had said.

Mrs. Shaw coughed. "As I was saying, all this wolf business started about a week after I arrived here."

Hattie removed the towel. Blood oozed from the cut. Vampires must drink blood. Blood gives them life. She shifted her gaze toward Mrs. Shaw. The woman sat calmly and continued to talk while Hattie cleaned the wound with soap and water.

"I was almost ready to leave, but my husband always said running away was no way to live your life."

Mrs. Shaw paid no attention to the fresh blood only a few feet away from her. Hattie felt sure the old woman in the wheelchair was no vampire.

"Of course," Mrs. Shaw said, "this situation probably wasn't what my husband had in mind when he said it, but I have no desire to return to that hellhole of Chicago."

The woman kept talking. However, Hattie had stopped listening. Mrs. Shaw had said she had arrived at the hotel a week before the wolf attacks began. Maybe there *was* a way to find this fiend.

Hattie took the soaked gauze from the pan

of carbolic acid, placed it on Will's hand, and wrapped a bandage around it.

"Come see me tomorrow so I can change the bandage," she told him. "And be careful with that hand."

After he had left, Mrs. Shaw said, "I thought he could use the stitches, but I suppose you know better."

"Mrs. Shaw," Hattie said, "you were saying something before about the week you arrived here. When was that? The date, I mean."

"The twenty-fifth of June. Why do you ask?"

"For the nurse's journal I have to keep. Some of the entries got ruined," Hattie said.

The twenty-fifth of June was a week before the Fourth of July, and two days later the killings began. Hattie needed to find out who else was still at the hotel.

She wheeled Mrs. Shaw into the lobby and asked one of the bellmen if he would take her for a little walk.

The assistant desk clerk was alone at the front desk. Hattie asked how long Mrs. Shaw and Mr. Quince had been guests. "The former nurse didn't make note of it, and I'd like to know."

The clerk took out the register and turned back a few pages. He confirmed Mrs. Shaw's arrival date in June. Quince, he said, arrived at the hotel three days later, on the twenty-eighth of June.

Hattie thanked him and started to go but suddenly turned back. "Tell me, I'm just curious, have they been here the longest?"

The clerk frowned, but checked, running his finger down the columns.

"There was Mr. Prescott. And Mrs. Harvey and her children, of course. No, I'm mistaken. Mrs. Harvey and family arrived the week after the Fourth of July." He turned a couple of pages and sighed. "Just our lungers remain as the long standing guests. So many guests left much sooner than anticipated. We have barely ninety guests still with us at this moment. Maybe things will improve since they caught the wolf."

Hattie asked the clerk for a piece of paper and an envelope. Borrowing a pen, she wrote a brief note, slipped it inside the envelope, then wrote DEPUTY VALDES on the front.

"Is anyone from the hotel going to town soon?" she asked the clerk.

He said Duke was leaving on the next train to pick up some overdue supplies.

"It's very important that this gets to Deputy Valdes," she said, handing him the envelope.

"If it's that important, the telephone is right over —"

"No, if Duke could deliver it that would be fine." She did not want to chance the operator in town overhearing her request.

"Service!" the clerk called out, and one of the uniformed boys appeared at the desk. Giving him the envelope, the clerk instructed him to hurry to the depot and give it to Duke. "Tell him he needs to deliver it to the jail."

"Make certain he gives it to Deputy Valdes, or one of the other deputies if he's not there," Hattie said. "But tell them Deputy Valdes needs to see it right away."

CHAPTER THIRTY-ONE

His black valise held tight in his hand, Lanigan left the rectory. He was in a hurry. And a little drunk. For what he had planned, he knew he needed that liquid fortification.

Down on the dusty street, the hack he had called Mendenhall's Livery to send waited. The driver, smoking a pipe, sat hunched over in his seat.

The train depot was on the other side of town, a good mile away. Lanigan needed to catch the four o'clock train that was leaving shortly for the Montezuma. There was no time to walk to it now, and he would not risk riding his horse. What if he dropped the valise? No, those bottles of poisoned blood he had prepared were too vital. Far too vital.

"¡Padre!"

Lanigan glanced in the direction the voice came from and nearly tripped over his own feet. It was Deputy Valdes trotting down the street on his horse. God, what did he want?

"I am sorry to bother you," Valdes said. "But I have a favor to ask."

Lanigan noticed the deputy winced as he eased down from his horse. He was favoring his right leg.

Valdes reached inside his saddlebag and took out a small crucifix. It was a simple handmade cross. Twine held the cross bar in place.

Lanigan knew just about every Mexican household around had at least one crucifix hanging in their homes.

"I made this myself," Valdes said. "My wife, she would like it blessed. *Por favor.*"

"She's coming home?" Lanigan asked vaguely. He recalled hearing that she was away in Albuquerque with their children.

"Soon, I think," Valdes said.

Somehow Lanigan did not quite believe the deputy. Something in the way he said it. But he took the crucifix and spoke quickly in Latin as he blessed it, making a hasty sign of the cross with his hand.

He gave it back to Valdes, who thanked him.

Climbing into the hack, he held the valise on his lap and told the driver to hurry to the depot.

■ ■ ■ ■

"What'll it be?" the barkeep asked. His hair was slicked back, and he wore a tie and vest.

Virgil Thibodaux leaned against the bar and put his foot up on the rail. He was tired.

"Beer," he said, wiping his face with a faded bandana.

He noticed a table at the rear of the place where some cowboys were playing poker. Otherwise, the saloon was quiet. Behind the bar was a large mirror. Above it hung a painting of a naked woman reclining in a giant seashell with ocean waves swirling around it. A big glass jar of pickled hardboiled eggs sat at the end of the bar.

"Those fresh?" Thibodaux asked.

The barkeep grinned. "Yes, sir. Prepared them myself earlier today."

The big Ranger went over and took one from the jar. Biting into it, he savored the salty sweet taste. After paying the barkeep, he showed him his sketch and asked him if he had seen the man.

"Can't say as I have."

Thibodaux nodded, swallowed the rest of his egg, and followed it with the remainder of his beer.

"You got a big town here," he said.

The barkeep snorted. "Railroad did that."

"I've been looking for this man." He showed him the sketch again. "You sure you haven't seen him."

"Nope, but we've had a lot of people in here. I can't remember them all. You some kind of law?"

"Texas Ranger. This fellow's wanted." Thibodaux slipped the sketch inside his shirt.

"You look just about wore out," the barkeep said and put another glass of beer on the bar. "On the house."

"I appreciate that. And you're right. I've been all over this town. The St. Nicholas Hotel, the Exchange, the Sumner House, the European, the Plaza."

"How about Wagner's and Baca's?"

Thibodaux gave him a weary nod. "And every other hotel and boardinghouse, saloon, and house of joy I can find. Nobody seems to have seen him."

"You try the Montezuma?"

"The what?"

CHAPTER THIRTY-TWO

Hattie's years as a Pinkerton operative had taught her that everyone was a suspect until they were not one. Admittedly, she found it hard to believe that Quince might be this vampire anymore than she thought Mrs. Shaw was the vampire. Or poor Mr. Prescott, if he were still alive. How could anyone suffering from consumption be such a thing?

She had been unable to find Quince. No one could quite recall whether they had seen him. She had gone to his room, but he did not answer when she knocked.

Meanwhile, it had been a busy afternoon at the nurse's station. Eleven guests came calling for treatment of various ailments. Most complained of soreness after taking the three-hour burro ride. Hattie gave each of them a small vial of liniment to apply to their inflamed areas. She treated a few others for sunburn, applying a camphorated tincture of opium to their faces and hands to lessen the pain. And to one young boy she gave a cup of peppermint tea to relieve his stomachache after eating too much pineapple ice cream in the dining room.

Now it was late afternoon, and she looked for Quince again. There was no answer when she knocked on his guest room door. She listened for a moment but heard no sound from inside. Turning to go, she hesitated. A fiend, a monster was on the loose. Everyone was a suspect, and Quince had been a guest at the hotel when that first killing took place back in July. She glanced up and down the hallway. Seeing no one, she placed her hand on the doorknob and twisted. The knob did not budge.

He had to be somewhere.

She did not find him in the lobby, the reading rooms, or the dining room. She looked outside the dining room windows in case he was in the small courtyard. He was not. Nor was he in the bar, the barbershop, or anywhere else in the basement. No one there had seen him, either. She even tried the bowling alley door, but it was locked. The sign was still there, like the one up in the lobby, informing guests that the alley was closed for repairs.

Back upstairs, she looked for him on the veranda and found him in a rocking chair about halfway down the side. He was wearing his hat, gloves, and dark glasses.

"I thought you said this sun was too much for you later in the day," she said.

"Well, I'm trying to follow the advice I was given to take in more of this good air." He indicated the empty chair next to him.

She felt a cool breeze as she sat down.

"You look like something's on your mind," he said.

"Only that I was looking for you earlier to see how you were feeling."

"Better," he said and coughed. Taking a handkerchief from his pocket he covered his mouth. When his coughing stopped, he cleared his throat. "This damn disease wants to make a liar out of me."

The sun peeked underneath the veranda roof. Hattie brought her hand up to shield her eyes and looked out past the veranda railing at the beauty of the distant mountains. Dark clouds were gathering beyond the mountains.

"Pretty, isn't it?" she heard Quince say.

"It is," she said, and looked over at him. The cheeks of his pale face had turned bright red, his eyes welled, and blood began dripping from his nose. A few drops landed on his white shirt. Suddenly, blood streamed out his nose and splattered his shirt.

"Oh, hell!" he exclaimed, yanking his handkerchief back out of his pocket and jamming it under his nose.

Hattie leapt to her feet. "Tilt your head back."

"It's happened before," he said. "I just need to get inside."

His handkerchief was red with blood. It dripped from his gloved hand.

"You're coming to the nurse's station," she said. "Let me help you up."

"I need my hat," he said.

She reached down and grabbed it. Straightening up, she saw his whole face had turned a bright crimson color.

"Keep your head back," she said and led him along the veranda, a much quicker route than going back in through the hotel.

They turned the corner.

"This should teach me to stay out in the —" he was saying as a bright flash exploded.

Hattie halted, blinded by the white glare.

"I'm so sorry, folks, I didn't expect anybody to come around this way." Drummond stood by his camera and dropped the flash tray to his side. "Do you require any help, ma'am?"

"No, no," she said. "I just need to get him to my office."

"I was getting a photo and . . . and I'm sorry."

They hurried past the photographer. Hattie heard Quince moan, but then she wondered if it did not almost sound like a growl.

When the sheriff gets back to town he will not believe this, Valdes thought, as he ran his finger over the crucifix he'd had Father Lanigan bless. Valdes knew if he had not witnessed what he had at Marta Kolbe's house, he would not believe it, either. Something evil was here, that was true. But how to —

The jailhouse door swung open. Deputy Cuddy stepped in, followed by old man Gonzales, the owner of the cantina across the street. Gonzales held a tray of food covered with a cloth. His wife prepared the meals for prisoners, and he usually brought the food over.

"*Señor* Gonzales," Valdes said, sliding the crucifix inside his shirt, "this is a surprise."

"I'm sorry you and your deputies had to come get the meals the last couple of days," he said, setting the tray down on the desk, "but my son was ill, and things have gotten so busy at the cantina with all the hunters in town. But, they are leaving, so I can bring

281

the food again."

"*Muchas gracias,*" Valdes said.

"*De nada,*" the old man said, heading for the door. "We are all so very happy this *lobo* is dead. *¿No?*"

"*Como no,*" Valdes said, knowing full well it was not true.

After the old man left, Valdes told Cuddy to take the food to Charlie Ross and Phil Larson.

"If them two was smart when they go before Judge Baylor come Monday, they'd plead guilty and shake hands," Cuddy said. "But I know they ain't too smart."

Taking the tray, he suddenly stopped and reached into his back pocket.

"Almost forgot," he said and placed an envelope in front of Valdes.

"What is this?"

"Duke Pennick give it to me. He was coming from the train depot, headed this way. He seen me and said to put it in your hands."

Cuddy left to give Larson and Ross their meals while Valdes tore open the envelope and read the note: *Have possible way of finding killer. Get names of all guests and others at hotels, boardinghouses, and homes who arrived in town between May 15 and July 6 and are still here. Will explain later. S. An-drews*

Valdes had to admit that that nurse had been good in the fight at the German woman's place and helped save his life today, but he did not care much for her bossy ways. But he was damned if he had any better ideas for finding the vampire. He folded the note and put it inside his pocket.

As Cuddy came back into the office, Valdes could hear the two prisoners complaining, as usual, about nothing but beans for every meal.

Valdes asked Cuddy if he knew where Deputy Silva was. Cuddy said he did not.

"You better go find him," Valdes said. "We have some work to do."

"You're not finished yet?" Kenton asked.

The German worker with the bushy eyebrows looked at him, standing in the entryway of the observation deck.

"Fast," the German said, then apparently remembered Kenton did not speak German. "I mean almost, *Herr* Kenton."

"Well, hurry," Kenton said. "Mrs. Harvey is expecting friends from Kansas here tomorrow. We can't have this floor sticky."

Kenton hurried down the stairs.

The German turned to his Italian coworker and, mimicking Kenton, said in Italian, "The floor, it cannot be sticky."

The two men chuckled.

"I wish I had *zigarette,*" the German said.

They had been on their knees for the last hour, brushes in hand, putting a coat of linseed oil mixed with turpentine on a section of the wooden floor at the far side of the observation deck.

"We did this two months ago," the Italian said in Italian.

Mixing German and Italian, the German said, "*Ja,* but *Herr* Kenton tells us to do it again, so we do it again."

"But why? The floor looks good to me."

"Because the sun comes through the big windows there, and it beats down on the floor back here, so it must be treated every other month; otherwise the wood, it warps," the German said, applying the mixture on the boards. "See, it soaks up the oil, but it not dry too fast. Very important."

The Italian stuck his brush into the bucket and pulled it out, the mixture dripping heavily onto the floor.

"*Nien,*" the German said. "Too much. You make lumps on the wood." He threw the Italian one of his rags and told him to wipe up the excess.

"*Ja,* better. Brush now, make smooth."

When they'd finished, they took their brushes and buckets and walked to the storage room just off the top of the stairs. After washing their brushes in a pan of water, they set the buckets on one of the shelves and tossed their oily rags in a pile on the floor.

Starting down the stairs, the Italian told the German, "Now you can smoke your cigarette."

"Wait, I left the tarp on the deck floor. I must go back."

"We get it first thing tomorrow. I'm hungry. Have your cigarette."

He was right. It would not hurt anything to leave it. Taking his makings from his pocket, the German began rolling a cigarette.

CHAPTER THIRTY-THREE

It was dusk when Virgil Thibodaux, hot and dusty in his buckskins, rode his blue roan gelding up to the Montezuma Hotel. Seeing all that red stone and windows with lights shining through them, and that big tower catching that last bit of sunset, he thought someone sure had poured a hell of a lot of money into this place.

A liveryman appeared and asked if he was a new guest. Thibodaux said he was here on Texas Ranger business. The liveryman offered to take his horse and feed and brush him, if he would like.

"Go ahead," Thibodaux said and cocked his head at the hotel. "This place serve food?"

"The finest, sir. It's a Harvey House."

Thibodaux had eaten at other Harvey House restaurants and they did dish up a decent meal. Much better than the beans he so often cooked for himself. Maybe he would get something to eat while he was here.

A noise drew his attention to the E. F. Drummond Photography wagon standing off the driveway. Someone was climbing the steps at the back of the wagon.

"What's that about?" he asked.

"He's a big noise photographer taking pictures of the hotel. Going to make it famous, they say."

Thibodaux grunted.

"Welcome to the Montezuma Hotel," the doorman said and opened the door.

Thibodaux entered the lobby and spotted a fellow with slicked-down hair behind the front desk.

"May I help you, sir?" the desk clerk said.

"Name's Thibodaux. I'm a Texas Ranger, and I'm looking for someone." He unfolded the sketch and showed it to him. "Is this man here?"

"Hard to tell." The clerk studied the sketch more closely. "This is not a very good likeness."

Thibodaux gave him a long look. "Maybe your bellboys or maids or fancy waitresses have seen him. You won't mind if I go ask them."

"They are very busy with our guests."

If his man was here, the ranger wanted

him. Besides, he was tired and did not relish the idea of riding all the way back to town tonight. "Fine. How much for a room?"

The clerk cleared his throat. "And how long do you plan to stay with us?

"One night ought to do it. Maybe two."

"The daily room rate is four dollars."

"Four dollars? Hotels in town aren't that much."

"They are not the Montezuma Hotel, sir."

"No, they're reasonable."

"Is everything all right, Mr. Kenton?"

Thibodaux turned and saw a plump woman, well dressed. She spoke with a little bit of an accent. German maybe.

"Indeed, Mrs. Harvey," Kenton said. "This gentleman was making an inquiry about our accommodations."

"I am certain you would find them most hospitable, sir," Mrs. Harvey said. "We are happy to have you stay with us."

She waddled away.

Thibodaux blew out a long breath. "Give me the register."

"Father Lanigan!" Kenton said. "We didn't expect to see you here."

Thibodaux looked up and saw a priest dressed in his long black cassock. He carried a black leather valise in his hand. Thibodaux noticed he was gripping the handle tightly.

"Yes, I promised a couple of guests I'd be back to . . . to hear their confessions."

"Perhaps you could help this Texas gentleman."

"Father," Thibodaux said, nodding his head. "I'm trying to find someone." He showed him the sketch.

The corners of the priest's mouth turned down, and he shook his head.

"I thought there might be a slight similarity to one of our consumptives," Kenton said.

"No. Not him."

"Appreciate you taking a look," Thibodaux said.

He watched the priest hurry away.

Inside his wagon, E. F. Drummond, his sleeves rolled up, stared at the silvery image on the thin photographic glass plate. It made no sense. Not at all. The image was the one he had taken late that afternoon out on the hotel veranda. The view of the timbered valley in the distance was ideally framed through the veranda walkway with its white painted posts on one side and the red hotel walls on the other. The thunderclouds roiling in the distance against the bright blue sky offered a perfect contrast of light and shadows over the valley at exactly the right moment. And then the nurse and that poor man with the bleeding nose came around the corner, just as he took the picture.

This cannot be. Did something go wrong with the camera? Were all the other photos taken today marred like this one?

There was a knock at the door. Probably the bellboy with his supper.

"Coming," he called out.

He could not take his eyes off the image. The nurse was there. She was leading the man along the veranda, one of her hands on the man's free arm, the other holding his hat. But the man was not there. His coat, shirt, trousers, gloves, boots were, even his dark glasses, but not him. And the bloody handkerchief Drummond remembered seeing the man holding to his upturned face was there all wadded up where his face ought to be. But there was no blood on the handkerchief. No blood on his glove, or on his white shirt. Not a single drop.

CHAPTER THIRTY-FOUR

Father Lanigan saw a look of mild surprise on the creature's face when it opened the door of its guest room.

"I wasn't expecting you," Quince said and glanced at the valise in the priest's hand. "And you came prepared, it appears." He gestured for him to come in.

Lanigan's heart pounded. He knew he should have taken a drink from his flask while he was still out in the hallway.

A sliver of dusk peeked through the parted curtains. Lanigan knew the bright glow of gas light, or any light, irritated Quince.

"I wanted to try to make up for not coming here last week," Lanigan said as he sat down by the table. "I really was sick. Here." He opened his valise and pulled out a bottle. "I brought five. All fresh today."

"That's very decent of you," Quince said, sitting opposite him. "It makes up for your lie about being sick."

"But I swear I didn't lie."

Quince made a gruff sound and pulled the cork from the bottle.

Lanigan tried not to look at Quince for fear the creature would somehow know what he had done. But the priest could not help a furtive glance. Quince brought the bottle to his mouth, hesitated, and then lowered the bottle, a pensive look on his face.

Oh God, it knows about the poison in the bottle.

"Something's bothering you," Quince said. "What is it?"

He tried to think. "There's . . . you . . . you should know there's a man looking for you."

"What man?"

Lanigan pointed at the bottle. "You should go on and drink first and —"

"What man?"

"At . . . at the front desk. A Texas gentleman. He's got a drawing of you. Your . . . your face."

"Did he say why he was looking for me?" Quince seemed unconcerned.

"No. But I saw him signing the register. I think he's staying here."

"What does he look like?"

Lanigan described him as a big man with

a thick moustache and dressed in buckskins.

"That's good to know," Quince said quietly.

A knock at the door startled Lanigan.

"Mr. Quince?" The voice was gentle but firm coming from the other side of the door. "It's Miss Andrews. I came to see how you're feeling."

Another knock.

"Are you there?"

Looking back at Quince, Lanigan saw him sitting calmly and watching the door. Lanigan felt like his heart was about to pound through his chest.

A few moments passed.

"She's gone now," Quince said.

Relieved, Lanigan watched as Quince brought the bottle up to his mouth. It was nearly to his lips when he paused, holding the bottle there, and smiled. It was a malevolent smile the priest had seen many times before.

"You look like you could use a drink," Quince said.

He knows he knows he knows! Lanigan stiffened, his mouth dry. *God, he's going to kill me. He's going to make me drink that blood! Please, no!*

Quince's smile faded into a look of concern. "Didn't you bring your flask?"

Lanigan yanked out his whiskey flask. Squeezing his eyes shut, he tilted his head back and took a long pull from it. The amber liquid burned but soothed his frayed nerves.

"Better?" Quince asked.

Lanigan nodded once and drew a ragged breath.

"Good," Quince said and set the bottle of blood down on the table. "There's something I need you to do for me." He chuckled. "Should be easy."

The priest made himself look away from the bottle of blood. "Is it about the man from Texas?"

"I'll deal with him. It's the photographer."

"Drummond?" Lanigan frowned, confused.

"There's something he has I want you to get for me. You'll do that, won't you?"

Sitting at his table in the dining room, Thibodaux noticed a comely woman with dark-red hair pulled back on her head. She stood at the entrance to the dining room and was craning her neck, like she was looking for someone. One of the Harvey girls walked up to her, and they spoke. The red-haired woman wasn't a Harvey girl, for, while she wore a white apron, her dress was gray, not black. He figured she must work at the hotel. Maybe she was the nurse. He was about to go show her the sketch when one of the other Harvey girls appeared at his table.

"Did you enjoy the mountain trout au bleu, sir?" she asked as she picked up his plate. Only the head and tail of the trout remained.

"That was tasty, yes," Thibodaux said.

"It's the specialty of the Montezuma."

"Better than any fish I ever had." Looking back at the entrance, he realized the red-haired woman was gone.

"The secret is the boullion our chef prepares it in," the Harvey girl was saying. "Would you care for anything else? Our brandy flip pie perhaps?"

"No, that's fine. Just the bill."

She smiled. "Your supper was compliments of the management and Mrs. Harvey. A little thank you to the Texas Rangers."

"Well, please thank her for me."

She started to go.

"Just a minute," he said. "Tell me, have you seen this man."

He showed her the sketch.

"I haven't." Another Harvey girl passed. "Sadie, does he look familiar to you?"

Sadie studied the drawing. "Might be Mr. Stallings, but it's not a very good likeness."

"Is this Stallings here?"

"No. He and his wife left a few days ago."

Thibodaux thanked them. He had already spoken to several of the housekeepers and bellboys. A housekeeper thought the man looked a little like Mr. Quince, a consumptive, but she could not say with certainty. The doorman had said he should ask the daytime workers.

It was nearly nine o'clock, and only a handful of guests remained in the dining room. Thibodaux had heard that some guests enjoyed having coffee out on the veranda at night. He thought he would see if his man was there.

Getting up from the table, Thibodaux saw a man waiting at the elevator in the lobby. The man glanced in his direction. By damn, it looked like the man in the sketch. Thin face. Moustache.

The birdcage elevator arrived. The man slid the door open and stepped inside.

Thibodaux hurried out of the dining room. The elevator started down. The man faced straight ahead. The ranger nearly knocked over the bowling alley "closed" sign trying to reach the elevator. By damn it was him!

The elevator stopped. He heard the door slide open below. Thibodaux raced down the staircase.

The basement hallway was brightly lit. Thibodaux heard voices coming from the bar to the right and opened the door. The place was thick with cigar smoke. A few men played cards at a couple of tables. Others were trying their luck at Faro. Several gentlemen stood at the bar. The barkeep set drinks down in front of them. As Thibodaux made his way around the room, a couple of players looked over at him. He was aware that wearing his holster and a buckskin coat made him stand out. The other guests were all dressed in fine suits. Just like the man getting into the elevator. But he was not here.

"What would you like, sir?" the barkeep asked.

Thibodaux shook his head and left.

He found the Curiosity Shop was dark, the barbershop, too. A couple of men were leaving the billiard room. The manager there told Thibodaux he was closing up.

"Did a man just come in here?" the ranger asked.

"No, sir."

A printed sign standing on an easel in front of the bowling alley said it was closed.

There was another door at the far end of the hallway. Thibodaux rushed to it. It opened easily, and he discovered stairs leading up to the hotel grounds. Damn it! He had lost his man.

Back inside, he headed down the hallway. He would show the sketch to the billiard manager and the barkeep.

As he passed the "closed" sign at the bowling alley, he glanced at the double doors. One of the doors was ajar. They had both been closed before.

He moved the easel out of the way, got his ear close to the door's opening, and listened. *Silence.*

He opened the door carefully. Light inside spilled out into the hallway. He left the door open. Stepping inside, his boot made the wooden floor creak.

A long cabinet lined the nearby wall. Another long rack holding dozens of black bowling balls lined another. The ball returns at each of the eleven lanes stood empty. There were no pins at the ends of the lanes.

The flooring of the two alleys over by the far wall was partially replaced. Stacks of lumber were piled nearby.

Thibodaux pulled out his revolver, cocked it, and checked behind the counter. No one was hiding there. And he did not see anyone trying to hide in the pits at the end of the lanes.

Behind the lumber pile he found clothes. A suit. Like the one he saw the man wearing. What in the hell was —

The sound of a soft click spun him around. The door had closed shut.

"Come out!" he said. "I'm a Texas Ranger."

He waited a moment, started for the door, and the lights went out, plunging the place into darkness. His revolver still cocked and at the ready, Thibodaux crouched low, listening closely for any sound that might direct him. Someone was here. The ranger knew it. Damn it! He could not even see his hand in front of his face in this pitch black.

He needed to get to the doors. His heart thumping, he drew a shallow breath through parted lips. He knew the doors were about fifteen or twenty paces away and just to the right.

He took a couple of steps. The floor squeaked behind him. He spun around, his finger squeezing the trigger of his revolver. Something sharp clamped down hard on his wrist, biting through it, snapping bone, and severing his gun hand from his arm.

Thibodaux staggered back, his scream cut short as something slammed into him, knocking him down. The thing was on top of him, pinning him to the floor. Raising both arms, he pounded at it and felt hard, bristly fur against the side of his remaining hand. Blood spewed from the stump of his other arm. He opened his mouth to scream for help, but vicious teeth tore into his neck.

Blood filled his mouth and spilled out over his face.

His arms flailed.

His legs kicked.

The last thing Thibodaux heard was the lapping of blood.

"Just get the names," Valdes told deputies Cuddy and Silva, as he sat at the sheriff's desk.

"You want to know who got to town two and half months ago and is still here?" Cuddy snorted.

"Get them while you make your rounds," Valdes said. "I need them. Might be a situation coming."

Silva shrugged, then motioned to Cuddy to follow.

"Seems like a big waste of time to me," Cuddy mumbled as they left the jailhouse.

Reaching into the desk drawer, Valdes took out the long knife the sheriff kept there, the one he had taken from the big Apache some years before. Valdes rubbed his thumb over the blade, brought out a whetstone, and started putting a sharper edge on the knife. Something told him it would be a good idea.

Quince opened the door of the bowling alley a crack and peered out into the hallway. Muffled sounds drifted down from the bar.

A trickle of blood ran down his chin. Catching it with his finger, he licked it clean.

He straightened his coat, stepped into the hallway, and closed the door behind him. It was time to get back to his room, where he had told Lanigan to wait for him.

Halfway down the hallway, Quince stopped. Returning to the bowling alley, he moved the easel with the sign reading Closed for Repairs back to its spot in front of the door.

CHAPTER THIRTY-FIVE

Lanigan wiped his sweaty hands on his cassock. He wanted to take another drink from his flask, but he did not dare as he sat in Quince's dark room and stared at the bottle of poisoned blood. It was still on the table where Quince had left it.

The priest knew that he had to get Quince to drink it when he came back to the room. It was the only way he would ever be free of the creature. It had to be done. *Had to be.* But how? If only —

The door opened. Quince entered. The bright hallway light made him appear as a dark shadow as he came through the doorway. Lanigan held his breath.

"The photographer is in the dining room," Quince said, shutting the door. "Go now. Use the window. You won't be seen. Bring me all the photographic plates. Put them in this."

Lanigan felt the rough burlap in his hand.

It was likely a potato sack Quince had taken from the trash barrels behind the kitchen. Quince had told him earlier that the plates were small, about the size of a visiting card, so the sack would easily hold the thirty or forty plates Drummond had already exposed.

Quince peered out the window and then raised it open.

Lanigan wanted to ask him why he wanted all of the plates. What was he going to do with them? Did it matter? Quince owned him. The creature knew his secrets, his weaknesses, his failures as a priest and as a man.

Lanigan started out the window, then hesitated.

"I . . . I'm going to need matches, I think," he said. "So I can see inside the wagon."

"Drummond left a red light burning," Quince said. "He needs it so he can develop his pictures."

The priest slipped out the window into the night. Quince's room was almost at the very end of that wing. Fewer people around. Lanigan gathered up his cassock, crouched low, and made his way around to the other side of the wing where the veranda was. There was a gentle grassy slope along that side of the hotel. Following the slope, he would not be seen by any guests out on the veranda.

The half moonlight provided enough light for him to see. Voices from the veranda carried in the night, but only a few. Rounding the slope below, where the big tower stood, Lanigan glanced up. A couple of people stood out by the railing on the tower observation deck.

Coming up the slope near the hotel entrance, he was glad to find no one there. The doorman stood inside the front doors. Past the doors and across the driveway circle was Drummond's wagon.

Lanigan moved cautiously, swinging wide, all the while keeping watch for any guests coming up the veranda or out the front doors.

Reaching the wagon, he kept behind it and made his way around to the rear door. All was quiet. Not a person in sight. Wait. By the hotel something moved out of a shadowed corner near the front doors into the glow thrown through the windows. Quince! Lanigan saw him motion at him with his hand. He wanted Lanigan to go. Quince had to be keeping watch in case Drummond came back from the dining room. But why had Quince not said he was going to be there? It didn't matter. Quince had told him to do this.

Lanigan climbed up the wagon steps, turned the handle, and opened the door. The red light spilled out, startling him, for it could easily attract unwanted attention. He rushed inside, pulling the door closed behind him. Everything in the cramped wagon was bathed in red, the cameras, the tripod, shelves, a trunk, photographic paper, and bottles of chemicals Drummond used to develop his pictures. Lanigan figured that likely explained the odor in the wagon, a sweet yet pungent smell.

At the front of the wagon a red lamp sat on top of a work desk — an oil lamp with a four-sided red glass chimney. Maybe the glass plates Quince wanted were on that desk.

Starting up the narrow aisle, Lanigan heard something crack under his shoe. He looked down and saw what appeared to be tiny shards of glass. There were more on the floor near the desk. And the top of the desk was covered with shards. It was as if a window had shattered. But there were no windows in the wagon.

Stepping back, he slipped on something slick and lost his balance, falling backwards. He dropped the sack and put his arm out to try to brace his fall. He hit the floor and felt something wet. He brought his hand up. It glistened with blood!

Then he saw the arm sticking out of an open cabinet. Lanigan tried to scramble to his feet, but the floor was covered in blood. Slipping again, he hit the floor hard, landing on his side. Drummond's face, his eyes wide open in terror, stared at him. The photographer was stuffed inside the cabinet. He had been cut open. Gutted. Blood everywhere. Lanigan's hands were slick with it. The blood covered his cassock.

The rear door flew open. Lanigan jerked his head and saw Quince, an evil grin on his face, red in the lamplight. Lanigan felt himself dragged out into the night.

"Murder! Blood! Murder!" Quince shouted.

"What are you doing?" Lanigan cried, trying to pull free. Suddenly, he was staring into Quince's face.

"You thought I couldn't smell the poison you put in the bottles?" Quince whispered. "I smashed all the glass plates after I cut Drummond open. And now they'll think it was you who killed him."

Quince shoved him down. Lanigan's face struck the dirt, Quince's boot on his neck.

"Help! Murder!" Quince yelled.

Lanigan tried to move, but Quince pushed

his boot down harder. Lanigan heard shouting.

"Murder?"

"What is it?"

"Hurry!"

The front doors burst open. Men ran out. Lights came on at windows on the upper floors.

"What's all this?"

"Who's murdered?"

Quince jerked Lanigan to his feet. "Run!"

Lanigan stumbled as Quince pushed him away.

"Here! He's getting away!" Quince shouted.

"I didn't kill anyone!" Lanigan cried.

"There he is!" the doorman yelled.

"Come on!" others shouted. "Don't let him get away!"

Lanigan put his hands out. "I didn't kill anybody!"

A couple of men grabbed him by the arms. One was a liveryman he recognized. A Mexican fellow.

"Let me go!" Lanigan wailed. "I didn't do anything!"

"It's *Padre* Lanigan," the Mexican cried.

"My God, he's drenched in blood," the other man holding him said.

"He killed the photographer!" Lanigan

heard Quince shout. "Gutted him like a hog! Come look!"

Lanigan struggled to pull free.

"Oh my Lord!" someone shouted. "It's like a slaughterhouse in there!"

The crowd grew.

"Get the law!"

"He's got blood all over him!"

"Murderer!"

"Get a rope! That's what we do where I come from!"

Something hit Lanigan in the face. He dropped to the ground. Faces became a blur. Frenzied shouts echoed around him.

"I didn't kill anybody," he whimpered. "It was —"

A gun fired. Some of the men crouched down, others scattered.

Lanigan heard a woman's voice. "Everybody back away!"

He saw a big man coming toward him. Duke, the carriage driver. Beside him was the nurse, holding a smoking pistol in her hand and pointing it at the crowd. The look on her face said she was prepared to use it.

"Get him up, and get behind me," she told Duke. "Everybody, get back in the hotel. Now!"

Lanigan cowered behind the nurse. "I didn't do this, I didn't —"

"Shut your mouth," she told him.

Men grumbled but started for the hotel. Some women came out wanting to know what all the shouting was about.

Lanigan heard Duke tell the Mexican liveryman to go bring a carriage around fast. The nurse whispered to Duke, asking him if he had his knife on him. Duke nodded.

Kenton appeared. Beside him was Mrs. Harvey.

"What is going on here?" Lanigan heard her say and then saw her at the front of the crowd, her face suddenly horrified at seeing him.

"Father? Miss Andrews, what are you doing?"

Before she could answer, a lanky man in a frock coat pushed through the crowd.

"The priest killed Drummond!" he cried. "I saw inside the wagon. He butchered him. And I found this, too!"

"Oh, God, no," Lanigan moaned. The man held his valise. Quince must have given it to him! Lanigan's knees buckled, but Duke held him up.

"It's his bag, the priest," the lanky man said. "His initials are right here on top. *JFL.* There's bottles of blood inside."

"Lord!" a woman screamed.

"The photographer's blood!" the lanky

man shouted and turned to Lanigan, his face angry. "I confessed my sins to you, you bastard!"

"He's a monster!" Lanigan thought he heard Quince shout.

"Some kind of damn cannibal!"

"This is a matter for the law!" the nurse shouted. "No one else!"

"This ain't right!"

"Come on, men!"

The nurse raised her gun and fired over the crowd. They halted.

"I will shoot the next man who comes toward me," she said.

"That's enough!" It was Mrs. Harvey. She turned to the crowd. "She's right. We must let the law take care of this."

"Everyone go back inside," Kenton said.

A loud clattering sound approached. The Mexican drove up with the carriage.

Lanigan scrambled into it and curled up on the floor, trembling. *What have I done what have I done what have I done?*

The nurse got in. Lanigan saw she was still pointing her gun at the crowd. She told Duke to get the valise and called out for Kenton.

"Call Doctor Burwell," she told him. "Tell him to get to the jail."

Duke climbed into the driver's seat.
"Go," the nurse said.

CHAPTER THIRTY-SIX

Quince strolled the hotel grounds, savoring the quiet. It would be his last night here.

He knew the bar in the basement was still crowded with guests reliving the whole incident with the priest. And the dining room was staying open an extra hour. Orders of Mrs. Harvey. Food, he had heard her say, would help calm the nerves.

The entire business had gone better than he had hoped. That lanky hotel guest had come running by just in time for Quince to tell him about the bloody horror inside Drummond's wagon. And the guest had to take a look. That was human nature. The man nearly retched. And when he showed him Lanigan's valise, Quince let it fall open at just the right moment and pretended to be as appalled as the lanky guest at seeing the grisly contents. "The priest must've filled these bottles with that fellow's blood!" Quince had said and shoved the valise into the lanky man's hands.

Quince laughed. What a show it had been.

And it had helped that Lanigan was so weak. Of course, Quince knew the priest would tell the deputies about him. About the killings. About everything. Would they believe him? Probably not. It was too incredible a tale. But they might. That nurse might. If she was a nurse. She was truly something out there tonight, holding off the crowd. She would be back here all right. She was different. She had gumption. And she was smart. Maybe smart enough to end his pain.

The sound of voices, the clop of horses' hooves, and rolling wagon wheels drew his attention toward the livery. They were moving the photographer's wagon there. Mrs. Harvey had told them to put Drummond's body in the icehouse until it could be sent to the undertaker. The man's wife and family lived in Wichita, she had said.

Coming around to the front of the hotel, he looked up at the tower. He did like it up there and had said so to the nurse. Perhaps she would remember.

"They brought him in drenched in blood," Deputy Cuddy said, leaning on the cantina bar and nursing a glass of beer. "They've

313

been trying to get him to talk, but he ain't said nothing."

"Well, what's he doing then?" a cowboy asked.

"Just rocking back and forth on his haunches in his cell. But I'll tell you this, it gave me a case of the jitters when I opened that bag of his."

"Why's that?"

Cuddy looked around to see if anybody was standing too close and lowered his voice. "Nothing in it but bottles, each one filled with blood."

"No!" the cowboy exclaimed.

Cuddy winced. "Not so loud."

Old man Gonzales set a covered pot with a handle on the bar. "Here's your food. Chiles and beans and beef."

Cuddy downed the rest of his beer and reached for the pot.

"Wait one," the cowboy said. "What about them bottles? Whose blood is it?"

Gonzales frowned. "What blood?"

Cuddy motioned with his hands to quiet down, then leaned in close. "All I know is a carriage driver from up at the Montezuma said some photographer fellow staying there was butchered like a hog. It appears Father Lanigan done it, and then he put the man's blood in bottles. Now, don't tell nobody."

■ ■ ■ ■

Deputy Valdes stood in the doorway of the last cell at the far end of the jailhouse, his arms crossed. He and Nurse Andrews had been trying to get some answers from *Padre* Lanigan. Valdes's patience was wearing thin.

"I didn't do it I didn't do it," the priest mumbled over and over, curled up in the corner of his cot, his head on his knees.

Though the sheriff had reminded his deputies never to jump to conclusions, Valdes found it hard not to, looking at this priest cowering there with his cassock covered in dried blood. It was almost stiff with it.

"If you won't tell us what happened, we can't help you," the nurse said. She sat on the edge of the cot opposite him.

"No one can help me," Lanigan whispered. "No one."

"Then how did you get this blood all over you?" Valdes said.

Lanigan pushed his face deeper against his knees. "I didn't do it I didn't do it I didn't do it."

Disgusted, Valdes shook his head.

"But do you know who did?" the nurse said.

Lanigan glanced at her and shuddered.

Valdes heard footsteps coming and stepped aside to let Doc enter the cell.

"Good God," he said at seeing Lanigan.

The priest tried to draw back further into the corner.

"It's not his blood," the nurse said.

"Mr. Kenton called to say I was needed here, but that was all."

"Mr. Kenton had his hands full," the nurse said. "The blood belongs to the photographer at the hotel. Mr. Drummond."

Doc stood dumbfounded. "The photographer?"

"All the priest says is he didn't kill him," the nurse said.

"What do you think, Doc?" Valdes asked.

"I think he's scared to death."

Lanigan reached into his cassock and pulled out a whiskey flask.

"Give me that," Valdes demanded, reaching for the flask. "No whiskey."

"No, let him have a drink," Doc said. "Might help steady his nerves."

His hands shaking, Lanigan brought the flask to his mouth, but it was empty.

"Hey," the prisoner Charlie Ross shouted down at the other end of the cells. "How about me? I'd like a drink, too."

"And me," Phil Larson said, his hands grasping the bars of his cell.

Disgusted, Valdes headed toward them.

"Who'd the sin buster kill?" Larson asked, his voice low.

Valdes ignored him and walked out into the office, where Cuddy dished up food onto plates from a small pot. Silva was writing a report while Duke poured coffee into cups.

"Did he confess?" Cuddy asked.

Valdes shook his head, then looked at Duke. "Tell me again what he said."

"Just kept repeating he didn't do it."

"Man drenched in all that blood don't look to me like he didn't do nothing," Cuddy said.

"And what was he going to do with these bottles after he filled them?" Silva asked, cocking his thumb at the valise sitting behind the desk.

Valdes did not answer. He didn't like any of it. Lanigan refusing to tell them what happened only made things worse. And word of this killing would not be kept quiet for long.

Hattie watched as Doc pulled the small flask from inside his Gladstone bag.

"Medicinal purposes," he said and offered

it to Lanigan. "Just a sip now."

His hands shaking, Lanigan took a swallow.

"Easy." Doc took the bottle back. "You rest a bit."

Once again, Lanigan dropped his head on his knees.

Hattie glanced at Doc, his face etched with concern. Then Lanigan mumbled.

"Did you say something, Father?"

He raised his head and whispered. "I . . . I tried to kill him, but I failed."

"Tried to kill who?" she asked gently.

His chin trembled. "The creature."

"What creature?"

"He drinks blood."

Hattie and Doc exchanged looks.

"Say that again," Doc said.

"He drinks blood. To live."

"The vampire," Hattie said.

Lanigan stared at her. "You know what he is?"

She nodded gravely.

Lanigan swallowed hard. "He made me bring him blood."

"Whose blood?" Doc said.

"Animal blood." The priest squeezed his eyes shut. "But he needs human blood more."

318

Hattie leaned in closer to him. "Who is he?"

Tears ran down Lanigan's face. "Please stop him. He killed the photographer and the stableman and all the others."

"My Lord," Doc whispered.

"Tell me who he is," Hattie said.

Scared, his words tumbled out. "I told him about Emilio Analla, that he beat his wife. I knew what he would do to him. I tried to stop him, poison him. Strychinine. I put strychnine in the bottles with the blood. But he knew. He knew!"

"His name, Father!"

Valdes appeared at the open cell door. "We just found out men are coming. Armed."

"Vigilantes?" Doc asked.

Hattie saw Lanigan stiffen.

Valdes nodded. "Twenty. Maybe more." He motioned at Lanigan. "They want him. I need to —"

"No!" Lanigan sprang off the cot, running headfirst into the cell bars, splitting his head open. Blood gushed.

"Damn fool!" Doc shouted.

Hattie snatched the blanket off the cot and held it to Lanigan's head, trying to stop the bleeding.

"Help me get him on the cot," Doc said.

Hattie tried to help the priest, but Lanigan gripped her shoulder, pulled her close, and whispered in her ear. She felt his hand slip from her shoulder as his head fell back.

"He's dead," Hattie said.

"What did he say?" Valdes asked.

She stood up. "He said Morgan Quince is the devil's creature."

"The consumptive?" Doc said. "I don't believe it."

"It was his dying confession," Hattie said. "We need to get back to the Montezuma right away. I only hope we're not too late."

CHAPTER THIRTY-SEVEN

Outside the jail, Valdes, cradling a double-barreled shotgun in his arms, told the mob of men, some of them bearing torches, that Father Lanigan was dead.

"Don't lie to us, Valdes!" one of the men shouted, a rifle in his hand. His name was Charlie Baker, a gruff man with hard eyes.

"Doc is inside. Said he had injuries we did not know about until he got here," Valdes said.

"Bring him out. Show us!"

"That's right!" others shouted. "Let's see him!"

"Quiet down!" Valdes said.

The mob settled some, and Valdes stared at Charlie Baker. "Charlie, are you calling me a liar?"

Before Baker could speak, Valdes cocked the dual triggers of the shotgun and leveled it at the gruff man.

The crowd backed away, clearing a wide

path behind Baker.

"Ain't right, deputy," Baker said.

"It is tonight. Go home. All of you! This is none of your business."

Grumbling, Baker and the others turned and walked away. A few jerked their heads around to see if Valdes was still there. He was.

Once he saw they were well past the courthouse, Valdes went back inside the jail, where Nurse Andrews and Doc were having a talk with Duke over in the corner by the pot-bellied stove. Doc drew on his cigarette.

Valdes laid the shotgun on the desk. Going down to the cell where Father Lanigan's body was, he helped Cuddy cover it with a blanket, and then the two of them carried it out behind the jail where Silva waited with the buckboard. As they placed it on the wagon, Valdes told Silva to take it to Wyman's Mortuary.

"Wake Wyman if you have to," Valdes said, knowing it was already past eleven o'clock, and Wyman tended to turn in early most nights. "And do not let anybody stop you."

Silva snapped the reins and wheeled the wagon around.

"What about me?" Cuddy asked.

"I need you to stay here and keep the peace."

"But where are you going?"

"To the Montezuma."

"Now you know what we're up against," Hattie said to Duke. "If you say no, we'll understand."

"You say this vampire fellow killed my friend, Zach Barrow?"

"That's right."

"I killed murdering Jayhawkers back during the war. Close enough to feel their last breath on my face."

"This won't be like that, Duke," Hattie said.

"It's not like anything you've ever seen," Doc said and opened the stove and threw the remains of his cigarette inside. "This thing is strong, let me tell you. And it can change into things. We weren't making that up."

"I ain't scared of what it can do," Duke said, drawing his Bowie knife from behind his back. "But it sure ought to be scared of what I'm going to do."

The front door opened, and Valdes came back in with Cuddy.

"Duke's coming with us," Hattie said.

"*Bueno,*" Valdes said, then asked Duke if he wanted a gun.

Duke said he did not.

"Well, I do," Doc said, picking up the double-barreled shotgun from the desk and taking a handful of shells from Valdes. "Maybe I can disable him long enough for the three of you to get at him."

Cuddy frowned. "What's going on here? You forming a posse without me?"

"I will explain when I get back," Valdes said. He opened the desk drawer and pulled out the long knife he had sharpened earlier. Slipping it into its sheath, he then strapped it to his side.

Hattie noticed a broom in the corner. Taking it in her hands, she broke the wooden handle across her knee, pleased that it split diagonally, leaving her with a piece of wood about two feet in length with a long, sharp end.

"What do you think you're doing, missy?" Cuddy said. "What the hell is this?"

"Do you have your revolver?" Valdes asked her.

Hattie patted her leg. "Let's go."

Hattie and Doc, holding the shotgun across his knees, sat in the hotel carriage driven by Duke, while Valdes rode ahead of them on his horse.

No one spoke a word. Hattie guessed she was as grim faced as Doc.

Rounding the bend, the hotel loomed. The grounds appeared peaceful. The lobby lights shown. Most of the guest room windows were dark. Hattie saw a faint glow at the observation deck at the top of the tower.

They pulled around to the front doors.

Doc hastily rolled a cigarette and lit it.

Hattie glanced up at the tower.

"If he hasn't run, he's up there," she said.

"How can you be so certain?" Valdes asked.

"Something he said to me."

Entering the lobby, she saw Kenton behind the front desk. He looked up from whatever he was writing.

"What's going on here?" he said. "Doc, what are doing with that shotgun?"

"A killer may be in the hotel," Valdes said. "Stay here."

Hattie said they should use the stairs. "Better than all of us in the elevator if Quince should try to attack us."

Valdes drew his six-shooter. Doc gripped the shotgun. Duke held his Bowie knife. Reaching under her skirt, Hattie drew her Swamp Angel revolver, holding it in one hand and the broken broom handle in the other.

They started up, watchful, keeping to the walls. Lights from the chandeliers burned brightly. With every flight of stairs climbed, Hattie felt more confident that Quince would not attack them yet. He was waiting for them on the observation deck. They stopped on the fourth floor landing.

"We know what we have to do," Hattie said.

"*Sí,*" Valdes said.

Duke nodded, watching the stairs above them.

His cigarette nearly down to nothing, Doc wiped his hands on his shirt.

"Doc?" Hattie said.

"Fine, fine," he said. "Nervous is all."

On the fifth floor landing, Hattie saw the storage room door ajar. *Was he in there?*

The pungent smell of turpentine was strong. Using the blade of his knife, Duke pushed the door open. Light from the landing chandelier revealed brooms, mops, and a few shelves with folded towels, paintbrushes, buckets of paint, turpentine, and linseed oil. Some oily-looking rags were in a pile on the floor.

Hattie saw a toolbox with a mallet on top. She took the mallet.

A creaking sound alerted her. She thought she saw Doc hastily throw the last of his cigarette away.

Valdes tapped her on the shoulder and

pointed at the observation deck.

Cautiously, they stepped inside. The lights hanging from the ceiling were turned low, making it hard to see. Hattie found the gas valve, but something was wrong.

Duke tried it. "The handle's bent into the wall. I can't move it."

"Quince doesn't want us to see him," Doc said, his voice quivering.

"We can see fine," Valdes said.

The room appeared empty. Outside the big windows was only darkness. Valdes went to the right, Doc to the left. Duke kept close to Hattie.

She glanced up at the beamed ceiling. Quince might have changed into a bat and was waiting to swoop down on them.

Where was he?

Over on the far side, a tarp lay crumpled on the floor.

Did it just move?

Behind her came Quince's voice, very calm. "What did the priest tell you?"

Spinning round again, Hattie saw him standing by the wall next to the bent gas valve. That low light kept part of his face in shadow.

Hattie took a breath. "He said you killed the photographer."

"Yes. I did."

"Why?"

"He took my picture."

Valdes drew back. "You killed him for taking your picture?"

"Let me show you why," he said. He took hold of the valve and turned it, filling the room with light, then walked past the windows, moving toward the front of the deck.

Hattie gasped. She saw her reflection and the others, but only Quince's clothes stood reflected in the windows. There was no head on top of his shoulders. He raised his arm. In the reflection, the sleeve of his coat went up, but no hand showed at the end of the sleeve.

"Shit," Duke said low.

"Keep steady," Hattie said. "Marta Kolbe said vampires show no reflection."

Even as she said it, Hattie realized it was one thing to hear it but more than unsettling to see it.

Doc coughed and took a step back, though Valdes stood firm, still holding his revolver at the ready. Hattie was glad of that.

"Since all of you know what I am, let's get to it," Quince said, stopping in front of the far window and turning to face them. "You've come to try to kill me."

"There'll be no trying about it," Duke said.

Quince settled his gaze on Hattie. "I never wanted this, to be this . . . creature. I want you to know that."

There was sorrow in Quince's voice, she thought. It sounded genuine.

Duke snorted loudly.

"Let's hear him out," she said. "But be ready."

"I do not trust him," Valdes said.

"I know," she said.

"Miss Andrews, you remember I said my wife and child died, and then I went to Europe? It began when I was in London. Late one night, I started walking. Didn't care where. I just wanted to get away from my grief. Somehow, I ended up at the docks. Fog rolled in, making it hard to see. I heard somebody hollering for help and in the lamplight saw three men holding another on the ground. I couldn't allow that and jumped into them. I carried a Bowie knife under my coat, like the one you have, Duke."

Hattie saw Duke chewing on his lower lip.

"I held my knife to one man and told the other two to back away. The fellow on the ground had a face white as chalk, his mouth and chin smeared with blood. I thought it was from the others beating him. But he started laughing and said, 'Life is blood, and blood is life.' Then he ran off into the fog. The one I had hold of told me I had set free a monster. He pointed to the body of a woman lying on the ground. Said the monster had killed her and drained her blood. I lowered my knife. The fellow was holding a gold cross in his hand. I didn't know why then. He said his name was Karl van Dalen. Claimed he was a doctor.

"He told me he and his men had been after the 'vampire' for some time. I couldn't believe it when he said the monster drank blood to live. Said this thing was called Dracula, which meant 'son of the devil.' "

"And you're a son of a bitch," Duke spat, trying to goad him.

Quince smiled. "I offered to come with them, help them find Dracula, since it was my fault he got away. And the fight had made me feel alive again, at least for the moment."

Hattie thought of her son, Tim.

"We chased Dracula across Europe. Caught up with him on a mountain road in some forsaken place. Gypsies had him in a wagon, protecting him. We were armed and on horseback. One of the wagon wheels hit a rock, and the rig flipped on its side. I got to it first and pulled my knife. While the others picked off the gypsies, I yanked open the wagon door. Dracula sprang on me, but I stuck him in the belly. I never heard such screaming. He was strong as a bull but bleeding like a stuck pig. He took a bite of my neck and wouldn't let go, and a strange feeling came over me. Warm and cold, like life and death together. Everything went black.

"When I came to, I felt weak as a newborn. Van Dalen told me Dracula was dead, but my life was in danger. That's when I saw the tube running out of his arm into my arm. He said a vampire secretes its own blood from its mouth when it feeds. He said Dracula's blood was in me, and he was giving me a blood transfusion. Soon I started retching up blood. Van Dalen said that meant the transfusion wasn't working. I heard the others say they ought to kill me, that I was becoming a vampire."

"What did you do?" Hattie asked.

"Ran like hell. Traveled at night. Any sunlight then would have killed me. The next day the blood fever came over me, like a wind swirling everything into a frenzy. I needed blood. It was the only thing I could keep down. Not food, not even water. I caught vermin and foxes and such. Anything to stop my insides from burning. But no people.

"I got passage home aboard a ship. Stayed below in my cabin. At night I caught rats and fed on them. I wanted to kill myself, but this damn 'curse' wouldn't let me. My body started wasting away. I needed human blood."

"You killed that woman," Hattie said and immediately regretted it. She was getting ahead of herself. Unwise for a Pinkerton detective. Too late now.

"What woman?" Quince asked.

"In Kansas City."

"The pickpocket. She was quick, but I caught her. She tried to stab me. Her intention was to kill me."

Valdes said, "But you kill people."

"Only ones who won't be missed," he said, adding that, after arriving back in America, it was easy finding proper prey.

"What do you mean 'proper prey'?" Hattie said.

"A drug addled whore in New York, a swindler in Cincinnati, the pickpocket in Kansas City, a pimp in Texarkana, a murderer on the run in Fort Worth. And more here. And after I fed on them, I tore out their throats. To hide the bite marks."

"But you didn't do that to the woman in

Kansas City," Hattie said. "Her neck showed the marks."

Doc spoke up. "And you turned Gretl Kolbe into a vampire."

"That wasn't my intention. I only wanted her blood, but her sister came looking for her before I finished."

Hattie felt a chill when he shifted his gaze back to her and said, "As to the Kansas City pickpocket, I was taught to respect women. I don't desecrate them, even the worst of them. I left her body at the depot because I was in a hurry. The train was leaving, and I had no time to drag her down to the river."

"The river?"

"I use rivers to dispose of the bodies. When I returned to the United States, I traveled by train from New York to Fort Worth. There's a river at each of those towns. I found proper prey. Cincinnati, Kansas City, all of them. After I consumed the blood of those scoundrels and thieves, I threw the bodies into the river. The currents did the rest. Even if they were found, I was miles away. The blood from one body satisfied me for several days. I did the same when I left Fort Worth to come here."

She saw his lips curl into a smile.

"Is something funny?"

"I remembered it was a dry spell from

Austin to El Paso."

"Mother of God," Doc said, his voice shaking.

Quince took a step toward him. "There's something else funny, Doc. Drinking all that blood, I'd get a kind of rosiness back in my cheeks for a short while. After I got home, friends noticed how pale and rawboned I was. Told me I ought to see a doctor. This sawbones in Fort Worth said I had symptoms of consumption and needed treatment. Dry air and all. An opportunity is what it was. It meant places I'd fit in, like here, where they welcome consumptives, without questions."

"Damn you," Doc said.

"Why? Because I fooled you?"

"No. Because you make a mockery of people's suffering."

"Believe me, Doctor, I suffer," Quince said evenly. "I felt dead and empty after my wife died. I'd give anything, *anything* to go back, but now I am cursed with living death, something a thousand times worse than anything you've ever seen. And there's no remedy, no —"

"Aw, shit, you're going to make me bust out crying." Duke shook his knife at Quince. "You killed my friend, you son of a bitch."

The vampire met Duke's accusation with

a cold stare. "You mean the liveryman I saw beating the horse."

"Zach Barrow never did any such thing!"

"A man beating a horse is nothing but a coward."

"You don't know what you saw!"

Quince's eyes turned red. Blood red. "I've seen plenty," he said low. "Right here in this town I saw a drifter put a knife to a shop-keeper's wife's throat, then take all their money. In Austin, I saw the son of a Texas senator lure a young boy into a back alley. I saw the pickpocket gal steal. And I saw your friend whip a horse."

"You saw wrong!"

Hattie smelled smoke. She glanced about but could see no evidence of it.

"I also saw the look on every one of their faces when they knew they were dying," Quince said, then looked at Valdes. "Like that Texas Ranger."

"You killed the ranger?"

Hattie knew nothing of any ranger, but she saw Valdes reach inside his shirt.

"You can find him in the bowling alley when we're done here," Quince said, "if you're still able."

Taking his hand out of his shirt, Valdes held up a crude-looking crucifix and ran at him, cocking his revolver. "You are going to

335

hell!" He fired at Quince, hitting him in the stomach.

Quince burst out laughing and, in an instant, wrenched the gun from Valdes's hand and threw it down, the barrel now crushed and bent. Then he caught the deputy by the throat with one hand and snatched the crucifix in his other hand.

"I wager you had Lanigan bless it," the vampire said.

Valdes struggled to pry Quince's hand from around his neck.

Quince's lips curled into a malevolent smile as he broke the crucifix into pieces. "There's nothing sacred about a cross blessed by a faithless priest."

Pulling the long knife, Valdes took a swipe at Quince. In one quick move, he released Valdes's throat, grabbed his arm and twisted. Valdes screamed, dropping the knife. Quince kicked it away, then hurled the deputy across the room like a child's doll. Valdes crashed through one of the plate-glass windows and slammed hard against the wooden railing outside, snapping some of the balusters loose. Shards of glass showered him. He did not move.

Hattie aimed her Swamp Angel, knowing it would do nothing to stop Quince but might distract him so Duke could get at him with his Bowie. She fired, hitting Quince in the chest with no effect. Doc brought his shotgun up and fired both barrels. The sound of the blasts filled the room. Quince darted out of the way. Some buckshot tore into his side, but most of it shattered the large glass window behind him. At the same instant, flames roared out of the storage room.

Ducking low, Hattie spun around. The fire reached up toward the ceiling of the staircase landing. Turning, she saw all that remained of the shattered window were jagged pieces of glass jutting out from the frame.

Doc cracked opened the shotgun to reload.

"Look out!" Duke shouted.

Quince jerked the shotgun from Doc's hands and threw it out the shattered window.

Hattie took aim again at Quince, who grabbed Doc, using him as a shield. Suddenly, Duke, his Bowie ready, slammed into Quince from the side. Doc fell away. Duke and Quince tumbled into the wall by the entryway where smoke swirled. Hattie heard Duke groan, saw his Bowie drop from his hand.

From out of the smoke, Quince came at

her. She fired her revolver. The bullet pierced Quince's chest. He kept coming. She cocked the hammer back. Quince's hand covered her face. She pulled the trigger, felt the revolver jerked from her grasp, and heard it clatter across the floor.

"You'll have to do better than that," Quince whispered in her ear.

Still clutching the mallet and stake in her other hand, she swung her arm as hard as she could, striking his head. Snarling, Quince yanked the mallet and stake from her and hurled them out the broken window.

His arms wrapped around her, his face only inches from hers. She struggled, saw his mouth open and two vicious-looking fangs lowering toward her neck. Desperate, Hattie raised her foot and jammed it down on top of his boot. Quince laughed. She felt his breath on her skin. Her flesh crawled.

"No!" she cried. Getting one arm free, she clawed his face, drawing blood.

More flames burst out of the storage room. The cans of paint and turpentine exploded. Startled by the blast, Quince released his hold on Hattie.

He backed away, glancing from side to side. Hattie saw Doc coming up on the left and Duke — thank God he was alive —

circling around from the right. Something glinted in Doc's hand. He had found Valdes's knife! Duke held his Bowie, low and ready.

"Come ahead," Quince said, his tone taunting. His body suddenly jerked, his head flew back, mouth sagging open. A jagged piece of wood burst out of his chest, covered in crimson and gore.

"*¡Bastardo!*" Valdes shouted.

The deputy was not dead! His face streaked with blood from glass cuts, Valdes had come up behind Quince, using a broken baluster from the railing outside as a wooden stake.

Quince's grotesque howl filled Hattie's ears. Blood spewed from his mouth. His body lurched again as Valdes thrust more of the bloody baluster through his chest.

"Kill him now!" Valdes shouted.

Doc and Duke started for Quince, then stopped as the vampire grabbed the end of the baluster in both his hands and pulled it out of his chest, blood spurting. He threw the baluster away, spun around to Valdes. Raising his arm, his hand turned into a black wolf's paw, sharp claws bared. The black paw flew down, the claws tearing out Valdes's throat.

Blood poured down the deputy's shirt as

he fell, dead.

"No!" Hattie screamed.

Doc and Duke came at Quince from opposite sides. His hand normal again, Quince stood, his legs unsteady. He backhanded Doc, sending him staggering across the room. Hattie heard the knife skitter across the floor.

Before Quince could spin around, Duke let out a yell and drove Quince backward, toward the shattered window Doc had shot out. They hit the floor, Quince on his back. Duke drove his Bowie deep into the vampire's bloody chest. Quince's face grew long, trying to change into the black wolf. One of his hands became a wolf's paw again, the other into something deformed.

Duke shouted, "He's weakened! Kill him!"

Hattie heard Doc moan. She could not see him.

Quince clawed Duke, ripping his shirt, tearing open his back. Duke screamed and pushed the Bowie deeper.

"Fire! Get the water hoses!" came a cry from below.

Smoke billowed, stinging Hattie's eyes. She scrambled across the floor, searching for Valdes's knife. The flames cast an eerie light. She found Doc tangled in the tarp by the far wall but couldn't find the knife. Wiping her eyes, she looked back and saw Duke slumped on top of Quince. The vampire let out a mournful sound and pushed the big man off. Quince's face became normal, then his hands. On his feet again, he teetered in front of the shattered window.

Hattie ran toward him. She had to stop him, somehow.

"Hurry," Quince said, lifting his arms out to his sides. "Please."

Quince turned his back, facing the shattered window and the darkness beyond.

Good God, he was changing into something else. Hattie saw his body began to shrink inside his clothes. *He can't get away! Don't let him get away!*

She threw herself at him, pushing him into the broken window. His neck came down on a large jagged piece of glass, severing his head from his body. It rolled to a stop against the railing.

Crimson covered the front of her dress. She was lying in a pool of Quince's blood, spreading across the floor. She put her hand into it. It felt cold on her skin.

"Everyone get out!" came another cry from down below. "Fire!"

Doc grasped Hattie's arm and helped her up. Going to Duke, Doc put his ear to his chest.

"He's alive," he said. "Help me get him to his feet."

Duke groaned.

The fire had spread onto the landing and down the elevator shaft. There was hardly room to get past it to the stairs.

Hattie remembered the tarp.

"Where are you going?" Doc called to her. "We need to get out of here!"

"We have to get the bodies down." She grabbed the tarp. Her legs wobbled. She coughed and covered her mouth. Smoke stung her eyes and lungs.

The gas light flames flickered and went out.

"Good! They must have shut off the gas," Doc said.

Hattie turned. The remaining plate-glass windows reflected the storage room flames, as though hell itself burned outside and inside.

Quickly, they rolled the bodies of Valdes and Quince on to the tarp. Even with two windows gone, the thickening smoke gathered, making it hard to breathe. Doc placed Quince's head between the two bodies.

Duke could hardly stand, his back badly clawed and bleeding. "Let's go," he said.

They heard voices, and the sound of footsteps charging up the stairs.

"Get the water hoses!"

"There are no water hoses up here!"

Men appeared on the landing carrying blankets and coats to try to beat out the fire.

"There's people here!" Hattie heard a man shout. "Help them!"

"We're all right." Doc coughed.

Hattie and Doc took one end of the tarp while Duke took the other end as they made their way past the men trying to put out the storage room flames. Thick smoke made it almost impossible to see.

Shouts echoed up the staircase.

"Everyone out!"

"Water! We need water!"

"We need more help!"

"Get the furniture out! Hurry!"

"What's wrong?"

"The water hoses won't reach, damn it!"

Down in the lobby, Hattie, Doc, and Duke hurried outside. No one needed to see what was in the tarp. No one should. Reaching the other side of the pathway, they stopped and placed the tarp on the ground.

Raging flames engulfed the top three stories of the tower. Half the roof of the third floor was burning. Windows billowed thick smoke and orange fire.

Panicked guests ran out the doors to

safety. Hattie saw Mrs. Harvey getting her children out with Kenton's help. Guests, some in robes and others wearing hastily donned clothes, cried and shouted and complained as hotel employees helped them down toward the terraces and safety. Hattie was relieved that Mrs. Shaw in her wheelchair was among them.

Exhausted, she helped Doc clean Duke's wounds. Her head pounded. She realized Doc was speaking to her, but his voice sounded far away.

"We'll need to bury Quince like the Kolbe woman said."

"Doc!" someone hollered, and he left her there.

A soft breeze brushed Hattie's face. So did the heat of the fire. A loud groan made her look up. The tower turret, consumed in fire, collapsed. Great flames burst upward into the night sky as myriad sparks flew out and drifted down.

"My God, woman! Get away from here!" a man shouted. "This whole place is going up!"

Hattie realized he was speaking to her. She recognized his face from the day she had arrived on the train, the man with the fretful wife. She was next to him. Both wore robes cinched tight, and he had on his hat.

She clutched her daughter against her chest, and he carried his son in his arms.

"Aren't you scared?" the woman cried, her eyes pleading, looking at Hattie as they ran past.

The edge of the tarp came loose. Hattie quickly tucked it under to cover the bodies. *One of them was a good man and the other a man who —*

A cold shiver took hold of her. She realized the truth of the matter and wondered if she would ever be scared again. Morgan Quince had ceased being a man. She had fought a creature — no, a monster — and survived.

EPILOGUE

Doctor Nathan Burwell

An inquest was held into the fire at the Montezuma Hotel and the deaths of Deputy Valdes and Morgan Quince. Doc, Hattie Lawton, and Duke Pennick testified that Deputy Valdes wanted to question Quince regarding the horrible deaths around town for the past few months. When asked why all of them went with Deputy Valdes, each said that Valdes had told them he needed his other two deputies to keep any citizens from trying to break into the jail to take Father Lanigan's body. They went on to say that Valdes had asked them to come, believing Doc might be needed in case someone got injured, Duke because Quince might put up a fight, and Miss Lawton since she was a Pinkerton detective and therefore an asset to the sheriff's office. All three stated that Quince admitted to the killings. Doc said that Valdes told Quince he was under arrest. "He and Quince struggled, and Quince pushed Valdes so hard he crashed through one of the observation windows," Doc explained. "The rest of us went after Quince, and that's when the fire broke out in the closet. Flames shot out and engulfed Quince as he ran past it. Duke got to him first and tried to put out the flames, but Quince fought him off rather than be taken alive."

When asked how Quince, being on fire, could possibly fight off a big man like Duke Pennick, Doc pondered a moment, then said, "I saw men in the war, their bodies torn and bloodied, still fighting when all my training and expertise as a doctor told me it wasn't possible. In Mr. Quince's case, what I witnessed was a man consumed by monstrous desire and then by the flames." Doc went on to say that Quince's body had suffered such terrible burns as to be unrecognizable.

Asked what he had done with Quince's body, Doc stated with a straight face he had sent word to a lawyer in Dallas, Texas, asking if he would look into Quince's will and any requests about burial. The lawyer responded, saying that Quince left no will, and he was not a church-going man. "So, I buried him in a little field outside of town.

No call to make a fuss. The man had confessed and was dead."

The inquest in the matter of the deaths of Deputy Valdes and Morgan Quince was closed.

There had been no inquest into the death of Father Lanigan. He had gone crazy, it was said. People did not even want to mention his name. His family in Philadelphia had sent word to the archbishop in Santa Fe. They requested his body be shipped back home. They said they would pay all the costs. Doc had seen to the embalming of Lanigan's body at Wyman's Mortuary, then he and Wyman placed it in a coffin and put it on the train.

Every Sunday Doc made a point of going to the cemetery at Our Lady of Sorrows Church where Deputy Valdes was laid to rest and placing a small handmade cross on his grave. He had sent a wire to the deputy's wife, still in Albuquerque with her children at her father's home, informing her of her husband's death. The next day a wire arrived from the father-in-law, saying someone would be coming to get his daughter's things. Valdes had told Doc of his father-in-law's contempt for him, so it came as no surprise that the old man added neither he nor his family would be attending the funeral of "a man cursed with so little ambition."

As for Quince, Doc and Hattie had taken his body to a crossroads well away from town and buried it exactly as Marta Kolbe had said, so it would not rise again to wreak havoc on the living.

Doc never slept peacefully again and never spoke to anyone of the events of that terrible night of fire and death.

Duke Pennick

Offered a job to help rebuild the Montezuma Hotel that fall, Duke accepted, being it was steady work, what with winter coming soon. He was on foot guiding a horse team when one of the two ropes tied around the ends of a stack of lumber that workers were lifting via a pulley gave way and sent the load crashing down. The sound and commotion spooked one of the horses, and it kicked, catching the back of Duke's head, knocking him out cold. He was taken to Doc's house, where he died three days later. The Santa Fe Railroad and Fred Harvey split the cost of the funeral expenses. The railroad allowed the entire construction crew the day off to attend the funeral. Doc gave the eulogy. Everyone said it was beautiful. Later that night, sitting at home

349

in the dark, Doc recalled Duke waking only once in the three days he was in Doc's care. Duke blinked at Doc, grinned, and said, "That was quite a time we had getting that vampire fellow, wasn't it?" He closed his eyes. They were Duke's last words.

Millard Kenton

Fred Harvey asked Kenton to stay on and continue as the manager of the new Montezuma Hotel, once it was completed. Kenton knew if Mr. Harvey asked, one did not turn him down. However, a telegram arrived on Christmas Eve, informing Kenton of the death of a wealthy aunt in New Canaan, Connecticut, who had left him her entire estate worth $150,000. The day after Christmas, Kenton sent Mr. Harvey his regrets, saying he would not be taking the job as the manager as his "situation has changed." He added that he greatly appreciated having been part of the Fred Harvey Company. After packing his belongings, he purchased a train ticket to head back East. During an evening stop in La Junta, Colorado, difficulties with the locomotive resulted in a long delay. Kenton and a couple of other passengers decided to take a walk into town. A fracas inside a saloon began when Miss Sadie Cathcart, the saloon owner, holding a revolver in her hand, shouted that no damn card cheater cowboy was welcome in her place as she chased the cowboy into the street. She fired a shot into the air to scare him off for good. Laughter and cheers erupted from inside the saloon. Angered, the cowboy turned, drawing his pistol, and fell backwards, tripping over his own feet as he fired. His shot went wild and struck Kenton through the heart, killing him instantly.

Mrs. Florence Shaw

Remaining in Las Vegas, Territory of New Mexico, she resided at the Plaza Hotel while the new Montezuma Hotel was being built. She wrote a letter to the president of the Atchison, Topeka and Santa Fe Railroad with "a suggestion" that a casino be added to the hotel. "I cannot tell you how boring some nights can be out there," she wrote. "Even for a lunger like me, a casino would be a welcome respite now and then." The president of the railroad responded with a letter, saying he would take her suggestion under advisement. When the hotel re-opened, she moved back into her former guest room, disappointed there was no casino. But, two years later, with fewer guests coming to the hotel, the Santa Fe

Railroad needed to do something to entice wealthy patrons and did build a casino adjacent to the hotel. It could hold one thousand people and included a stage for shows. Mrs. Shaw passed away in her sleep the night before it opened.

William Pinkerton and Robert Pinkerton

The brothers worked tirelessly, following the legacy of their famous father, tracking criminals from the United States to the remotest corners of Latin America and Europe. There were successes, such as the retrieval of the Thomas Gainsborough painting *Portrait of Georgiana, Duchess of Devonshire,* stolen by Adam Worth, known as "The Napoleon of the Criminal World," a nickname given him due to his short stature rather than his volume of crimes. And there were unfortunate incidents such as the Homestead strike, also known as the Homestead massacre. It occurred in the summer of 1892 in the town of Homestead, Pennsylvania. Hundreds of striking steel workers clashed with some three hundred Pinkerton agents. Both sides were armed. When it was all over, nine strikers lay dead, along with three Pinkerton agents.

Nonetheless, respect for the Pinkerton

Detective Agency remained in the eyes of many.

Marta Kolbe

Some months after the Montezuma Hotel fire, Marta, on her way to deliver eggs to the Plaza Hotel restaurant, encountered Wilhelm Gottschalk, a stout Fort Union commissary sergeant who was on leave for ten days and traveling to visit a cousin who lived in Kansas. Sergeant Gottschalk had spent the night in the Plaza Hotel, having missed his train the previous evening. He was rushing out the door to get to the depot early the next morning when he ran into Marta, knocking the basket of eggs from her hands. She spoke in German calling him a *dummkopf.* At the same moment Gottschalk, also speaking in German, begged her pardon. They looked into each other's eyes, and they were married three months later, the day after Gottschalk retired from the army. Within the year they opened Gottschalk's Fancy and Staple Groceries on the south side of the plaza, advertising, "Eastern fruits, vegetables, and local eggs our specialty."

Sally Harvey

Within hours of the fire being extinguished, Sally sent a wire to her husband, still in Europe, telling him of the catastrophe. Fred Harvey immediately booked passage aboard the *Etruria,* joining his wife and family in Las Vegas less than three weeks later. On hearing from her of the tragic deaths of E. F. Drummond, Deputy Valdes, Father Lanigan, and a hotel guest named Quince, he was devastated and offered his personal condolences to the Drummond, Valdes, and Lanigan families. Quince, he was told, had no family. He thanked Doctor Burwell for his efforts.

Ever the businessman, Fred agreed with the decision of the Atchison, Topeka and Santa Fe Railroad, the owners of the hotel and surrounding property, to rebuild the hotel, duplicating the previous design with a few minimal alterations.

Almost a year to the day after the fire, the Montezuma Hotel, renamed the Phoenix Hotel, in honor of the mythical bird that rose from its own ashes, opened its doors for the third time on August 16, 1886. However, the name conjured bad memories for many, and the hotel once again became the Montezuma. Sadly, the new Montezuma was never profitable, losing forty thousand dollars a year for the next seven years. Then the Panic of 1893 drove many businesses into receivership, but not the Fred Harvey Company. It continued to prosper well into the twentieth century. The railroads, however, were not so fortunate. The Santa Fe Railroad, facing bankruptcy, closed the Montezuma on September 1, 1893.

When her husband bemoaned the demise of the jewel of both the Santa Fe Railroad and the Harvey Houses, Sally told him she thought it was for the best. He asked her what she meant. "I'm so sorry to say this to you," she said, "but I believe that place was cursed."

Hattie Lawton

A few days after the inquest, Hattie boarded a train to journey back home to Baltimore, unaware of what her future held. No doubt, unsavory tasks would most certainly arise. But were there more such supernatural manifestations, other such monsters, or worse, waiting in the shadows? She prayed there were not. She hoped there were none. And she also knew that praying and hoping were not at all the same as being convinced.

AUTHOR'S NOTE

A vampire in the Old West.

How to tell such a tale?

Sometimes authors get an idea that just won't write, as the saying goes.

But this one kept rolling around in my head. There had to be a way to make it play. The problem was the vampire. Who was he? How did he become a vampire? Why was he in the Old West? How did he get there?

While doing research on vampires, I read Bram Stoker's classic novel, *Dracula.* One of the characters who joins Dr. Van Helsing in chasing Count Dracula is Quincey Morris, a wealthy Texas adventurer. In Stoker's novel the count kills Morris during the final fight. I thought, *what if Morris doesn't die? What if Dracula bit him?*

Looking into Stoker's background, I discovered that in the winter of 1884, (thirteen years before *Dracula* was published), this brawny Irishman, who handled the business affairs of famed British actor Henry Irving's Lyceum Theater in London, sailed to the United States with the theater troupe for their first American tour.

What if, during that voyage across the Atlantic, Stoker met a man one night who appeared nearly devoid of color and who told him a story that seemed almost beyond comprehension? The man was a rich Texas cattleman who had gone to Europe to escape a tragic memory and found himself caught up in chasing a monster, a vampire, and, being bitten by this vampire, became one himself?

I believed this had strong possibilities, though I decided to drop Stoker as a character in my tale.

I found inspiration in an intrepid young woman named Hattie Lawton, who joined the Pinkerton Detective Agency and was sent as a spy to Richmond, Virginia, shortly after the start of the Civil War. She and her fellow detective, Timothy Webster, were later captured and thrown into prison. Timothy was hanged as a spy; Hattie was released after serving one year. Nothing is known of her after that. I proceeded to create her story from there.

The setting for the tale came when I discovered that, on the night of August 8,

1885 (about a year and a half after Bram Stoker arrived in America), the Montezuma Hotel, also known as the Montezuma Castle, located near the town of Las Vegas in the Territory of New Mexico, burned down. No lives were lost, but the cause of the fire remains uncertain. Some say it may have been an electrical short in a storage room near the observation deck at the top of the five-story tower. Others believe it was due to a clogged gas line in the tower. Another possibility could be that someone carelessly tossed a match in the wrong place. About all that remained after the fire was put out were the exterior red stone walls of the first three floors, the first floor veranda, and the chimneys. A fiery climax in a fairy tale-like castle that actually existed in the Old West was too good to resist.

Historical events, circumstances, and conjecture all combined to bring *Blood West* to fruition.

However, this is a work of fiction. Hattie Lawton, Robert Pinkerton, his brother, William Pinkerton, Mrs. Sally Harvey, and her son Byron all did exist. But their words are mine.

The books written by Allan Pinkerton about the cases he took on helped with understanding the workings of the Pinkerton Detective Agency. They include *The Detective and the Somnambulist. The Murderer and the Fortune Teller,* Toronto, ON, Canada, Belford Brothers Publishing, 1877; and *Spy of the Rebellion,* Lincoln, University of Nebraska Press, 2011. I also found useful information at www.brilliantdeduction .info.

Little is known about Hattie Lawton. After her release from Castle Godwin prison, she disappeared from history. A fire destroyed the records of the Pinkerton Agency in the 1880s. However, *The Pinks: The First Women Detectives, Operatives, and Spies with the Pinkerton National Detective Agency* by Chris Enss, TwoDot, 2017, provided some important and appreciated details regarding Hattie's early days with the Pinkertons.

For the background on the Montezuma Hotel, I am grateful to Everett Apodaca in Santa Fe, New Mexico, for his expertise and knowledge about the history of the hotel and his gracious willingness to share it with me. Also, thank you to Kathy Hendrickson at Southwest Detours in Las Vegas, New Mexico, for a tour of the Montezuma Hotel and grounds, now the Armand Hammer United World College, founded in 1982.

Works I consulted about the Montezuma Hotel are: *Montezuma: The Castle in the*

West, Jon Bowman, Editor, *New Mexico Magazine,* 2002; *Appetite for America: How Visionary Businessman Fred Harvey Built a Railroad Hospitality Empire That Civilized the Wild West* by Stephen Fried, Bantam Books, 2010; *Harvey Houses of New Mexico: Historic Hospitality from Raton to Deming* by Rosa Walston Latimer, The History Press, 2015; *Montezuma: A Biography of the Building* by Carl D. Sheppard, Patricia H. Sheppard, 2002; *A Room for the Night: Hotels of the Old West* by Richard A. Van Orman, Indiana University Press, 1966; and *Montezuma Memories: An Anthology* by Tom Wiley, Montezuma Club, 1972.

For an understanding of tuberculosis and how it impacted New Mexico Territory in the 1880s, I thank Dr. James Kornberg for sharing his expert knowledge on frontier medicine, particularly tuberculosis and its early treatments. Other sources I consulted are: "History of Tuberculosis, Part 1 — Phthisis, Consumption and the White Plague," by John Firth, *Journal of Military and Veterans' Health,* Volume 22, No. 2, June 2014, online at www.jmvh.org; and *Chasing the Cure in New Mexico: Tuberculosis and the Quest of Health* by Nancy Owen Lewis, Museum of New Mexico, 2016.

So much has been written about vampire history and lore, in fiction and nonfiction, that it seemed overwhelming at first. However, I soon discovered that much of the history and lore was rewritten for novels and the movies to accommodate whatever telling the authors and filmmakers wanted to do. (Full disclosure: I did the same with this book.) But I needed to try to understand the vampire and its beginnings. For that I went to two sources: *Vampires, Burial, and Death: Folklore and Reality* by Paul Barber, Yale University Press, 1988; and the book that started it all, *Dracula* by Bram Stoker, Grosset & Dunlap, 1897.

I'm most grateful to Tiffany Schofield, senior editor at Five Star, and her splendid team for all their tireless work. I'm also indebted to my developmental editor, Deni Dietz, as well as Erin Bealmear, content project editor, Kathy Heming, cover designer, and Cathy Kulka, copy editor, for their superb expertise.

My thanks to Shannon Hensley at Shannon Hensley Law Offices for all her help and guidance.

And a very special and heartfelt thank you to my wife, Marilyn. Being married to a writer, she lives with the stories I tell as much as I do. As my first reader, she offers her support and advice. I'm thankful every day for her love, understanding, patience, and humor.

Thomas D. Clagett
Santa Fe, New Mexico

ABOUT THE AUTHOR

Thomas D. Clagett spent twenty years as an assistant film editor in Hollywood. His credits include *The Two Jakes,* Jack Nicholson's sequel to *Chinatown,* and the TV series *St. Elsewhere.* His novels include *Line of Glory: A Novel of the Alamo,* a Spur Award Finalist for best historical fiction, *West of Penance,* winner of the Will Rogers Medallion Award for best inspirational novel and also winner of the New Mexico-Arizona Book Award for best historical fiction. His first novel, *The Pursuit of Murieta,* was named a Will Rogers Medallion Award honorable mention winner. A member of the Western Writers of America, Clagett lives with his wife, Marilyn, in Santa Fe, New Mexico. His website is www.thomasdclagett.com.

The employees of Thorndike Press hope you have enjoyed this Large Print book. All our Thorndike, Wheeler, and Kennebec Large Print titles are designed for easy reading, and all our books are made to last. Other Thorndike Press Large Print books are available at your library, through selected bookstores, or directly from us.

For information about titles, please call:
  (800) 223-1244

or visit our website at:
  gale.com/thorndike

To share your comments, please write:
  Publisher
  Thorndike Press
  10 Water St., Suite 310
  Waterville, ME 04901

CPSIA information can be obtained
at www.ICGtesting.com
Printed in the USA
BVHW041025210723
667593BV00010B/21